The Series: The Chronicles of Erenor

AN OVERVIEW

In *The Chronicles of Erenor*, readers are pulled into a captivating world of magic, adventure, and destiny. From the first introduction of Lysandra in *The Last Mage* to the cosmic rift that distorts reality in *Erenor's Dawn* and the climactic battle against the evil sorcerer Malachor in *Erenor's Destiny*, this epic fantasy series weaves a compelling tale of intricate characters, rich world-building, and thrilling action.

Every page is filled with tension and wonder, inviting readers to embark on a journey where ancient prophecies, untamed magic, and the power of courage and friendship hold the keys to survival and victory. *The Chronicles of Erenor* is a must-read series that guarantees an unforgettable adventure, seamlessly blending romance, profound themes, and the eternal struggle between light and darkness.

KIM BOCK

ERENOR'S DESTINY

BOOK 3

The Chronicles of Erenor

Contents

Erenor

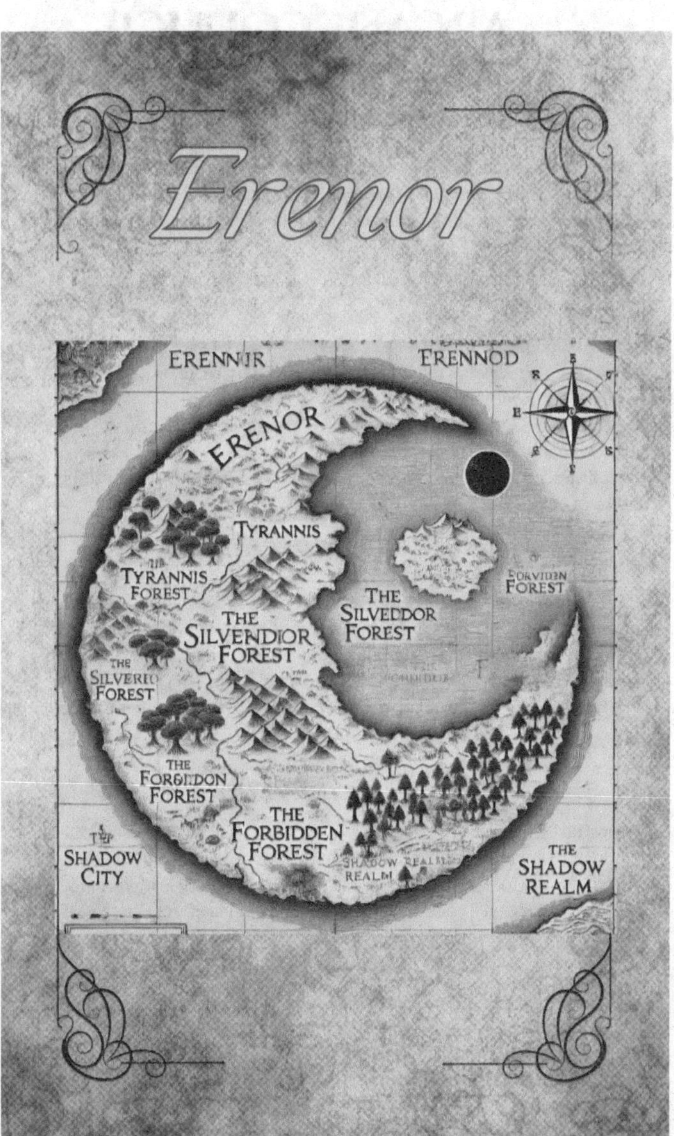

CODE OF ERENOR ARCANE COUNCIL

Preamble

We, the undersigned members of the Arcane Council of Erenor, do hereby affirm our commitment to safeguarding the balance of magic and preserving the integrity and safety of our realm. United by our shared values and the sacred duty entrusted to us, we establish this Code to guide our actions, define our responsibilities, and ensure the secrecy and efficacy of our Council.

Purpose and Mandate

The Arcane Council exists to:

- Protect Erenor: Serve as the guardians against dark magic and other threats that endanger the realm.
- Regulate Magic: Oversee the ethical use of magic, ensuring it serves the greater good and does not harm the balance of nature or society.
- Maintain Secrecy: Operate covertly to protect the identity of our members and the nature of our work.

Membership

- Eligibility: Membership is open to all who possess magical abilities and demonstrate a commitment to our principles, regardless of origin or background.
- Duties: Members must actively participate in the Council's missions, adhere to this Code, and maintain the secrecy of the Council.
- Oath of Secrecy: Every member must swear an oath to protect the Council's secrets upon joining. Breach of this oath is punishable by expulsion and magical nullification.

Leadership

- Supreme Leader: The reigning King of Tyrannis shall be the nominal head of the Arcane Council, overseeing its alignment with the realm's laws and interests.
- High Council: Composed of founding members and key leaders, responsible for strategic decisions, policy-making, and crisis management.

Ethics and Conduct

- Integrity: Members must act with honesty and integrity, prioritizing the welfare of Erenor and its inhabitants.
- Respect: Treat all beings, magical or otherwise, with respect and fairness.
- Prohibition of Dark Magic: The use of dark magic is strictly forbidden unless specifically sanctioned by the High Council for controlled purposes.
- Neutrality: The Council remains neutral in political conflicts, intervening only when the use of magic poses a threat to peace and balance.
- Sanctions: Members found in violation of the Code may face sanctions including suspension, expulsion, or magical containment.

Prologue:

THE WAR OF SHADOW

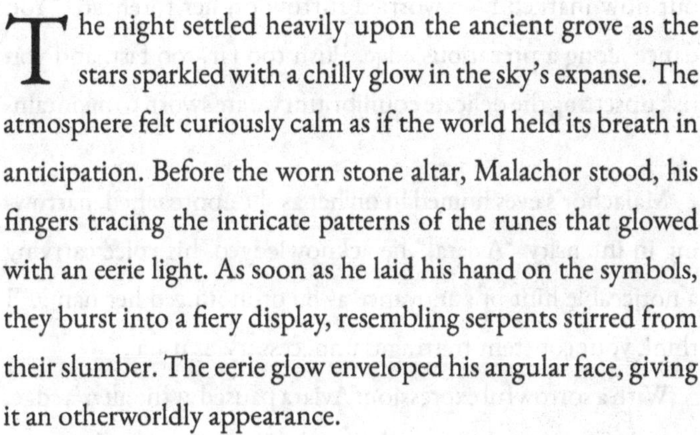

The night settled heavily upon the ancient grove as the stars sparkled with a chilly glow in the sky's expanse. The atmosphere felt curiously calm as if the world held its breath in anticipation. Before the worn stone altar, Malachor stood, his fingers tracing the intricate patterns of the runes that glowed with an eerie light. As soon as he laid his hand on the symbols, they burst into a fiery display, resembling serpents stirred from their slumber. The eerie glow enveloped his angular face, giving it an otherworldly appearance.

"The fearful hold on to boundaries, much like a child clinging to their favorite blanket," reflected Malachor, his resonant baritone filled with unwavering conviction, like the unyielding standing stones that encircled the clearing. "Only those brave enough to surpass our constraints achieve power and true mastery."

His eyes, once a mesmerizing emerald reflecting the lush

forests he and Aviara had cared for, now shone with a vibrant brightness as though an internal blaze was on the verge of engulfing him. The intensity of his gaze revealed an almost tangible hunger, a predatory force lurking beneath his outward demeanor.

"Be careful, Malachor." Aviara's warning emanated from the encroaching shadows, her voice gently admonishing as it floated over the murmuring grass. A shimmering, iridescent glow that seemed to hold off the approaching darkness illuminated her slender figure as she entered the open space. The gentle glow illuminated a face of otherworldly beauty, ageless and peaceful but now marked by a worried furrow on her forehead. "You dance along a precarious edge. Push too far, too fast, and you risk upsetting the delicate equilibrium we are sworn to maintain-"

Malachor's eyes homed in on her as she approached, narrowing in intensity. "Aviara," he acknowledged, his voice carrying a noticeable hint of annoyance as he pronounced her name. "I think your constant fretting is unnecessary, as usual."

With a sorrowful expression, Aviara paused at the altar's edge, her gaze fixed on her once-beloved friend. She gazed upon a cherished tree, its life draining away from an unseen toxin, its once vibrant leaves wilting, and its roots decaying beneath the bark. "Malachor, you are not the same anymore."

The response came with a humorless laugh. "Aviara, you are mistaking ambition for an illness." He looked back at the altar, where a swirling mass of powerful energies materialized above the stone covered in ancient symbols, a tumultuous tangle of fundamental forces pushing against reality's delicate, ethereal nature. With an ecstatic fervor, Malachor declared, "Today, I am breaking free from the shackles that hold back our potential." "Today, I will reshape the very firmament of our world!"

"Malachor, this is utter foolishness!" Aviara's composure shattered as she cried in genuine fear. To save him from the edge, she lunged towards him with her slender fingers outstretched as if trying to wrench him back forcefully. However, just as she was about to reach him, an invisible force crashed into her with incredible power, causing her to lose her breath and stumble backward. The glade quivered in terror as the earth rumbled with a deep-rooted dread while Malachor's dark enchantments pierced the very essence of reality.

"Experience the beginning of a new era!" With a powerful, piercing cry, Malachor's voice broke through the din of tortured space and the roaring emptiness. Using a precise motion, he positioned the last component of the spell, channeling all his determination into the pulsating energy field.

The world's balance hung in the air momentarily as powers beyond mortal comprehension strained against their containment. A loud noise echoed, resembling the agonizing cry of a deity, as the Cosmic Rift tore apart, violently ripping a jagged hole in the fabric of reality. Shadows erupted from the abyss like a tide of ravenous, writhing darkness, obliterating the glade's meager illumination with the same certainty as a hurricane destroying a candle.

Malachor stood unwavering amidst the turbulent storm, his laughter resounding—a distorted hymn of triumph and rebellion against the very essence of life.

"Put an end to it!" The loud noise of uncontrolled chaos drowned out Aviara's desperate plea while the encroaching darkness swallowed her outstretched hand. Her only option was to observe, filled with horror and disbelief, as Malachor became engulfed by the forces he had unleashed. Dissolving into the swirling shadows, the voracious rift expanded, devouring everything in sight.

Once the unnatural storm finally subsided, the clearing was filled with eerie stillness. In the absence of stars, the ancient trees stood as skeletal remnants, their branches stretching towards a sky devoid of life, while the once beautiful and vibrant grass had transformed into lifeless ash. The center of the destruction revealed a hideous scar on the ground, marking the spot where the altar once stood. The land served as a haunting reminder of the chaos and betrayal that had unfolded.

Aviara found herself in a desolate setting, tears streaming down her face like glistening rivulets. The dark genesis that Malachor had brought into existence had devoured him completely, but she felt a profound sadness, knowing that this was the start. With the balance destroyed, Erenor faced the threat of destruction, and Aviara stood alone against the growing darkness.

Struggling to get up, she felt the wind strengthen, carrying faint whispers that encircled her like serpents, ready to suffocate her hope.

Beyond the veil, Malachor's voice echoed, offering both a scornful challenge and a menacing pledge. "Aviara, mourn the disturbance of your precious equilibrium."

Stealing her resolve, Aviara squared her shoulders and took in the view of the devastated land. The War of Shadow had begun, and she knew that the upcoming conflicts would decide the destiny of their world. Regardless of how the night grew darker, she refused to give up. Until her last moment, she will fight fiercely for hope and the sake of Erenor.

With this, the Chronicles of Erenor begin, recounting the fabled exploits of the courageous heroes who united against the shadowy forces, bringing about a radiant future for the Land, its cities, its enchantments, and the myriads of creatures and people that call it home.

ERENOR'S DESTINY

BOOK 3

The Chronicles of Erenor

Chapter 1

RUMORS OF BLACK MAGIC

Golden rays of sunlight poured through the open window, illuminating Lysandra's features and casting a warm glow on her sleeping form. She slowly stirred and opened her eyes, taking in the familiar sight of her bedroom. Her long silver-blonde hair cascaded down her back like a shimmering waterfall.

She felt a tingling sensation from the dark energy inside her as a surge of resolve rushed through her veins. It reminded her of her demonic ancestry and the immense power she wielded as the last mage of Erenor. Closing her eyes, Lysandra focused on the light within, pushing back against the darkness threatening to consume her.

She couldn't let it win. Not when Erenor needed her more than ever before. Rumors of black magic emerging in pockets across the land had reached their ears, and the looming return of Malachor—a powerful sorcerer who had once brought Erenor to its knees—hung in the air like a gathering storm.

With determined purpose, Lysandra slipped out of bed and padded her bare feet across the cool stone floor. She dressed quickly in a simple tunic and breeches, securing her sword belt around her waist. The weight of the blade was a comforting reminder of her inner strength.

In the kitchen, Aerin stood by the hearth, stirring a pot of steaming porridge. The earthy scents of herbs and spices filled the air, mingling with the aroma of freshly baked bread. As she approached him in the doorway, Lysandra couldn't help but take in his appearance—tall and robust, with tousled dark hair ruffled from sleep.

He was her companion, rock, and love on this journey.

"Good morning, my love," Aerin said with a smile that made Lysandra's heart beat as she entered the room. "Breakfast is almost ready."

Lysandra crossed the room, slipping her arms around Aerin's waist and resting her chin on his shoulder. "Smells delicious."

Aerin turned, gathering her close. His lips brushed her forehead, a tender gesture that spoke volumes. "How did you sleep?"

"My dreams were a mess," Lysandra admitted, frowning. "They were full of dark shadows and whispers. The threat is getting stronger, Aerin."

Aerin's expression mirrored her concern. "I know, it's troubling news about Malachor's return. But we'll figure it out together, Lysandra. You're not alone in this."

Lysandra nodded, grateful for his support. "I was thinking we should go see Master Elarion today. Maybe he can help me control my powers and give us insight into Malachor's plans."

"Good idea," Aerin agreed. "Elarion always knows what to do. And maybe he can help us figure out who or what we're up against."

A loud bark interrupted their conversation, and they both turned to see Shadow, their loyal wolf companion, lounging in the sun outside. His sharp, amber eyes scanned the area, ever watchful.

"We should bring Shadow with us," Lysandra suggested. "He might sense something we don't."

Aerin nodded as he served them bowls of porridge. "Excellent idea. Shadow's instincts have saved us before."

As they ate, the weight of their mission hung heavy in the air. They quickly finished, eager to get going.

Before they left, Aerin took Lysandra's hand and looked into her eyes with unwavering love. "No matter what happens, I want you to know I love you more than anything. I'll stand by you through everything; our love is a beacon of hope in the darkest times."

Tears welled in Lysandra's eyes at his words. "I love you too, Aerin. More than anything else in this world."

She leaned in for a kiss that promised a future together, no matter how uncertain.

"Let's go," she said with determination after they broke apart. "Master Elarion is waiting, and we have a world to save."

They stepped out into the sun, hand in hand, with Shadow by their side. The road ahead was dangerous and uncertain, but they were ready to face whatever came their way. Failure was not an option when it came to protecting Erenor and all that they loved.

Lysandra and Aerin weaved through the bustling streets of Tyrannis, hand in hand. The city was well-known for its bustling markets and diverse population, but dark energy pulsed through Lysandra's veins and consumed her mind. She could feel it, like a shadow lurking beneath her skin, waiting to be unleashed.

Aerin squeezed her hand, reminding her she wasn't alone in this struggle. "Are you okay?" he asked.

"I'm fine," Lysandra said with a forced smile. "Let's just hurry to Master Elarion's cottage."

As they navigated the lively crowds, merchants shouted about their wares, and street performers vied for attention with their juggling and dancing skills.

Suddenly, a cloaked figure stepped out from the shadows of a narrow alley. "Step right up, my friends, and have your fortunes read," the cloaked figure called out in a mysterious, melodic voice. "I can tell you of the secrets that lie ahead and the twists of fate that await you. A silver piece is a small price for a glimpse into the unknown."

Lysandra shook her head while holding onto Aerin tighter. "No, thank you. We're in a hurry."

The fortune-teller's eyes glinted beneath his hood. "But who knows what secrets the future holds? Are you sure you don't want a glimpse?"

Before Lysandra could respond, Aerin spoke up. "She said no. Now, if you'll excuse us,

The fortune-teller bowed and disappeared back into the shadows. Lysandra shivered, feeling an odd sense of foreboding wash over her. Glancing at Aerin, she saw the same unease reflected in his eyes.

They continued down quieter streets until they reached Master Elarion's cottage, a familiar yet anxiety-inducing sight for Lysandra. Tucked away in a grove of ancient trees in the SilvernDeor Forest, the cottage's thatched roof and whitewashed walls were a welcome sight.

As they approached, Lysandra's heart hammered in her chest with the weight of her concerns. "I hope Master Elarion can help us," she said to Aerin.

He gave her a reassuring smile. "Don't worry, we'll figure it out."

A knock on the door interrupted the stillness of Master Elarion's home.

The weathered door swung open with a creak to reveal his

wizened face.

"Ah, Lysandra and Aerin! I've been waiting for you," he said with a twinkle in his eyes, welcoming them into the cozy house.

The scent of herbs and old books filled the air as they followed him into his study, where ancient tomes and artifacts cluttered every surface. Master Elarion settled into an armchair while Lysandra and Aerin sat on the plush sofa.

"Now, what brings you two here?" he asked kindly, his gaze locking onto Lysandra's troubled expression.

Lysandra took a deep breath before confessing her struggles with controlling her dark powers. "It's like a raging storm inside me, threatening to break free at any moment."

Aerin added, "With Malachor's return, we fear for Lysandra's safety."

Master Elarion's expression turned grave. "Malachor has returned? This is troubling news indeed."

Lysandra nodded, her voice tight. "We don't know what he's planning, but it can't be good. And my powers are becoming more unstable by the day."

Understanding filled Master Elarion's features as he rose from his chair and went to one of the bookshelves lining the walls. He returned with a few dusty tomes in hand.

"These books contain ancient techniques for harnessing and controlling dark magic," he explained as he laid them out before Lysandra and Aerin. "But I must warn you—it will not be easy. It will require great strength and unwavering commitment to the light."

Lysandra carefully caressed the spine of one of the ancient tomes, running her fingers over the rough leather cover and tracing the embossed designs. The pages felt cool and smooth under her touch, but they seemed to pulsate with a magical energy that made her skin tingle. She could sense the weight of their knowledge and power within their very being.

As she looked up at Master Elarion, his piercing gaze met hers with pride and determination. Lysandra could feel Aerin's hand in hers, grounding her as they prepared for what was to come. She knew this journey toward mastering dark magic would be treacherous, but she was ready to do whatever it took to protect Erenor and those she loved.

With a nod from Master Elarion, they began their training. He carefully opened one of the books, its crackling pages filled with faded text and illustrations. "The key to controlling your magic lies in finding balance and unity within yourself," he explained. "You must learn to embrace both the light and the dark without letting either overwhelm you."

Lysandra leaned in closer, her eyes scanning the words as Master Elarion continued. "Through meditation and focus, you can tap into the energy that flows through you and the world around you."

She closed her eyes and followed his instructions, letting herself sink into deep concentration. With each breath, she could feel Aerin's presence beside her, anchoring her even further.

And then it happened. A spark ignited within her mind, setting off a swirling vortex of light and shadow—an untamed force threatening to consume her. But Master Elarion's voice brought her back: "Do not fight the power, but do not let it control you. Find the balance within yourself."

Lysandra took a deep breath and focused on the steady beat of her heart, slowly finding harmony within the chaos. Beside her, she could feel Aerin doing the same—his earthy magic pulsing with life and growth.

"Now," Master Elarion said, breaking the silence, "reach out to each other. Let your powers mingle and intertwine, finding harmony in their unity."

As they extended their palms towards each other, Lysandra opened her eyes and met Aerin's gaze. Their combined magic crackled and sparked between them, a rush of energy threatening to sweep them away. But together, they found balance and control, their powers intertwining in a dance of perfect harmony.

Thanks to the unbreakable bond their love had created, they clung to one another amid the confusion and upheaval. Slowly but surely, they gained control over their magic, learning to wield it as a tool instead of fearing it as a force. Lysandra could feel the intensity of their bond like a raging fire burning inside her. Aerin stood firm beside her, his presence a solid pillar of support as they faced each challenge together. At that moment, she knew that nothing could tear them apart.

As if sensing her thoughts, Master Elarion spoke again. "Remember," he said, his voice wise and kind, "your true strength lies not in your powers alone but in the unity you share." Lysandra and Aerin nodded in agreement, their gazes never wavering from each other. They were aware of the dangers on their journey, but together, they felt invincible.

Master Elarion's eyes shone with pride and nostalgia as he settled into his old armchair. "You know," he began, his voice filled with reminiscence, "when I was your age, I also struggled with my magic."

As their mentor's words captivated them, Lysandra and Aerin exchanged surprised looks.

"I had to learn to embrace both the light and dark aspects of my powers," Master Elarion continued, his gaze drifting off as if lost in memory. "It was no easy feat. Sometimes, I feared the darkness would consume me, and I would lose myself completely."

Bringing his attention back to the present, Master Elarion locked eyes with Lysandra and Aerin again. "But you two have something I did not have back then," he said gently. "Each other." He smiled warmly at them. "Your bond is a rare gift, a strength that will guide you through even the darkest times."

Aerin and Lysandra nodded, their hands entwined tightly. "We got this," Aerin said, his voice full of conviction.

Lysandra's eyes lit up with determination as she looked into Aerin's gaze. "Nothing can stop us when we're together," she promised.

Master Elarion beamed at their resolve. "Don't forget, real power comes from love and trust," he reminded them. "Keep your hearts open for each other, and you'll always find a way."

Aerin gave Lysandra's hand a reassuring squeeze before turning to Master Elarion. "Thanks for everything, Master," he said gratefully. "We wouldn't have made it this far without your guidance."

The old mage chuckled softly. "You two have grown into amazing sorcerers," he praised. "Now go out there with courage and faith, knowing that your bond will guide you."

As if sensing their newfound determination, Master Elarion got up from his chair and gestured toward the door. "You've learned a lot today," he said proudly. "But remember, your journey is far from over. You'll face challenges and darkness that will test your bond."

Lysandra and Aerin stood tall, ready for whatever came next. "We got this," Lysandra confidently declared, echoing Aerin's earlier statement. "Together, we can handle anything."

Master Elarion nodded with a slight smile on his lips. "Then off you go," he said, motioning for them to leave. "Your destiny awaits, my young friends. And know that the fate of Erenor lies in your hands."

Lysandra and Aerin left the cottage, gratefully nodding to their mentor. The sun set, casting a warm glow over the land.

"We need to find Feyla and Eolande," Lysandra stated, already focused on their next move. "They'll know what to do about Malachor. Together, we can defeat him. We have to."

Aerin reached for her hand again, his eyes shining with love and determination. "Together," he whispered.

Lysandra's fierce smile grew wider as she nodded. "All of us together again," she replied, grabbing Aerin's hand. Her sadness appeared briefly in her eyes. "Except for..."

Aerin squeezed her hand. "We all miss him, my love, but Harrow will always be right here," he said, covering his heart with his left hand.

She nodded. "I know. We need to ensure that his sacrifice wasn't for nothing. We can beat Melachor and save Erenor." She cleared her throat and lifted her head high. "This time, it must be forever. We can't go on like this—putting out one brush fire after another. We must put out the roaring flames that started it all. Malachor."

Golden rays of sunlight poured through the open window, illuminating Lysandra's determined features as she fastened her sword belt around her waist. The weight of the blade was a reassuring presence, a tangible reminder of the battles she had fought and the challenges ahead.

"Ready to go?" Aerin asked, his voice cutting through the morning stillness.

Lysandra turned to face him, a smile playing on her lips. "Definitely."

They made their way through the bustling streets of Tyrannis, the city's vibrant energy starkly contrasting with the looming threat of Malachor's return. Shadow, their loyal wolf companion, trotted alongside them, his keen senses alert for any signs of danger.

A cloaked figure stepped out from the shadows as they navigated the crowded marketplace. "Care to have your fortune told, my friends?" the figure rasped, his eyes glinting beneath his hood.

Lysandra's hand instinctively went to her sword hilt. "We don't have time for games," she said, her tone sharp.

The figure chuckled, a sound that sent shivers down her spine. "Ah, but the future waits for no one, young mage. Especially not for those who bear the weight of a dark legacy."

Aerin stepped forward, his stance protective. "We'll make our future, thank you."

As they pushed past the fortune-teller, Lysandra couldn't shake the unease in her gut. The remnants of her dark power pulsed beneath her skin, a constant reminder of the fine line she walked between light and shadow.

They arrived at Feyla's workshop with a heavy scent of oil and metal. Eolande greeted them at the door, her elven grace a welcome sight.

"Thank the gods, you're here," Feyla said, her brow furrowed as she hunched over her workbench. "I've been working on a device to disrupt Malachor's magic, but I need a rare crystal from the Caverns of Lumina to power it."

"The Caverns of Lumina?" Aerin asked, his eyebrows raised. "Aren't there ancient sentinels watching over that area?"

Feyla nodded grimly. "Yes, but it's our only chance. Malachor's power grows stronger every day."

Lysandra met Aerin's gaze, a silent understanding passing between them. "We'll get the crystal," she said, her voice filled with resolve. "Failure is not an option."

Eolande placed a hand on Lysandra's shoulder, her touch gentle yet firm. "Remember, Lysandra, your magic is a gift. Embrace it, and let it guide you through the darkness."

Lysandra swallowed hard, the weight of responsibility heavy on her shoulders. "I won't let you down," she promised.

Shadow nudged Lysandra's hand as they prepared to leave, his amber eyes filled with unwavering loyalty. She kneeled, burying her face in his thick fur. "We'll be back soon, boy," she whispered. "Keep them safe while we're gone."

The journey to the Caverns of Lumina was treacherous, with the path winding through dense forests and over jagged mountain passes. Lysandra and Aerin pushed forward, their determination fueled by the knowledge that the fate of Erenor rested on their success.

As they made camp for the night, huddled around a small fire, Aerin broke the silence. "Do you ever wonder what life would be like if we weren't constantly fighting against the darkness?" he asked, his gaze distant.

Lysandra poked at the embers with a stick, watching the sparks dance in the night air. "Sometimes," she admitted. "But then I remember all the people counting on us, and I know we can't give up."

"You're right," Aerin said, his voice filled with conviction. "We're in this together, no matter what."

The next day, they reached the entrance to the Caverns of Lumina, the crystal formations casting an eerie glow in the darkness. Lysandra felt a chill run down her spine as they stepped inside, the ancient magic of the place palpable in the air.

Suddenly, a figure emerged from the shadows, its form shifting and twisting in the dim light. "Who dares enter the domain of the guardians?" it demanded, its voice echoing off the cavern walls.

Lysandra stepped forward, her hand on her sword hilt. "We come seeking the Crystal of Lumina," she said, her voice steady despite the fear coursing through her veins. "To protect our land from the darkness that threatens it."

The guardian regarded them for a long moment, its eyes glowing with an otherworldly light. "The crystal is not easily won," it warned. "Only those who prove themselves worthy may claim it."

Aerin glanced at Lysandra, a silent question in his eyes. She nodded, her resolve unwavering. "We'll do whatever it takes," she said.

As they ventured deeper into the caverns, Lysandra could feel her magic growing more substantial, the light within her pushing back against the darkness that threatened to consume her. With Aerin by her side, she knew they could overcome any obstacle.

Finally, they reached the chamber where the Crystal of Lumina rested, its brilliance nearly blinding in the gloom. As Lysandra reached out to claim it, a voice whispered in her mind, ancient and powerful.

"Remember, young mage," it said, "the true strength lies not in the crystal but in the bonds that unite you. Trust in your friends and in the love that guides your path."

With the crystal in hand, Lysandra and Aerin returned to Tyrannis, their hearts lighter despite the challenges ahead. They knew that with their friends by their side, they could face anything Malachor threw at them.

As they entered Feyla's workshop, the inventor's face lit up with relief. "You did it!" she exclaimed, embracing them.

Eolande smiled, her eyes shining with pride. "I never doubted you for a moment," she said.

Lysandra handed the crystal to Feyla, watching as the inventor carefully placed it into the device she had been working on. "With this, we stand a chance against Malachor," she said, her voice filled with determination.

Lysandra felt a sense of hope rising within her as they gathered around the workbench, the glow of the crystal illuminating their faces. They had faced the darkness before and would face it again, united in their love for each other and their land.

The road ahead was uncertain, but one thing was clear: together, they were unstoppable.

Chapter 2

SHADOWS OF THE PAST

Under a sky awash with the pastel hues of dawn, the air vibrated with the hum of magic. Aerin kneeled on the grass, his palms hovering above the earth as tendrils of green energy spiraled into the soil. Beside him, Lysandra mirrored his actions; her eyes focused intently on the wildflower she had coaxed back to health.

"Like this?" Aerin asked, uncertainty threading through his deep voice.

"Deeper," Lysandra instructed, her tone firm yet encouraging. "You've got to feel the life in the earth; connect with it."

Aerin's brow furrowed as he channeled more power, and the once-withered plant before him gradually unfurled its petals. The sight should have filled him with pride, but all he felt was disquiet.

"Good," she said, a smile touching her lips. "You're a natural, you know."

"I don't feel natural," he admitted, allowing the magic to ebb away. "This... healing. It's a world apart from what I used to do. My hands..." He trailed off, staring at the scars crisscrossing his skin—reminders of a darker time.

"Your hands are capable of so much good now, Aerin." Lysandra reached out, her fingers brushing against his. "The past doesn't have to define us."

"Easy for you to say," he muttered, pulling away to stand. "You haven't haunted people's nightmares."

"Maybe not," she conceded, rising to join him. "But I've fought against the darkness in my blood daily. We both have shadows to overcome."

Aerin sighed, his gaze locked on the horizon where light battled the remnants of night. "I keep thinking about those I hunted. How can I ask the world for forgiveness when I can't forgive myself?"

"Because everyone deserves a chance at redemption," Lysandra said softly, touching his shoulder. "Even former witch-hunters turned healers."

"Especially them," he replied, a wry smile tugging at his lips despite the turmoil inside.

"Let's try again," she suggested, gesturing to a patch of trampled grass. "There's plenty of healing left to do."

As they settled back into their practice, Aerin couldn't shake the weight of his past. But with Lysandra by his side and the warmth of the rising sun on his face, he began to believe that maybe, just maybe, there was hope for him yet.

"Focus on the wound, Aerin," Lysandra urged, her voice a gentle nudge. "Let your magic be the salve, not just the intent."

Aerin closed his eyes, drawing in a deep breath. A soft glow emanated from his hands as he hovered them over the gash on the practice dummy. The edges of the flesh-like material began to knit together, slowly at first, then with more confidence.

"See? You're getting there," Lysandra said, a smile playing on her lips as she watched the transformation. "Healing is part of who you are now."

"I just wish I could heal my scars as easily," he admitted, the light fading from his touch as the task was completed.

"Scars are reminders," she replied. "They teach us lessons and make us stronger. The real healing happens here." She tapped a finger against his temple, then placed it over his heart.

Before Aerin could respond, a burst of laughter echoed through the clearing.

Feyla and Eolande strode into view, the former's gear clinking with each step, the latter moving with elven grace.

"Hope we haven't missed all the fun," Feyla quipped, adjusting the goggles perched atop her head.

"Never too late to join," Lysandra welcomed them, gesturing towards the array of training elements scattered across the field.

"Show us what you've been honing, Feyla," Aerin said, eager for a distraction from his thoughts.

"I thought you'd never ask." With a grin, Feyla pulled out a small gadget. At the flick of a switch, it whirred to life, projecting a shield of pulsating light around them. "My latest defense charm—Malachor won't see this coming!"

"Your mind is a treasure trove, Feyla," Lysandra beamed, examining the device with interest.

Eolande, quiet until now, unsheathed his sword, the blade singing as it cut the air. "And I've been perfecting a few new maneuvers. I'm used to my bow and arrow. This sword is new and hopefully more deadly. It will come in handy when we face Malachor's minions," he said, demonstrating a series of swift, elegant strokes that left trails of shimmering energy in the air.

"It looks like we're building quite the arsenal," Aerin remarked, impressed despite himself.

"Indeed," Lysandra agreed. "Each of us brings something unique to this fight. Together, our strength is multiplied."

"Teamwork is our greatest enchantment," Eolande said, sliding his sword back into its sheath.

"And with every challenge we face, we grow closer and stronger," Feyla added, deactivating her charm. "I repeat, Malachor won't know what hit him."

"Thanks to both of you," Aerin said sincerely, feeling renewed camaraderie. "I'm starting to believe we can do this."

"Belief is the first step," Lysandra affirmed, reaching for his hand. "Now, let's prepare. We have allies to rally and a shadow realm to get to and conquer."

"Lead the way," Aerin said, a spark of determination lighting his dark eyes as they set off together. Their path ahead was woven with trust and the promise of adventure.

Aerin swung his sword in a wide arc, the whoosh of the blade mingling with the hum of magic in the air. Lysandra deflected it gracefully, her sword meeting his with a resounding clang that sent vibrations down Aerin's arm.

"Good form," she praised, a smile tugging at her lips as she danced back, preparing for another exchange.

"Trying to keep up with you," Aerin replied, feinting left before lunging right, only to find Lysandra no longer there. She had anticipated his move, stepping aside with the ease of flowing water.

"Predictable," she scolded, though her eyes sparkled with mischief.

"Think so?" Aerin's response was a gust of wind magic, conjured with a flick of his wrist, aimed not to harm but to startle.

Lysandra's laughter rang out as she countered with a shield, her sea-green eyes alight with the thrill of their mock battle.

"Nice try, but you'll have to do better than that," she called out, sending a ripple of earth magic towards him. The ground beneath his feet shuddered, and he jumped back just in time.

"Is that what we're doing now? Using magic?" Feyla interjected, her mechanical devices whirring as she joined the fray, a mischievous glint in her eye. A small orb flew from her hand, releasing a net of light that splayed across the clearing like a spider's web.

"Gotcha!" Eolande's voice echoed as he slipped through the

shadows cast by the tall trees surrounding them, emerging just behind Aerin. His blade, glowing with enchanted light, stopped a hair's breadth from entering Aerin's throat.

"Yield," Eolande declared with a smirk.

"Alright, alright," Aerin conceded with a laugh, surrendering his hands. "You got me."

As the sparring wound down, the group caught their breath, grinning and exchanging congratulatory nods and claps. They worked as a unit because of their mutual trust and zeal for battling the darkness that threatened their world.

"Hey," Lysandra said, touching Aerin's shoulder as the others dispersed to tend to their gear. "You did well today. Both with the sword and your magic."

"Thanks," he replied, his smile fading as he looked down at his hands—the hands of a healer, yet still those of a former witch hunter. "Sometimes, I'm unsure if I'm cut out for this... this healing path."

"Because of your past?" Lysandra asked gently, her gaze locking on his.

"Yeah." Aerin exhaled slowly, the weight of memories pressing down on him. "Hunting those I now protect... it haunts m e."

Lysandra nodded, understanding flickering in her eyes. "But you are more than your past, Aerin. You've grown. You've changed. That guilt shows you care and that you have a good heart. Don't let it anchor you to who you once were."

"Easy for you to say," he muttered, though part of him knew

she was right.

"Is it?" Lysandra tilted her head, her expression softening. "Every day, I fight the darkness within me, remember? We each have our demons. It's how we face them that defines us. Yours led you to a new purpose—one of healing, of making amends."

"Maybe." Aerin sighed, the burden inside him easing slightly under the warmth of her words.

"Trust in who you are now, not who you were," she encouraged, squeezing his shoulder. "You're a healer, Aerin. You bring light to the shadows. That's something to be proud of."

"Thanks, Love. I... I needed to hear that," he admitted, a small smile returning as he met her steady gaze.

"Anytime," she replied, her smile widening. "Now, come on. Let's join the others. We've got a quest to plan, allies to rally, and adventure ahead."

"Together, then," Aerin said, feeling a surge of determination.

"Of course, what else?" Lysandra affirmed, and they returned to rejoin their friends, ready to face whatever lay ahead.

Lysandra's fingers traced the intricate patterns etched into her leather bracers, a subtle glow emanating from the runes. She looked up, locking eyes with Aerin, who had just shared his tumultuous past and doubts about his path as a healer.

"Your journey reminds me of my own," she began, her voice steady despite the tempest always raging within her. "I was born from darkness, a lineage I neither chose nor wanted. But it's a part of me, as much as the air I breathe."

Aerin leaned against a moss-covered boulder, watching her intently. "How do you deal with it? The constant push and pull?"

"By accepting both sides," she said, letting her hand drop to her side. "By understanding that my power doesn't define me, but how I use it does. I choose light daily, even when shadows claw at my soul." She offered a wry smile. "It's an ongoing battle, one that makes me stronger."

"It sounds exhausting," he replied, but his tone held respect.

"It is." Lysandra nodded, and then her gaze shifted beyond Aerin's shoulder to where Feyla and Eolande were packing their gear.

"Hey, you two! Would you be willing to share your wisdom on embracing who you are?" she called out to them.

Feyla trotted over, a bundle of rope slung over her shoulder. Her brown eyes sparkled with an irrepressible spirit. "Oh, you mean how I'm the only non-magical bean in this magical stew?" She laughed, waving her free hand dismissively. "Magic or no magic, I have brains, guts, and gadgets. That's enough for me."

"See?" Lysandra pointed it out. "Feyla might not have spells at her fingertips, but her inventions are as potent as any incantation."

Eolande joined them, his quiver secured to his back and his new sword at his hip. "Each of us has our unique strengths," he added smoothly. "Mine lies in my heritage, bow, and ability to see things others might miss. We're all different, and that's not just okay—it's necessary. Together, we form a balance."

"Exactly," Lysandra agreed. "We can't escape who we are, nor should we want to. Our differences give us strength, and our friendship binds us together. That's how we'll face whatever comes."

Aerin absorbed their words, a sense of camaraderie swelling within him. "Thank you, all of you. You're right; we're stronger together. And maybe, just maybe, that's enough to tip the scales in our favor."

"Of course it is," Feyla chirped, punching Aerin lightly on the arm. "Now come on, let's get moving. Adventure waits for no one!"

"Nor does destiny," Eolande remarked, offering a reassuring nod.

"Or love," Lysandra added quietly, glancing at Aerin with a meaningful look that spoke volumes.

"Then let's not keep them waiting," Aerin concluded, standing tall as they gathered their belongings, ready to enter the unknown as one unified force.

The wind howled through the craggy peaks of Mount Eldar as Aerin and his companions huddled around a flickering campfire, the night air biting into their skin. The flames danced and cast elongated shadows against the rocks, mirroring the group's tense expressions.

"Malachor won't be expecting a direct assault," Lysandra said, her eyes reflecting the firelight. "That might give us the element of surprise."

"Aviara's intel was clear," Eolande murmured, running a hand through his blonde hair. "Malachor's stronghold is fortified with dark magic. We can't just storm in."

"Nor should we," Feyla said, fidgeting with a small piece of gear she'd pulled from one of her many pockets. "We'll need a distraction. Something to draw his forces out."

Lysandra nodded, considering. "A frontal attack could serve that purpose, but it's risky. We don't have the numbers for a prolonged battle."

"Then we'll need allies." Aerin leaned forward, the light softening the hard lines of his face. "I might know a few entities who owe me a favor. And they're not exactly on friendly terms with Malachor."

"Entities?" Feyla raised an eyebrow, intrigued.

"During my... witch-hunting days," Aerin explained with a grimace, "I crossed paths with magical beings. Some I fought, others I aided. It's time to call in those debts."

"An alliance of convenience, then," Lysandra mused, her hair glinting like quicksilver. "But will they be willing to fight alongside us?"

"Desperate times, right?" Aerin met Lysandra's gaze, a silent plea for understanding there. "If Malachor isn't stopped, it won't just be humans suffering under his tyranny."

"True enough," Eolande conceded, his tone even. "The whole

of Erenor would fall into darkness."

"Besides," Aerin added, a faint smile tugging at the corner of his mouth, "there's something poetic about former foes standing together against a common enemy."

"Poetic or not," Feyla said, her eyes sparkling with mischief, "it beats going in alone."

"Agreed. We reach out to these allies of yours, Aerin," Lysandra decided, her voice carrying the weight of command. "We forge a united front and strike when Malachor least expects it."

"Then it's settled," Aerin said, satisfaction lacing his words. "Tomorrow, we begin anew. For Erenor, for freedom—and the future we all deserve."

As the fire crackled between them, the friendship and shared purpose bonds drew them closer. Together, they were more than just a band of rebels; they were a beacon of hope against the encroaching darkness.

"Alright, I've also got something in mind," Lysandra announced, breaking the contemplative silence over the group. Her eyes held a glint of strategy as she leaned forward, her fingers drumming rhythmically on the map spread before them.

"Hit us with it," Feyla prodded, her gaze flicking up from the intricate gears of a contraption she was tweaking. It was one of her less imposing inventions, designed for communication rather than combat, but its purpose was no less vital.

"Remember the band of rebels we ran into a fortnight ago?"

Lysandra's question was met with nods around the circle. "They've been raiding Malachor's supply lines for months. They know the Shadowrealm's ins and outs."

"More than we do," Aerin interjected with respect and concern. His hands, which once would have clutched his weapons in suspicion, now rested calmly on his knees.

"Exactly." Lysandra's expression softened momentarily at Aerin's admission. "If we can get them on our side, they could be invaluable. They're familiar with the terrain, the traps, and the dark magic at play. We need that edge."

"Are you suggesting an alliance?" Eolande's voice was calm, yet the slight raise of his eyebrow betrayed his intrigue.

"More than that," Lysandra continued, her tone firm. "We team up. Combine forces. They give us intel, and we give them extra muscle. And magic." She shot a pointed look at each of them, acknowledging their strengths.

"Seems sound," Aerin mused, rubbing his chin thoughtfully. "We share a common enemy. And there's power in numbers."

"Then we're agreed?" Lysandra asked, seeking confirmation from each member of their tight-knit cadre.

"Agreed," they chorused, with varying degrees of enthusiasm.

"Let's not forget the risks," Feyla chimed in, her brown eyes serious for once. "This isn't just a stroll through the woods. Those rebels are playing a dangerous game."

"Which is why we'll approach cautiously," Lysandra assured her, reaching out to clasp Feyla's shoulder with a reassuring squeeze. "But we won't win this fight alone. With the rebels, we stand a chance."

"Then let's not waste time," Aerin declared, rising to his feet with a new purpose. "Those rebels won't find themselves."

"Nor will they wait for us if they believe we're not coming," Eolande added, standing gracefully. "Time is a luxury we don't have."

"Then it's settled," Lysandra said, rolling up the map with a snap of her wrists. "We set out at dawn. Rest up; tomorrow, we face the unknown."

As the night deepened around them, the four companions exchanged resolute looks. There was comfort in their unity, and determination sparked within each heart like flint to steel. They were ready to face whatever the treacherous terrain might throw their way—with each other and the rebels, whom they hoped to call allies.

Dawn had barely kissed the sky with its timid light when the quartet set out, venturing into the treacherous terrain between them and the rebels. The map had warned of perils, but the reality was far more daunting: ravines yawned like open wounds in the earth, rivers frothed with untamed ferocity, and dark forests whispered secrets that could unsettle the bravest of hearts.

"It looks like we've got a choice," Aerin said, eyeing the chasm before them. "Either we find a way across or take the long route around."

"Let me check my pack," Feyla murmured, rummaging

through her gadgets. With a triumphant "Aha!" she pulled out a compact grappling hook device. "This should do the trick."

"Trust Feyla to come prepared for a siege," Lysandra quipped, her sea-green eyes twinkling with approval as she watched Feyla expertly attach the hook to a sturdy-looking tree across the gap.

"Give it a test," Aerin suggested, his protective instinct flaring despite his knowledge of Feyla's competence.

"Already on it," Feyla replied, tugging on the rope with all her might. Satisfied, she looped one end around a tree on their side. "Who wants to be the guinea pig?"

"Guess that's my cue," Lysandra volunteered, stepping forward confidently.

With a running start, she clipped onto the rope and swung across the ravine, landing nimbly on the other side.

"Show off," Aerin called after her, but he couldn't suppress the proud smile that crept onto his lips. One by one, they followed until all four stood on the far side of the chasm, breathing heavily but unscathed.

"Next challenge?" Eolande asked, brushing a lock of hair out of his face.

"That would be the river," Feyla pointed out. A roar reached their ears, signaling the presence of rushing water nearby.

"I can't swing over this one," Aerin muttered, squinting at the white-capped rapids.

"Perhaps not, but..." Feyla trailed off, digging into her bag once more. This time, she produced several inflatable bladders and a coil of rope. "We can make a raft. It won't win any prizes but will get us across."

"Your mind is a treasure trove, Feyla," Lysandra said, helping to tie the bladders together and reinforce them with binding spells. Magic met mechanics in a symphony of survival as the impromptu raft took shape.

"Is everyone ready? We'll need to paddle hard and keep our balance," Feyla instructed as they pushed the raft into the tumultuous water. The river fought them every inch of the way, waves crashing over the sides and soaking them to the bone, but their determination held firm.

"Stay focused! We're nearly there!" Lysandra shouted over the roar, pushing against the current with an oar fashioned from a broken branch.

"Look out for that eddy!" Aerin warned, his voice laced with urgency as he pointed downstream.

"Got it!" Eolande called back, leaning her weight against the swirling pull of the water.

Finally, with muscles burning and hearts racing, they landed on the opposite bank, dragging their makeshift craft ashore.

"Nice work, team," Feyla said, shaking water from her hair. "But I'm hoping the next part of the journey involves less swimming."

"Agreed!" Lysandra laughed, squeezing water from her hair. "I think we've had enough baths for one day."

"Let's hope the forest is kinder to us," Aerin said, leading the way into the ominous blanket of trees that marked the final stretch of their journey to the rebels' hiding place.

The group pressed on through the thick, looming shadows, staying close together as they navigated the eerie landscape. Now and then, a distant howl or the faint rustle of unseen creatures would pierce the silence, making them acutely aware of the lurking dangers. Because of their friendship, they were steadfast in facing whatever danger lay ahead in the heart of darkness.

As they trekked through the dense undergrowth, Lysandra's boots sank into the spongy moss, leading them to a clearing shielded by twisted trees and cascading vines. The atmosphere was already eerie, but the lingering effects of fey magic and the palpable sense of relief from her allies gave it an uncanny edge.

"Could this be it?" Aerin's low voice rumbled as he surveyed the surroundings, his eyes betraying a weariness from countless battles.

"Lysandra, look," came a calm voice as Eolande pointed to a discreet emblem carved into a tree trunk—the rebels' mark. "This is our destination."

The symbol was a subtle signal that the uninitiated could easily miss, but to the group, it was a sign of hope. Feyla nodded and brushed past the symbol with her fingers, acknowledging its significance.

"Good eyes, Eolande," she said, a smirk playing on her lips despite the exhaustion that clung to her like a second skin.

Lysandra approached the tree and pressed her palm against the bark, murmuring a few words under her breath. The ground beneath them rumbled, and a passage slid open, revealing a hidden entrance bathed in the soft glow of enchanted torches.

"I always loved a good secret door," Feyla mused, stepping forward and descending into the earthen tunnel without hesitation.

The group followed, their steps echoing lightly as the passage sealed behind them, plunging them into a world where shadows danced with light. They emerged into a hollow chamber where the rebels had made their sanctuary, a place teeming with life and quiet determination.

A woman wearing leather armor with fiery curls in her hair greeted them with the words, "Welcome, friends." "I am Sylvi. You've been expected."

"Expected?" Lysandra raised an eyebrow, exchanging a glance with Aerin.

"Word travels fast when the wind carries it," Sylvi replied with a knowing smile. "Especially when it concerns those who stand against Malachor."

"Then you know why we're here," Eolande stated, his tone steady.

"Indeed. Come, there's much to discuss." Sylvi gestured for them to follow her deeper into the stronghold.

They were led to a round table covered with maps and scrolls, the walls adorned with weapons and wards against dark magic. These rebels were no strangers to battle; the air hummed with the energy of warriors ready to fight for their cause.

"Malachor's stronghold is fortified by spells ancient and vile," Sylvi began, tracing lines across a map shadowed with ominous markings. "But we've found a weakness."

"Let's hear it," Feyla said, leaning forward, her eyes alight with curiosity and the spark of challenge.

"Here," Sylvi tapped a location on the map, "a hidden pathway through the Shadowrealm. It's treacherous, but it leads straight to the heart of his domain."

Aerin frowned, his protective instincts flaring. "How can we be sure this isn't a trap?"

"Because I've walked it myself," Sylvi replied, meeting his gaze squarely. "And returned to tell the tale."

"Then we have our way in," Lysandra said with resolve. She looked at each group member, seeing the mixture of fear and bravery in their eyes. "Together, we'll face whatever darkness awaits us."

"United, we stand," Eolande affirmed, his voice a soft echo of their resolve.

"It looks like we've got ourselves a plan," Feyla added, a grin creeping onto her face. "Time to show Malachor what happens when he messes with the wrong crew."

"Indeed," Lysandra nodded, a fierce smile curving her lips. "Let's begin right now."

Chapter 3

MEETING WITH AVIARA

The flickering firelight cast a restless dance of shadows across the craggy walls of the mountain hideaway, where Lysandra and her companions huddled with the rebel faction they had joined forces with. The atmosphere was thick with tension and disquiet, broken intermittently by the murmurs of rebels sharing uneasy speculations.

"Could be she's not coming," one gruff voice muttered.

"Malachor wouldn't dare show his face again, not after last time," another countered with a hint of bravado that fooled no one.

Lysandra, however, barely heard them. She paced before the flames, each step a silent echo of the turmoil within her. Aerin watched her, his dark eyes following her movement. He understood her well enough to offer support without words, yet close enough to intercept if the weight of the world she carried became too much.

"Easy, Lys," he said softly, momentarily reaching out to still her. "She'll come."

"Will she have answers, though?" Her voice was steady, but her eyes betrayed her concern. "Every minute we wait, Malachor grows stronger."

Before Aerin could reply, a figure stepped into the circle of light, as silent as the mountain breeze. Aviara's appearance was like the arrival of a storm cloud over a tense sea—ominous and filled with the promise of turbulence.

"Aviara," Lysandra breathed deeply, relief mingling with fresh concern. "What news do you have?"

"Grave tidings, my friends," she said, her voice sad as her gaze swept over the gathered group. "Malachor has indeed resurfaced. His darkness spreads even as we speak, and if left unchecked, it will consume Erenor in its entirety."

A collective shiver ran through the rebels at his words. Lysandra clasped her hands tightly, steeling herself against the dread that threatened to overwhelm her.

"Tell us what must be done," she demanded, her resolve hardening like ice.

Aviara nodded gravely, locking eyes with her. "You need to act quickly. Your mission is twofold: we must unite the fractured alliances of your world and completely heal the celestial fracture itself. Too many evil entities have appeared since you dealt with the Ethereal Wells." She sighed. The rift has not healed completely. It would be best if you dealt with that once and for all. Only then can we hope to banish Malachor's shadow and others like him from Erenor."

"Then let's not waste any more time," Lysandra said, addressing the rebels with a commanding presence. "We've battled evil before and won. We can do it again. Our world will be saved if it's the last thing we do."

The fire seemed to burn brighter with its renewed purpose, casting a warm glow on determined faces. With Aviara's guidance and the strength of their unity, they prepared to face the darkness ahead.

"Who is Malachor, exactly?" Lysandra's voice cut through the crackling of the fire, sharp and commanding, as she fixed Aviara with an intense stare. "And how does he tie into the celestial fracture? We need to understand our enemy before we can attack."

Aerin's hand found her shoulder, a silent vow of solidarity. She could feel the warmth of his palm through her tunic, grounding her.

The flickering fire cast eerie shadows on the rough walls of the mountain hideout. Tension now hung heavy in the air, broken only by the murmurs of rebels speculating nervously after everything Aviara had said.

Let's not waste any more time," Lysandra said, addressing the rebels with a commanding presence. "We've battled evil before and won. We can do it again. Our world will be saved if it's the last thing we do."

The fire crackled, sending sparks into the ink-black sky as Lysandra's gaze hardened on the dancing flames. She imagined each spark symbolizing their unyielding determination to face whatever came next.

"Thank you, Aviara," Lysandra said, her warrior's heart ignited with newfound determination. "With your help, we'll end this threat once and for all."

"Then prepare yourselves, for tomorrow brings a challenge like no other," Aviara declared before fading away as gracefully as she appeared, leaving behind a trail of divine energy that danced like fireflies.

"It looks like we've got a plan," Aerin murmured, his grip on Lysandra's hand tightening.

"Let's make sure everyone's ready," she responded, her spirit emboldened. Together, they turned back to their allies, the glow of the impending dawn already looming on the horizon.

Lysandra's fingers traced the pommel of her sword, a rhythmic pattern that echoed the cadence of her troubled thoughts. The chill mountain air did little to cool the burning uncertainty within her.

"Are you sure we can trust her?" She asked, not daring to look into Aerin's eyes. "Aviara was our enemy not so long ago."

"Enemies become allies when the world is at stake," Aerin replied, his voice steady and grounding. He reached out, gently turning her chin to meet his gaze. "We need her knowledge,

Lysandra. Malachor won't go down without a fight."

"Indeed, he will not," interjected Master Elarion, stepping closer with a furrowed brow. "I share your doubts, but Aviara's insight is invaluable. This threat... it's beyond anything we've faced before."

Lysandra let out a slow breath, the weight of her destiny pressing down on her shoulders. She looked between the two men who had been pillars in her tumultuous life. "Alright," she conceded, her voice firm, "we'll take all the help she offers. But I'm keeping my guard up."

"Good," Eolande nodded, approval shining in his eyes. "A wise warrior never fully lowers her shield."

"Let's get moving then," Lysandra said, brushing off the lingering unease.

The group buzzed with nervous energy as they gathered their belongings. Swords clinked, potions rattled, and packs thudded against the rugged terrain as each member prepared for the journey ahead.

"Here," Aerin said, handing Lysandra her cloak, "the nights are getting colder."

"Thank you," she murmured, noticing how his fingers lingered a moment longer than necessary, a silent promise of support.

"Everyone ready?" Lysandra called out, her voice cutting through the crisp air.

One by one, affirmations were voiced, a chorus of resolve echoing among the craggy peaks.

Lysandra took a deep breath, her eyes alight with the fire of purpose. As she exhaled, a gust of wind caught her hair, whipping it into a dance around her face. "Let's make history," she declared, her tone laced with the strength of her elemental magic.

"Or rewrite it," Aerin added with a wry smile, stepping beside her.

"Either way, we're doing it together," she said, squeezing his hand, feeling the power of their intertwined destinies.

With a nod from Aviara, the group set off. The encroaching darkness gradually swallowed their silhouettes, leaving only the embers of their campfire—a small beacon of hope amidst the towering stone giants.

With a final wave, Aviara turned and vanished into the shadowy underbrush, her presence lingering like the last note of a mournful ballad. Silence settled over the group, heavy as a tapestry woven from the threads of destiny.

"I never thought I'd miss this place," Lysandra whispered, her gaze sweeping over the rocky alcove that had been their refuge. The mountains stood indifferent to their plight, ancient guardians keeping their secrets.

"Change is the only constant," Aerin replied, his voice steady. "But some things remain." He squeezed her hand, and her skin tingled.

"Ready?" she asked, though it was less a question and more a call to arms.

"Of course," he answered, and there was a promise in his

words—a vow that extended beyond the battlefields they were marching toward.

They stepped forward together, a motley crew of rebels and romantics, their faces etched with the fierce determination of those fighting for survival and a future worth fighting for. Lysandra led with the confidence of one born to stand against the tide, her hair a banner in the wind.

"Remember, we're not just fighting for ourselves," she said over her shoulder. "We're fighting for what Erenor could be."

"Freedom from tyranny; love triumphing over hate," Feyla chimed in, her eyes glinting with the fire of shared conviction.

"Let's not get ahead of ourselves," Eolande cautioned, though his stance was as resolute as any warrior's. "One step at a time."

"Right." Lysandra grinned, feeling the familiar surge of adrenaline. "First step: kick Malachor's ass."

"Second step: celebrate," Aerin added with a crooked smile, eliciting a round of laughter that cut through the tension like a well-honed blade.

"Third step: figure out how to heal the celestial fragment without getting ourselves killed," Lysandra finished, her humor belying the gravity of their quest.

"Details, details," Aerin teased, earning him a playful glare from Lysandra.

"Let's keep those details in mind, shall we?" She retorted, though the banter lightened her heart.

"Of course, my love," he said, his endearment carrying on the wind like a whisper of hope.

Their path opened up in front of them, a winding trail fraught with unknown danger, but Lysandra felt the weight of fear lessen with every step taken in unison. The world might be teetering on the brink of chaos, yet within Aerin's embrace, she found an anchor, a reminder that no matter how dark the night, dawn always followed.

The jagged rocks beneath their feet seemed to claw at the sky, a problematic ascent that tested their will and endurance. "Watch your step," Lysandra called back to the group, her footing sure despite the treacherous ground.

"I wouldn't dream of spoiling our dance with Malachor by tripping over a stone," Aerin quipped, but his gaze was intensely focused on the path ahead.

"Your humor never falters," she said, a small smile playing on her lips even as she summoned a gust of wind to steady a loose boulder before it could tumble onto the path of their companions.

"It feels like I'm holding back a storm with a whisper," Lysandra confessed, her eyes reflecting the elemental forces at her command.

"Sometimes a whisper is all it takes," Aviara murmured, her form wispy but unexpectedly present, her voice carrying the weight of ancient wisdom. "Trust in your strength, Lysandra, and in the bond you share with those around you."

Their journey continued, the relentless terrain giving way

to brief moments of respite where the group could catch their breath. During one such pause, Aerin pulled Lysandra aside, their hands finding each other's naturally.

"Are you holding up?" he asked, concern etching his rugged features.

"Better now," she admitted, leaning into his embrace. "With you here, I feel grounded."

"That's good because you're my anchor, too." His words were a soft rumble that resonated within her chest. "Together, we're unstoppable."

"Even against a sorcerer who plays with the multiverse like it's his toy box?" She couldn't help the flicker of doubt that crept into her voice.

"Especially against him," Aerin replied firmly. "We've faced darkness before and won. This time won't be any different."

"Because we have each other?" she whispered, resting her head against his shoulder.

"Exactly." He gently kissed the top of her head, a promise sealed in the simple gesture.

They stood there for a moment longer, two warriors seeking solace in the eye of an approaching storm. Their love was a silent vow to fight for Erenor and the future they dared to imagine together. The moment passed quickly, and they rejoined their friends, ready to face whatever challenges lay ahead, their hearts fortified by the love they felt for one another.

The mountain path narrowed, and the air around them was thick with the scent of magic and dread. Shadows clung to the craggy walls like dark whispers, promising danger with every step they took closer to Malachor's stronghold.

"Easy, does it?" Aerin murmured as he steadied Lysandra, her boot slipping on a loose stone.

"Thanks," she said, a tight smile on her lips. "I'm okay."

"I'm always ready to catch you," he replied, his gaze steady on her face. There was no fear, only the calm certainty of the battles they had fought and survived together.

"Focus, you two," Feyla called from ahead, her voice bouncing off the stony pass. "We're almost there."

They emerged onto a plateau, and the sight before them stole their breath away. The shadow realm stretched like a malignant dream, its skies swirling with ominous clouds. At its heart stood Malachor's stronghold, towers jagged like broken fingers clawing at the heavens.

"By the gods," Eolande whispered, his hand reaching the amulet at his throat.

"Gods have nothing to do with this place," Aviara responded, her form shimmering into view beside them. "This is a land shaped by Malachor's will alone."

"We've come too far to be afraid now," Lysandra said, her voice firm despite the chill that crept up her spine. She felt the hum of her power beneath her skin, a storm waiting to be unleashed.

"Right," Aerin said, stepping beside her. "Together, we can do this."

"Remember, we must heal the celestial structure," Aviara reminded them, her eyes scanning the dark horizon. "It's not just about defeating Malachor—it's about saving our world from the chaos he's unleashed."

"Then let's not keep our world waiting any longer," Lysandra declared, drawing her sword with a metallic ring. It glinted a streak of silver into the gloom. Shadow, who had been loping silently beside her, growled softly.

"Stay alert," Aerin instructed, his daggers appearing in his hands like extensions of his resolve. "Protect each other."

"Always and forever," came the chorus of replies, a patchwork of determination woven from their collective spirit.

"Aviara, can you get us inside?" Lysandra asked, turning to the nature goddess, whose presence had become as comforting as it was awe-inspiring.

Aviara nodded, her dark eyes bright with otherworldly light. "I will open the way. But once inside, my influence will wane. Malachor's magic is potent."

"Then we'll rely on each other," Lysandra stated, her eyes locking with Aerin's. They shared a nod, an unspoken promise echoing between them.

"Let's go end a reign," Aerin said, his voice low but fierce.

"End it and begin a new one," Lysandra added, squeezing his hand briefly before letting go.

With a gesture from Aviara, the air in front of them shimmered, and a gap appeared in the stronghold's defenses—an entrance that beckoned them forward.

"Stay close," Lysandra commanded, leading the charge as they crossed the threshold.

As the group moved into the belly of darkness, an oppressive and vast stronghold loomed over them. Yet they walked with heads held high, their bond a shield against the encroaching shadows.

"Love and light," Lysandra whispered under her breath, a mantra against the darkness.

"Courage and might," Aerin completed, his voice blending with hers.

Side by side, their hands no longer intertwined. Still, their hearts were irrevocably linked. Lysandra and Aerin stepped into the stronghold, the final confrontation awaiting them within the shadowed halls of Malachor's twisted sanctuary.

Chapter 4

ANCIENT SPELLS & LEY LINES

The rustling of leaves underfoot was the only sound as Lysandra led her companions through the dense underbrush, Shadow's sleek black form gliding silently beside her. The forest seemed to close around them, the twisted trees stretching their gnarled fingers toward the sky as if reaching for something beyond their grasp.

"Keep your eyes open," Lysandra whispered, her grip tight on the hilt of her sword. "Aviara predicted that magic would hide the grove."

The forest floor was a mixture of soft moss and crunchy leaves, with the occasional stick or root poking through Lysandra's boots. Her grip on her sword was tense, and she could feel the vibrations of Shadow's soft footsteps beside her as they cautiously moved through the enchanted forest, every sense on high alert for the hidden grove.

The rough texture of the tree bark scraped against Lysandra's hand as she brushed past. The leaves brushing against her skin left a slight tickle in their wake. The forest floor was a mixture of soft moss and prickly brambles under her feet.

Aerin nodded, his dark eyes scanning the shadowy thicket. His hand instinctively found hers, giving it a reassuring squeeze. "We'll find it," he said with a confidence that bolstered her wavering spirits.

"It feels like we're walking into a trap, though, doesn't it?" murmured Eolande, voicing the anxiety that hung tangibly in the air.

"Aviara wouldn't lead us astray," Lysandra replied, but her furrowed brow betrayed her doubts.

Suddenly, Shadow halted, sniffing the air. His ears perked up, and he let out a low growl. Lysandra's heart quickened as she followed his gaze. There was a shimmer in the air, like heat rising off a sun-scorched road.

"Here," she said, stepping forward and passing her hand through the distortion. The illusion wavered before dissolving entirely, revealing the hidden grove.

"By the gods," breathed Aerin, as they all looked in wonder at the sanctuary that unfolded before them—flowers glowing with ethereal light and trees whispering secrets of ancient days.

"Aviara should be here," Lysandra said, her voice barely above a murmur. She felt the familiar flutter of nerves, the weight of what was at stake pressing down upon her.

"Let's not keep her waiting then," said Aerin, giving her hand another squeeze before letting go.

Together, they stepped into the grove, and each was lost in their thoughts about the impending battle and the counsel they sought from their enigmatic guide, Aviara. With every step, anticipation built within Lysandra's chest, a crescendo drowning out the whispers of fear—at least for the moment.

Shadow's muscles tensed beneath Lysandra's touch, the grove's tranquility doing little to ease the wolf's alertness. Lysandra shared his tension, her gaze scanning the shadows between the light and dark. Then, as if materializing from the very essence of the forest itself, Aviara stood before them.

"Aviara!" Aerin exclaimed, relief etching his features.

The deity's presence was like a warm embrace, her power an unspoken promise in the cool air. They all felt it—felt her—an anchor in the upheaval that brewed on their horizon.

"Children of Erenor," Aviara's voice cascaded over them, "I am here, as I have always been and promised."

"Thank the stars," muttered Eolande, his usual stoic demeanor momentarily forgotten.

"Your guidance..." Lysandra began, but Aviara raised an elegant hand, silencing her with gentle authority.

"Time is a river swiftly flowing," she said. "Malachor's shadow lengthens with each passing moment. You must be the light that cleaves the darkness."

"Then you'll help us?" asked Lysandra, hope threading through her words.

"More than help, Lysandra. I will stand with you against Malachor." Aviara's gaze was unwavering, the depth of her eyes holding centuries of sorrow and determination. "My past demands it—my redemption lies within your victory."

Their chests swelled with courage, and the deity's commitment ignited a fire within their hearts.

"Whatever it takes," affirmed Aerin, his voice firm.

"Whatever it takes," echoed the group in unison, their resolve hardening like forged steel.

"Let us prepare, for the path that lies ahead is fraught with peril, and our time is limited," Aviara solemnly declared.

As the weighty words hung in the air, each group member felt a sense of foreboding settle over them, realizing that the most challenging part of their journey was about to begin.

Lysandra took a step forward, the trailing edge of her cloak gently rustling the damp, dew-laden leaves of the grove. By her side, Shadow moved in sync, his fur seamlessly blending with the dusky hues of the twilight enveloping the secluded sanctuary. Every nerve tingled with heightened sensitivity as they eagerly awaited Aviara's forthcoming revelations.

"Malachor," Aviara began, her voice a melody of strength and sorrow, "was not always the harbinger of doom we know now." She moved among them, her form barely disturbing the air. "He was once a guardian, much like myself. However, he succumbed to the lure of dark magic while I chose the light.

"Is there a way to bring him back?" Aerin asked, his eyes filled with hope as he sought a solution that didn't involve destruction.

"Too much time has passed, and too much blood has been

spilled for redemption," Aviara replied, her voice tinged with regret. Even the loyal companion, Shadow, let out a soft, understanding whine.

"Then how do we stop him?" Lysandra's voice shattered the silence, her unwavering determination reflected in the steely resolve of her gaze.

"His origins lie within the Heartstone, an ancient relic tied to the lifeblood of Erenor itself." Aviara's hands wove through the air, conjuring ethereal images of a crystalline heart pulsing with energy. "It is the source of his strength but also his greatest weakness."

"An Achilles' heel," murmured Feyla, her words indicating that her mind was already racing with strategies.

"Exactly," said Aviara, nodding at Feyla.

Looking back at Lysandra, her fingers suddenly danced, and the image shifted, revealing runes and symbols of lost magic. "I will teach you the incantations needed to sever his connection to the heartstone. These are ancient spells that many people have forgotten but which the deity of nature has preserved for this occasion.

"Will we be strong enough to wield such power?" The seriousness of their task overshadowed Lysandra's question, which hung heavy in the air.

"Your lineage, Lysandra, is key," Aviara said, her eyes locking onto hers. "The darkness you fight within yourself will become your weapon against Malachor."

"Darkness to fight darkness," whispered Lysandra, feeling the familiar stir of energy within her veins.

"Balance," Aviara corrected softly. "You and Aerin, together, are the embodiment of balance. His light complements your darkness. Together, you shall tip the scales in our favor."

Aerin reached out, taking Lysandra's hand in his own, their combined strength an unspoken vow.

"Teach us," he said, and Aviara smiled, the warmth of a thousand sunrises breaking through the shadows of doubt.

"Very well. Listen closely, for we have much to cover and little time to spare."

"Aviara," Lysandra started, looking serious, "you're talking about ancient spells. But how do we know they'll work against Malachor's power?"

"His power is old, but so is the magic I offer you," Aviara replied, a shimmering aura of confidence surrounding her. "These spells have been safeguarded for an age, woven into the fabric of this very forest. They await your command."

"Can we practice them here, in safety?" Aerin asked, his voice steady despite the flicker of concern in his dark eyes.

"Indeed. This grove is shielded from prying eyes," Aviara assured, her gaze sweeping across them. "Here, you may hone your skills until the incantations are as natural as breathing."

"Will there be signs that we are ready?" Eolande inquired, his fingers tracing the bow unconsciously.

"Trust in yourselves and each other," Aviara advised, her voice as soothing as a balm. "Your unity will be your strength."

"Speaking of strength," interjected Feyla, her brow furrowed with curiosity, "you mentioned your realm is healing. How does that change our approach?"

"Ah, yes." Aviara nodded, her hand gracefully reaching up toward the lush green forest canopy above, her fingers spread wide as if to encompass the entire expanse. "The life force of my domain is flowing again. As it flourishes, so does the energy you can draw upon. It's a reserve of power you can use during your battle with Malachor and his minions."

"Is it like a source of magic?" Lysandra asked for clarification, her warrior's mind piecing together the tactical advantage.

"Exactly," Aviara confirmed. "As Erenor's lifeblood rejuvenates, it feeds into the ley lines that cross beneath us. You will find that your spells carry more force and enchantments more resilience."

"Then our timing couldn't be better," Aerin said, a hint of a smile playing at the corners of his mouth. "We strike with the land itself as our ally."

"Nature's resurgence is a beacon of hope," Aviara agreed, her smile mirroring Aerin's. "Harness it well, and even Malachor's dark heart will falter."

"Hope," echoed Lysandra, her resolve hardening like steel tempered in fire. "That's something we could all use more of."

"Let us begin," Aviara declared, her hands outstretched as light gathered around them. "The battle for Erenor beckons, and we must answer its call with courage and the full might of the magic entrusted to us."

Their warriors, united by destiny and a fierce desire to save the world, drew closer together. With Shadow's watchful amber eyes upon them and the hidden grove pulsating with ancient power, they prepared themselves for the trials ahead.

Lysandra stepped forward, her eyes meeting Aviara's deep, dark gaze with an intensity that spoke volumes. "Aviara," she began, her voice steady and full of warmth, "we can't begin to thank you enough. You've given us more than guidance; you've given us a fighting chance."

"Seriously," chimed Feyla, her usually cheerful face etched with sincere respect. "You've turned the tide for us."

Aerin nodded, his hand finding Lysandra's and squeezing it gently. "Erenor owes you a debt that can never be fully repaid."

Shadow, silent as ever, gave a soft huff, his amber eyes fixed on Aviara, echoing the sentiment of gratitude.

Aviara's lips curled into a gentle smile, her aura shimmering softly around her. "My dears, your thanks are heartfelt, but I should be grateful. You have allowed me to right the wrongs of my past." Her eyes swept across the group. "I will not leave you to face Malachor alone. My divine guidance and protection are yours, as sure as the moon guides the tides."

"Your support means everything," Lysandra replied, her grip on Aerin's hand tightening. "With you by our side, we'll return Dawn to Erenor."

"Remember," Aviara said, stepping closer, her presence enveloping them like a calming breeze, "you carry the light of Erenor within you. Trust in it, as I trust in all of you."

"Trust," Lysandra echoed, feeling the weight of the word

settle in her heart. She exchanged glances with her companions, each face reflecting determination and the comfort of Aviara's promise. With the help of an ancient deity's light, they were prepared to face the darkness.

"Alright, let's break this down," Lysandra said, focusing intently on the map unfurled before them. The grove was silent, but for the rustling leaves and the occasional snort from Shadow as he lay nearby,

Feyla leaned in, pointing to a swirling mass of ink that signified Malachor's stronghold. "If Aviara's intelligence is right, there should be a series of hidden tunnels leading into the heart of the Shadowrealm."

"Which are, no doubt, crawling with his minions?" Aerin interjected, his brow furrowed. "We'll need to be stealthy."

"Or clever," Feyla chirped, tapping the side of her head. "Give me time, and I can whip up gadgets to give us an edge."

Lysandra smiled, acknowledging Feyla's knack for invention. "We'll take every advantage we can get. But it's not just about getting in; we must consider how we will face Malachor once we're there."

"Head-on isn't exactly subtle," Aerin muttered, rubbing at a scar on his hand absentmindedly.

"Subtle won't defeat Malachor," Lysandra countered. "Aviara said his power source is his vulnerability. We strike that, and we strike him."

"Then it's settled," Feyla declared, rolling up the map with a wrist snap. "We go in armed with knowledge, gadgets, and brute force."

"Let's not forget Aviara's divine protection," Aerin added, his voice softer now. He caught Lysandra's gaze, and something unspoken passed between them—a promise to protect each other against all odds.

"Indeed," Lysandra agreed, standing tall. She turned to face the deity, who had been a quiet sentinel during their planning. "Aviara, we are prepared to do what must be done."

"Your courage warms my heart," Aviara responded, stepping forward. Her dark hair seemed to absorb the dappled sunlight, casting her face in an ethereal glow.

"Before we part," Lysandra began, "is there anything else you can offer? Is there any final word of advice?"

"Remember that strength lies not only in your blades and spells but also in the bond you share." Aviara's voice resonated with the wisdom of the ages. "Trust in one another as you trust in me. That unity will be your greatest shield."

"Thankful doesn't cover it, Aviara," Feyla said, her voice tinged with emotion. "You've given us a real shot at ending this nightmare."

"Go now, children of Erenor," Aviara instructed, her tone gentle yet unwavering. "And know that my spirit walks with you."

With a collective nod, the group gathered their belongings. Shadow rose, shaking his fur, ready to follow where Lysandra led.

"Let's move out," Lysandra commanded, her sword resting

in her hand, not as a threat but as a symbol of the fight ahead. They turned their backs to the grove, stepping into the unknown with determined hearts.

"Goodbye, Aviara," Aerin said over his shoulder, his voice carrying the weight of gratitude and resolve. "Until we meet again."

"Until then," Aviara whispered, watching them disappear into the forest. Her divine presence lingered in the shadows they left behind; she was a comfort.

The canopy of the darkening forest closed behind them as Lysandra led her companions away from Aviara's hidden grove. Once thick with ancient magic and secrets, the air buzzed with the electric charge of impending action.

"Can you believe it?" Feyla breathed, her brown eyes alight, "We're going to do this."

"We are," Lysandra affirmed, a smile tugging at the corner of her mouth, her eyes focused on the path ahead. Shadow padded silently beside her, his black fur blending into the shadows.

"Aviara believes in us," Aerin added, his voice steady and reassuring. "We've got more than just hope on our side."

"Still," Lysandra mused aloud, "it's not just about believing. We have to be smart and precise. Malachor won't go down easily."

"Nor will we," Aerin said, reaching for her hand. His touch was grounding, reminding her she wasn't alone in this fight.

"Hey, lovebirds," Feyla teased, breaking their momentary connection. Let's keep the pace up. The others will worry if we don't show up soon."

"Right," Lysandra agreed, giving Aerin's hand a final squeeze before letting go. They hurried their steps, moving through the forest with a quiet urgency, their silhouettes like ghosts among the trees.

"Think Aviara's right, then?" Feyla asked after a while, her gaze flickering between them. "About unity being our shield?"

"Without a doubt," Lysandra responded without hesitation. "Together, we're stronger than any one of us alone."

"Especially with your gadgets, Feyla," Aerin said, offering a supportive nod toward the inventor. "Your mind is as sharp as any spell."

"Flatterer," Feyla retorted, but her lips curled into a pleased smirk.

They continued, bantering and lightening their steps, until the encampment appeared. The rebel group's fires were tiny flickers of hope against the growing darkness.

"Time to rest up," Lysandra announced as they approached. The companions nodded, each feeling the weight of the day's revelations and the promise of tomorrow's dangers.

"To think," Feyla mused, glancing back at the shadowy forest, "this time tomorrow, we could be... well, let's just say things will be different."

"Let's focus on the now," Lysandra suggested. "Rest, prepare, and be ready for anything."

"Anything and everything," Aerin agreed, his arm brushing against hers.

Shadow gave a low, contented growl as if in agreement, and the trio crossed the threshold into the camp. Around them, faces turned, expressions ranging from concern to curiosity, but as Lysandra, Aerin, and Feyla passed by, those looks transformed into nods and smiles of solidarity.

"Sleep well," Lysandra called out to the gathering. "Tomorrow, we fight for Erenor."

"Tomorrow!" echoed Aerin, and Feyla nodded, her eyes shining with fierce determination.

They each found their space among friends and fellow warriors, the warmth of the fire seeping into their bones. As they settled down, a calm settled over Lysandra's spirit, a whisper telling her that no matter what lay ahead, they were ready—ready to confront Malachor, prepared to save Erenor, and ready to face whatever future awaited them together.

She snuggled up to Aerin, and his arm instinctively wrapped around Lysandra's shoulders. His fingers traced soothing circles on her arm as she snuggled into him.

Lysandra could feel the warmth of Aerin's body seeping into her own as she leaned into him. She sighed and closed her eyes. Tomorrow was another day; now, they could enjoy each other's presence and rest.

Chapter 5

CUTTING OFF THE HEAD OF THE SNAKE

The remnants of the night's fire crackled, its embers glowing feebly as dawn crept over the horizon. Lysandra sat on a fallen log, her keen eyes tracing the lines of fatigue etched into the faces of her companions. The weight of their recent battles hung over them like a shroud, and the absence of Harrow, their dragon comrade whose scales once shimmered like molten gold under the sun, felt like a void in their ranks.

"Another day, another slew of reasons to avoid what's coming," Aerin muttered, breaking the morning's silence as he poked at the dying fire with a stick.

"I can't say I'm thrilled about marching headlong into Malachor's trap," Eolande added, his arms crossed as if warding off the chill of their uncertainty.

"Are we even sure we stand a chance?" Feyla's voice was barely even a whisper, but it resonated with the doubt clouding each of their thoughts.

Lysandra let out a slow breath, feeling the familiar tug-of-war within her soul. Her dual heritage, a blend of celestial light and shadowy abyss, granted her extraordinary power, yet the same lineage cast a pall over her confidence.

"Every time I close my eyes, I see the darkness waiting to consume me," she confessed, her gaze distant. "It's like walking a tightrope between two abysses, knowing one misstep could be catastrophic."

Eolande shifted uncomfortably, his eyes reflecting a storm of emotions. "We all have our demons, Lysandra. But you've never let yours win before."

"Your strength is more than just the magic coursing through your veins," Feyla chimed in, her hand reaching out to squeeze Lysandra's shoulder in a silent show of support.

"Besides," Aerin said with a wry grin, attempting to lighten the mood, "we wouldn't have gotten this far without your light guiding us. And your dark side's not too shabby when it comes to kicking ass."

A thin smile tugged at Lysandra's lips. They were right; she couldn't let her fears dictate their path. However, the idea of facing Malachor and having either the light or the darkness within her consume her sent a chill down her spine.

"Malachor will not wait for us to resolve our inner conflicts," she said, standing up. "We must move forward despite our doubts."

"Then we'll face him together," Feyla affirmed, her tone

steady and determined. "As we always have."

Their shared resolve fortified Lysandra's spirit. Yes, the road ahead brimmed with danger, even death, but she would march right into the unknown with her friends by her side. The unyielding threads of fate that intertwined their destinies would cause them to rise or fall together.

"Let's pack up," Lysandra announced, her voice clear and unwavering. "We have a world to save."

And with those words, the group began their preparations, their camaraderie a beacon of hope amidst the encroaching shadows.

"Okay, let's get to it," Lysandra said, her fingers drumming on the weathered wood that had become their makeshift council table. Her companions and the new allies from the rebel faction gathered around, the air thick with anticipation and the scent of the pine trees that surrounded their encampment.

"Aviara was clear," she continued, her gaze meeting each pair of eyes. "Malachor's power grows, but he's not invincible. There's a pattern to his spells, a rhythm we can disrupt if careful and precise."

"Like finding the flaw in a piece of armor," Jagger from the Rebel Faction chimed in, leaning forward with interest sparking in his eyes. The accident that had marred his relationship with Sage seemed a lifetime away as he focused on the present threat.

"Exactly," Lysandra affirmed. "We hit him where it hurts, breaking his concentration. That's when he's vulnerable."

"Sounds like a plan," Aerin said, arms crossed, her expression of grim determination. "But how do we even get close enough?"

"Which is why we need to be smarter, faster." Sage's voice was steady despite the memories that haunted her. She had lost much, but her spirit remained unbroken.

"Aviara mentioned the cosmic rift," Lysandra said, painting their task's gravity. "It's where Malachor draws his strength, deep within the heart of chaos. If we can reach it,"

"We cut off the head of the snake," finished one of the rebels, a burly man with scars that told tales of battles long past.

"Isn't that place swarming with his minions?" someone asked, voicing the concern that hung over them like a dark cloud.

"Sure, it's a death trap," Lysandra admitted her fear a silent undercurrent beneath her resolve. "But it's also our best shot. We've come through fire and shadow before. This time won't be any different."

"Then we'll need every advantage. Potions, charms, weapons... anything that gives us an edge," Feyla added, her mind already racing through the logistics.

"Agreed," said Lysandra. "Preparation is key. We leave at dawn."

"Guess it's time to sharpen my sword," Jagger muttered, half to himself, pushing back from the makeshift table.

"More than swords will be needed," Lysandra said softly, catching his eye. He nodded, understanding the weight of the magic they were up against.

"Tonight, we rest," she declared. "Tomorrow, we take the

first steps toward ending this nightmare."

They all rose from the makeshift table with a collective sense of purpose. The night may have been closing in, but the flame of hope—fueled by camaraderie and the thrill of an impending battle—burned brighter than ever.

As they dispersed to prepare, Lysandra felt the familiar dichotomy within her stir: light and darkness vying for dominance. Yet, there was no turning back. The path ahead was dangerous, but walking was theirs, and they would do so together.

The ground beneath their feet began to tremble as they approached the cosmic rift, a jagged scar on the earth where reality seemed to warp. Lysandra's boots crunched over the frosted grass, her breath misting in the air, her eyes fixed on the shimmering void ahead.

"Watch your step," she warned as the path narrowed and the air crackled with unseen energy. "The ley lines are twisted here. Malachor's been feeding off them."

"Feeding off them?" Jagger scanned the horizon, sword unsheathed. "How can you tell?"

"Can't you feel it?" Sage replied before Lysandra could, her gaze darkening. "It's like the magic's curdled."

"Exactly," Lysandra confirmed, her senses attuned to the disturbance. She could almost see the threads of power, corrupted and writhing like serpents in the sky.

"Then we tread carefully," Aerin said, drawing his bow with a steady hand. "We cannot allow ourselves to be ensnared by his sorcery."

"Agreed," Lysandra murmured, leading the way with a flicker of light at her fingertips, pushing back against the oppressive darkness.

As they navigated the labyrinthine terrain, illusions rose from the twisted landscape—phantoms of their deepest fears designed to fracture their resolve. Jagger's jaw clenched when a spectral image of a house on fire flickered before him, but he slashed through it with a grunt, dispelling the vision.

"Keep moving," he grunted, his eyes seeking out Sage's. "Don't let it get to you."

"Too many ghosts here," Sage muttered, though her voice held steady.

"Focus on what's real," Lysandra reminded them, her voice a beacon amidst the chaos.

Finally, they reached the entrance to Malachor's stronghold, a gaping maw of darkness that threatened to swallow them whole. The shadowrealm loomed before them; its very atmosphere was a pulsating mass of despair.

"Everyone ready?" Lysandra asked though the tightness in her chest betrayed her apprehension.

"Let's end this," said Jagger, gripping his sword tighter.

"Stay sharp," Aerin added, his eyes searching the shadows for movement.

"Whatever happens, we do it together," Feyla affirmed, reaching out to squeeze Lysander's hand briefly before letting go.

Taking a deep breath, they stepped into the stronghold, the

darkness enveloping them like a shroud. Malachor had laid devious traps: floors that gave way to pits of spikes, walls that suddenly sprouted deadly blades, and shifting corridors that seemed to lead nowhere.

"Left!" Lysandra called out suddenly as the floor beneath Jagger's foot crumbled. He pivoted, narrowly avoiding a fall into the abyss.

"Thanks," he said, his voice terse with adrenaline.

"Keep your eyes peeled for guardians," Eolande warned, nocking an arrow to his bowstring. "They'll be here somewhere."

No sooner had he spoken than a pack of shadow hounds materialized, their eyes glowing with a baleful light. With snarls that echoed through the twisted halls, they charged.

"Fire and ash!" Lysandra exclaimed, channeling her elemental magic. Flames danced around her hands, scorching the nearest beast as it leaped.

"Water and wind," Sage chanted, her incantation summoning a torrential gust that sent another hound tumbling end over end.

"Earth and steel," Jagger growled, swinging his sword in a wide arc to meet the onslaught, grounding himself in his physical strength against the supernatural menace.

"Air and flight," Aerin's voice rang out, his daggers finding their marks with deadly precision.

Together, they fought back-to-back, a seamless unit of magic and might. Each beast that fell seemed to dissolve into the shadows from whence it came, but the relentless tide of Malachor's guardians continued to surge.

"Never-ending, isn't it?" Jagger panted, wiping sweat from his brow.

"I can't give up," Lysandra grunted, dispatching another foe with a burst of light.

"I wouldn't dream of it," Sage replied, her determination fierce despite the odds.

"Forward," Aerin commanded, leading them deeper into the stronghold.

The Shadowrealm tested their every skill, bond, and will to press on. But with each step, they drew nearer to the heart of darkness, where Malachor awaited. His escape was again within reach, his power a storm on the verge of breaking.

"Circle up!" Lysandra's voice cut through clashing metals and sinister incantations as she launched herself at Malachor with renewed ferocity. The heart of the Shadowrealm pulsed like a malignant beat around them, shadows writhing in tandem with their master's rage.

"I love you," Aerin grunted, releasing a volley of arrows that glowed with a celestial light. They arced toward Malachor, slicing through the murk, only to be swallowed by a vortex of dark energy he conjured with a flick of his wrist.

"Your light is insignificant," Malachor sneered, his eyes abysses from which there seemed no escape. He raised his arms, chanting in an ancient tongue, and the ground beneath their feet trembled as if alive with malice.

"Feels pretty significant to me," Lysandra snapped back, her resolve hardening. She spread her palms wide, calling upon her heritage—the very veins of Erenor itself. Flames erupted around her, a fiery aura that pushed back against the encroaching darkness.

"Give him everything!" she cried out to her companions.

"Got your back," Sage replied, linking her magic with Lysandra's. A torrent of water spiraled from her hands, weaving with the fire to create a steam that seemed to cleanse the air of Malachor's corruption.

"Let's rock this," Jagger added, his voice steady. The earth responded to his call, roots and vines bursting forth to entangle the feet of Malachor's minions, tripping them into the inferno Lysandra conjured.

"Come on, you bastard," Eolande challenged, his bows finding their mark repeatedly, each striking with more force than the last, borne aloft by gusts of wind that Sage summoned with a whisper.

The elements danced at Lysandra's command, a power disruption rivaling the storm of darkness Malachor unleashed. Fire clashed against shadow, water quenched the flames of destruction, and the earth rose to defend its children.

"Is that all you've got?" Malachor taunted, even as he staggered under the assault.

"Hardly," Lysandra growled, feeling the surge of elemental magic course through her. With each spell cast, her confidence swelled. She was the Last Mage, the beacon of hope for Erenor, and she would not falter.

"Focus on your magic," she instructed, her voice now commanding. "We hit him together, now!"

Their powers converged, a symphony of the elements directed at the heart of darkness. Malachor's laugh turned into a roar of fury as the combined might of fire, water, earth, and air struck him, the impact echoing through the shadowrealm like the first crack of dawn dispelling night's deepest gloom.

"Back to back!" Lysandra shouted, her voice piercing the din of battle. She could feel the thrum of Eolande's bow as he loosed another volley, the arrows singing through the air like vengeful spirits.

"Got it," Sage called out, and even through the din, a smile was in her voice. With a flick of her wrist, a barrier shimmered into existence around them, deflecting a shadowy tendril that sought to trap them.

"Jagger, now!" Aerin yelled over his shoulder, ducking as a shadow blade whistled past where his head had been moments before.

"Watch this," Jagger grunted, slamming his fist into the ground. The earth responded, erupting a wave of stone upwards, throwing Malachor's minions into disarray.

"Nice touch," Sage complimented, twirling her staff, her movements fluid and precise, each strike imbued with light magic that left glowing trails in the darkened realm.

"Keep the pressure on!" Lysandra commanded, feeling the weight of leadership heavy on her shoulders but buoyed by the trust her allies placed in her. "We can't let him recover!"

"Recover?" Malachor sneered, emerging from the shadows like a serpent slithering from its den. "You think you have me cornered?"

"We know we do," Aerin shot back, his eyes never leaving their foe as he drew his bow.

"Your overconfidence will be your downfall," Malachor hissed, raising his hands. Dark energy coalesced between his palms, swirling and growing, threatening to overwhelm them.

"Divide and conquer," whispered Lysandra, locking eyes with Aerin. They had one chance at this—one opportunity to turn the tide. "On three..."

"Three!" they shouted in unison without waiting for the count.

Aerin's arrow was released, trailing a comet's tail of light, while Lysandra thrust her hands forward, unleashing a torrent of elemental fury. The fire roared like an enraged dragon, the water spiraled like a relentless whirlpool, the earth stood firm like an unbreakable fortress, and the air howled with the force of a hurricane. Their magics intertwined, a dazzling vortex aiming straight for Malachor.

"Impossible!" Malachor bellowed, his voice laced with disbelief, as the combined assault bore down on him.

"Nothing's impossible when we stand together!" Sage affirmed, reinforcing their attack with a radiant burst of her power.

"Take that, you dark-hearted fiend!" Jagger added, his earth magic lending solidity and strength to their combined spell.

Malachor staggered his cloak of shadows tearing at the seams, the raw energies clashing against his defenses. He roared a sound of pure malice and pushed back with all the darkness at his command.

"Push through!" Lysandra gritted her teeth, sweat beading on her forehead as she poured more of herself into the spell. Her heart raced; every beat was a war drum in her chest.

"Almost... there..." Aerin strained, his face set in a mask of determination.

With a final, collective surge of will, their powers broke through Malachor's barrier, striking true. A blinding explosion enveloped the Shadowrealm's heart, the shockwave shaking the very fabric of the dimension.

As the light dimmed, they stood panting, staring at the spot where Malachor had been. Silence fell in stark contrast to the chaos that had reigned moments before.

"Did we...?" Feyla began, hope mingling with uncertainty in her voice.

"We did what we came to do," Lysandra declared, though her gaze remained wary. They had struck a significant blow, but the battle for Erenor was far from over. "We've healed the celestial fracture."

"For now," Aerin said, touching her shoulder, his touch grounding. "But we'll be ready for whatever comes next. To-gether."

"Look out!" Aerin's shout pierced the cacophony as a bolt

of dark energy hurtled toward them. Lysandra rolled to the side, the ground searing where the bolt struck, leaving behind a charred echo of her shadow.

"I can't keep this up." Feyla panted, notching another arrow into her crossbow with trembling hands. Her shots were precise, each one finding its mark among the multitude of shadow creatures that swarmed about them like angry wasps.

Eolande stood back-to-back with her, losing arrows in tandem. "We must," he said through gritted teeth, his ordinarily calm face twisted in concentration. "For Erenor."

"Where did he go?" Sage scanned the murky horizon, her staff at the ready.

"Malachor's not one to retreat easily," Lysandra muttered, frustration edging her words. She could feel the toll of the battle weighing on her limbs, but the rush of combat kept her moving and alive.

"By the gods, we've been at this for hours," Aerin grumbled, his sword slicing through a wraith-like figure.

"Feels like days," Feyla quipped back, despite the worry carved deeply in her brow.

"Careful," Eolande warned. "He's cunning. He'll wait for us to weaken before—"

Before he could finish, the ground erupted beneath them, tendrils of darkness shooting upwards. The group leaped in different directions, narrowly avoiding being trapped. They rallied again, forming a tight circle, eyes darting about for any sign of their foe.

"Where are you, you coward?" Lysandra called out, her voice a challenge.

A laugh, cold and devoid of humor, echoed around them. Malachor materialized, his form flickering between planes. "You cannot hope to defeat me," he sneered. "I am beyond your petty magics!"

"Then why run?" Lysandra shot back, anger fueling her magic.

"Strategic retreat," he said, his grin widening. "But I grow tired of these games."

"Then come and face us!" Aerin roared, stepping forward.

"Enough!" With a wave of his hand, Malachor unleashed a maelstrom of dark spells, forcing the group to scatter once more.

"Stay together!" Lysandra shouted over the din, her command barely audible above the roar of magic and mayhem.

"Protect each other!" Aerin added, locking eyes with Lysandra, a silent promise passing between them.

The battle raged, relentless and exhausting, pushing them to their limits. But even as they fought with everything they had, Malachor's laughter rang out again. In a flash of darkness, he vanished, leaving only the echoes of his departure.

"Is he..." Feyla trailed off, gasping for breath.

"Escaped," Eolande finished for her, his expression grim.

"Next time," Lysandra said, determination hardening her features, "we end it."

"Let's regroup," Aerin said, glancing at the group worriedly.

"We need to plan. We need to be ready."

As they gathered their strength, the air crackled with unsaid fears and unspoken vows, and the knowledge that Malachor still lived hung heavy. The fate of their world, teetering on the edge of ruin, drove home the reality of their quest. They would have to face him again, and next time, there would be no escape—for either side.

"Whatever it takes," Lysandra whispered, meeting their gazes. "We will stop him."

"Whatever it takes," they echoed, their voices a unified resolve against the coming darkness.

With Malachor's lingering threat shadowing their path, they began the treacherous journey back to the rift, knowing that the actual climax of their saga awaited them, along with all the potential consequences of their desperate fight for Erenor's future.

Chapter 6

THE FORBIDDEN FOREST

"Great," Feyla muttered, her gaze locked on the towering trees of the Forbidden Forest as they loomed ahead. "Because normal forests are just too boring."

Lysandra couldn't suppress a smirk. "Where's your sense of adventure?"

"Stuck in my other pants, probably with my sanity," Feyla shot back, but a twinkle in her eye betrayed her excitement.

The foliage grew denser, and the air was thick with whispers of ancient magic. Each step they took was a silent pact with the unknown, an agreement to embrace whatever lay hidden within the gnarled branches and shifting shadows.

"Keep close," Aerin instructed, his voice steady despite the unease that flickered across his face like shadows from a flickering flame.

"Always the protector, huh?" Lysandra teased, though her heart warmed at his concern.

"Someone has to be," he replied with a half-smile.

That's when they saw it—the first elemental challenge. A labyrinth of fire erupted before them, crackling walls of hungry flames reaching high into the canopy as if challenging the very sky.

"It looks like a warm welcome," Feyla quipped, but her laughter danced nervously on the edge of fear.

"Okay, focus," Lysandra said, her eyes scanning the maze, searching for patterns in the chaos. "We must find the right path without turning into crispy critters."

"Any bright ideas?" Aerin asked, the weight of his previous life as a witch hunter momentarily darkening his tone.

"Let's not rush into this," Lysandra suggested, her eyes reflecting the leaping flames. She could feel the fire's rhythm—an erratic beat that thrummed in sync with her pulse. It was both a threat and a siren's call to the power she harbored within.

"Rushing leads to burning," Feyla added, pulling a small gadget from her belt. "Let me try something."

She fiddled with the device, which clicked and whirred softly. "This should give us a read on the heat flux. Might predict a safe passage."

"Smart," Lysandra acknowledged, impressed by Feyla's resourcefulness in the face of magic she didn't possess.

"Here goes nothing," Feyla said, tossing the gadget into the flames. They watched it blink green and red, charting a potential route through the inferno.

"Follow the green," Aerin decided, stepping forward with a

determination that made Lysandra's heart swell. He might fear the magic, but he'd never let it stop him from protecting what mattered.

"Right behind you," Lysandra assured, her resolve steeling as they entered the fiery maze together, the heat licking at their skin, a test of courage and trust in their quest through the Forbidden Forest.

"Stand back," Lysandra commanded, her voice cutting through the crackle of flames. With a fluid motion, she extended her arms toward the blaze. The fire danced and swirled at her command, parting to create a narrow path. "I can hold this for a while, but stay sharp."

"Your control is remarkable, Lys," Aerin said, his gaze fixed on the fiery corridor. He raised his hands, green energy glowing at his fingertips. "Let me shield us, just in case." A protective bubble encased them with each step, warding off the searing heat that sought to sear their skin.

"Nice teamwork," Feyla chimed in, her eyes twinkling with pride as she followed close behind, her earlier invention tucked safely away. "Who needs magic when you have these two?"

"Keep moving," Lysandra replied, though a small smile graced her lips. She dared not admit it aloud, but Aerin's presence bolstered her confidence, even as she fought to suppress the darkness within.

As they navigated the labyrinthine paths, the flames appeared to bow before Lysandra's silent command, retreating and roaring in frustration. Their progress was slow but steady, and the heat became a mere whisper against their protected skin.

"Look!" Feyla pointed upward, where a shadow detached from the canopy above. It descended gracefully, revealing itself as a large owl, its feathers a mosaic of browns and whites. Its wise golden eyes seemed to pierce through the forest haze, locking onto the group below.

"Travelers of Erenor," the owl said, its voice deep and resonant. You step on holy ground that is subject to untamed elements. Allow me to guide your steps henceforth."

"An ally or another test?" Aerin asked, suspicion narrowing his eyes.

"Both, perhaps," Lysandra responded, feeling an inexplicable trust toward the creature. "What guidance do you offer, wise one?"

"Beyond the flame lies a challenge of earth, where strength alone will not suffice," the owl intoned, ruffling its feathers. "I shall lead you to the water's edge. Observe the pattern of the land, for therein lies the key."

"Thank you," Lysandra said, nodding in appreciation. Her instincts told her the owl's intentions were pure, a rare occurrence in their perilous quest.

"Lead the way, then," Aerin agreed as the owl retook flight, its silhouette a guiding beacon through the remaining twists and turns of the fiery maze.

Together, they emerged from the flames, the sense of danger ever-present but tempered by the camaraderie and unspoken affection that bound them together. Ahead, the Forbidden Forest beckoned with new trials, but for now, they followed the owl into the unknown, ready for whatever lay ahead.

The owl's guidance had been cryptic at best, but as the group approached the riverbank, Lysandra's gut churned with the certainty that this churning expanse was their subsequent trial. She could almost hear the sly undercurrents whispering promises of a watery grave.

"It looks like we're going to swim," Feyla remarked, eyeing the water suspiciously.

"Swim?" Aerin frowned. "Those currents will tear us apart."

"Then it's a good thing I've been tinkering," Feyla said, rummaging through her pack. She pulled out what appeared to be a collection of leather pouches and corked bottles. "Air pockets," she explained, tossing one to each member. "They should keep us buoyant."

"Brilliant," Eolande praised, securing his device.

"Let's not waste time," Lysandra decided, stepping into the water. The cold bit at her skin, but she pressed on, her eyes scanning for movement beneath the surface.

"Stay close!" Aerin called out, his voice threaded with concern, but Lysandra surged ahead, her warrior instincts kicking in.

As they ventured more deeply, the river came alive with thrashing forms and elongated shadows darting between them. One lunged at Lysandra, its mouth agape, revealing rows of razor-sharp teeth.

"Look out!" Aerin shouted.

Lysandra sidestepped deftly, her sword cleaving through the water with lethal precision. Eolande's arrows found their marks, too, thinning the numbers that swarmed around them.

"Keep moving!" Feyla yelled over the chaos, her makeshift flotation device keeping her head above the turbulent waves.

"Watch your back!" Eolande warned as another creature snaked towards Aerin. With a swift dive, he intercepted it, his knife flashing through the murky depths.

"Thanks!" Aerin grunted, sparing him a quick nod before they both kicked forward, fighting the pull of the water.

"Almost there!" Lysandra called, spotting a calmer stretch of the river up ahead. Her muscles burned with exertion, but she wouldn't allow herself to weaken—not when the others depended on her.

"Stick together!" Feyla's voice wavered, exhaustion seeping into her tone, but her determination shone brightly.

Together, they broke through the final waves, emerging onto the far bank, gasping and soaking. They had faced the river's wrath and emerged victorious, their bond unbroken and their resolve steeling them for the trials yet to come.

"Everyone alright?" Lysandra asked, her eyes meeting each of theirs in turn.

"Better now that we're out of that," Aerin replied, squeezing the water from his hair.

"Next time, I'm inventing a boat," Feyla muttered, but her lips curled into a tired smile.

"Or wings," Eolande quipped, checking his bow for damage.

"Whatever comes next," Lysandra said, her hand finding Aerin's, "we face it together."

"Out of the water, now!" Lysandra's command sliced through the sound of rushing water. Scrambling onto the rocky shore, they scanned for the source of her urgency. A ripple in the otherwise placid surface caught Aerin's eye.

"Something's wrong," he murmured, his hand instinctively reaching for the hilt of his sword.

"Malachor's tricks," Feyla spat, nocking an arrow to her bow with practiced ease.

"Brace yourselves," Eolande said, his stance widening as the water bulged and swirled, a massive form rising from its depths.

The elemental water towered over them; its roar was a deafening cascade. Aerin felt the mist on his face, the raw power emanating from the beast sending chills down his spine.

"Divide and conquer?" Feyla suggested, her eyes darting between the monster and her companions.

"Agreed," Lysandra replied, her voice steady despite the surge of adrenaline. "Aerin, with me. Feyla, Eolande, flank it."

"Got it!" Feyla called out, letting an arrow fly. It zipped through the element's watery form, causing ripples but no damage.

"Useless," she cursed under her breath, backpedaling as the creature turned its attention towards her.

"Focus on the core!" Eolande shouted, drawing the creature's ire long enough for Aerin to rush forward.

"Keep it distracted!" Lysandra yelled, her hands weaving intricate patterns in the air. Flames danced around her fingers, starkly contrasting the watery behemoth before them.

"Careful, love," Aerin warned as he joined her side, ready to shield her if needed.

"Trust me," she shot back with a fierce grin, unleashing a stream of fire that sizzled against the elemental's swirling body.

"Hit it where it hurts!" Feyla cheered, finding her opening as the elemental reeled from Lysandra's attack.

"Keep it up!" Eolande was encouraged, slipping past the creature's thrashing limbs to strike at its heart.

With a concerted effort, they focused their attacks, fire, and fury on meeting the relentless onslaught of water. Finally, with a shudder that shook the earth beneath their feet, the elemental released one last torrential cry and collapsed into a harmless puddle.

"Nicely done," Aerin breathed, clasping Lysandra's shoulder with a proud smile.

"Let's not get cozy," Lysandra said, pulling away to survey the path ahead. "We've got more ground to cover."

Before them lay a terrain of jagged rocks and hidden crevices. The forest loomed, dense and foreboding, the next challenge already whispering through the leaves.

"Watch your step," Eolande cautioned as they crossed the uneven ground.

"Traps," Feyla muttered, eyeing the stones warily.

"Can you disarm them?" Lysandra asked, trusting Feyla's keen intellect.

"Give me a minute." Feyla kneeled, her fingers probing the rocky soil. She pulled a small device from her pack, wires glinting in the dappled sunlight.

"Here," she said after a tense moment, pressing something small and metallic into the stone. There was a click, and a section of the path ahead cleared, revealing a safe passage.

"Good work," Aerin said, offering her a quick nod of appreciation.

"Let's keep moving," Lysandra said, leading the way. "Stay alert."

"I always am," Feyla quipped, though her eyes remained vigilant.

Together, they navigated the treacherous terrain, each group member using their strengths to overcome obstacles and decipher the puzzles hidden among the rocks. With every challenge, their bond grew more robust, their trust deepening like roots in fertile soil.

"Almost through," Lysandra announced as they approached the forest's threshold, the shadows of the trees welcoming them into their embrace.

"Ready for whatever comes next," Aerin affirmed, his hand finding Lysandra's once more.

"Then let's end this," she said, determination blazing in her eyes as they stepped into the darkness together, united against the looming threat of Malachor.

"Watch out!" Lysandra's sharp command cut through the air as a stone slab jutted from the wall, nearly skewering Eolande.

"Thanks," he breathed, darting back to safety. The elf's ordinarily serene face was etched with concern as he scanned the surrounding rocks for more hidden threats.

"Can you sense any more traps?" Aerin asked, his eyes fixed on Lysander's face, seeking reassurance in her confident gaze.

"Let me focus." Closing her eyes, Lysandra extended her palms toward the ground. Her silver-blonde hair lifted slightly as she summoned her magic, connecting with the earth's energy. Slowly, the tumultuous terrain ahead shifted, with stones rolling away to create a safer path.

"Brilliant," murmured Feyla, watching in awe as the passage unfolded.

"Quick, before it resets!" Aerin urged, leading the way across the newly formed bridge. His hand brushed against Lysandra's as they crossed, a silent thank-you for her intervention.

As the group pressed forward, the puzzles grew more complex, demanding the best of their varied skills. The tension among them spiked at a particularly confounding juncture, where pathways twisted like serpents and dead ends loomed like gaping maws.

"Any bright ideas?" Feyla quipped, though her laughter didn't quite reach her eyes.

"Give me a moment," Lysandra muttered, her fingers tracing symbols in the air, seeking guidance from the arcane forces that whispered in her blood.

"Maybe I can help with that."

They all spun around at the sound of the new voice. Perched

on a moss-covered boulder sat a tiny figure no larger than a rabbit, with wings shimmering like dew in the morning sun. The forest sprite tilted its head, regarding them with a mischievous grin.

"Who are you?" Eolande asked, one hand on the hilt of his sword.

"Name's Pipp," the sprite chirped. "I know these puzzles like the back of my wing. Malachor's goons have nothing on me!"

"Can we trust him?" Aerin murmured to Lysandra, and his brow furrowed in suspicion.

"Got a better idea?" She retorted, her eyes sparkling with challenge.

"Alright, Pipp. Show us what you've got," Feyla said, stepping forward with a wry smile.

Pipp led them through the labyrinthine rocks with a series of playful flips. The sprite paused at intervals, whispering hints that would unravel the enigma of each obstacle.

"Press that stone, but not the one beside it," Pipp instructed, pointing to a seemingly innocuous rock.

"Here goes nothing," Lysandra said, placing her palm on the cold surface. A click echoed through the air, and a section of the pathway realigned, granting them passage.

"Amazing," Aerin said, his voice tinged with relief as they advanced unscathed.

"Stick with me, and you'll be fine." Pipp winked. "Just remember, the forest takes care of its own."

"Thank you, Pipp," Lysandra said, acknowledging the

sprite's aid. "We won't forget this."

"May the winds be at your back," Pipp called after them as they moved on, his laughter fading into the rustling leaves.

"Let's keep moving," Lysandra said, feeling a surge of hope. With new allies and their combined strengths, they were one step closer to facing Malachor—and whatever else lay ahead.

"Look out!" Feyla's sharp cry sliced through the dense air of the Forbidden Forest as a platform wobbled precariously beneath her feet.

"Got you," Eolande said, his voice steady as he reached out from his floating stone, steadying Feyla with a firm hand on her shoulder.

"Thanks. That was too close." She flashed him a grateful yet rattled smile.

"Everyone, focus!" Lysandra's command cut through the tension like a blade. "We need to move in sync, or these platforms will toss us off like fleas."

"Sync? We can do that," Aerin agreed, his gaze locked onto the platforms ahead. "On your lead, Lysandra."

"Right. Everyone, watch the rhythm of the stones," she instructed. Her hair danced around her face as she raised her arms, summoning a gentle breeze to test the stability of their path.

"See that larger one there?" Lysandra pointed towards a floating rock, slightly more significant than the rest. "It looks steady. Let's aim for that as our next step. On my mark... now!"

The group leaped together, carried by the gust conjured by Lysandra's magic. They landed with a unified thud, the stone beneath them holding strong.

"Nice call," Aerin said, catching his breath.

"Keep it up, and we might just survive this," Lysandra replied with a half-smile, her eyes scanning the sky for the next safe passage.

"Speaking of survival," Aerin murmured, eyeing a nasty scrape on Eolande's arm. "Let me fix that."

"Later," Eolande insisted, though his wince betrayed the pain.

"No, now. We can't afford distractions." Aerin's tone brooked no argument as he touched the injury, his earthy magic glowing softly, mending flesh and easing pain.

"Better?" he asked after a moment.

"Much. Thank you," Eolande acknowledged, flexing his healed limb.

"Alright, let's keep moving. Shadow, stay close," Lysandra ordered, referring to the wolf padding cautiously from stone to stone.

"Should've known these challenges wouldn't be grounded," Feyla quipped, trying to lighten the mood as they eyed the next platform.

"Keep your wit sharp, but your focus sharper," Lysandra retorted, then paused to feel the breeze. "This next part will require precise timing. Wait for my signal."

"Understood," they chorused.

"Go!" At Lysandra's shout, they leaped again, soaring across the chasm between the stones. A sudden shift in the wind made the jump treacherous, and Feyla stumbled upon landing.

Aerin was instantly at her side, his healing energy cocooning her twisted ankle. "You're alright, just a sprain."

"Thank goodness for your quick reflexes," Feyla said, testing her weight on the foot.

"Let's not test them any further," Lysandra interjected. "Stay close and match my rhythm. We're nearly through."

"Lead the way," Aerin said, his trust in Lysandra evident despite the ever-present undercurrents of concern.

"Next time, we pick a quest," Feyla muttered as they prepared for another leap. "Let's find one with less altitude."

"Agreed," Eolande chimed in, the corner of his mouth turning up in a rare, small smile.

"Here we go," Lysandra announced, and once more, the group sprang into action, carried forward by the unity of their resolve and the strength of their bond.

The air crackled with a charge, making the hairs on Lysandra's arms stand. She sensed it before she saw it—the whirl of dust and leaves shaping into a towering form. The air elemental, an envoy of Malachor, barred their path with a cyclonic screech.

"Damn it!" Aerin cursed under his breath, drawing his sword, the metal gleaming against the swirling winds.

"Steel won't cut it," Lysandra called over the roar, her eyes narrowing as she studied their enemy. "We need to combine our magic!"

"Got any bright ideas?" Feyla shouted, clutching her bow, useless against this whirlwind adversary.

"Create a vortex!" Eolande yelled back, his agile form braced for action.

Lysandra nodded, extending her arms wide. "Aerin, funnel your healing aura into the wind. It'll stabilize a core for my fire."

"Let's do it," he replied, joining her. Their powers intertwined, his soothing energy blending with her fiery essence.

"Focus on the eye of the storm," she instructed, feeling the raw power surging between them.

"Right behind you," Aerin assured, his confidence bolstering her resolve.

With a thrust of her hands, Lysandra sent a controlled flame spiraling towards the elemental. The blaze encased the swirling wind, creating a fiery twister that roared towards the sky.

"Keep pushing!" she urged, her muscles tensing.

"Almost there!" Aerin added, his voice strained but unwavering.

The elements wailed, piercing their ears like shards of glass, but they held firm. And then, as suddenly as it had appeared, the creature exploded into a burst of wind and embers, dissipating into nothingness.

"Is it... over?" Feyla asked, her voice tinged with disbelief.

"Seems so," Eolande said, glancing around warily.

"Good work, everyone," Lysandra said, her chest heaving. She locked eyes with Aerin, a silent acknowledgment passing between them.

"Let's get out of this forest," Aerin said, sheathing his sword and offering his hand to Feyla to help steady her.

"I couldn't agree more," Feyla replied, accepting the gesture.

The group proceeded cautiously, moving through the now-still forest. They passed under the ancient trees' canopy, the shadows retreating as they neared the edge of the forbidden forest. When they finally stepped out into the open, they were greeted by the golden rays of the setting sun, painting the sky in hues of orange and pink.

"Look at that," Eolande murmured, gesturing toward the horizon. "Freedom never looked so beautiful."

"It feels like we've been reborn," Feyla said, a small smile playing on her lips.

"Let's not forget what waits for us," Lysandra reminded them, her gaze turning steely as she faced the path ahead.

"Whatever it is," Aerin said, standing beside her, "we'll face it together."

"United," Lysandra agreed, feeling the weight of the challenges they had overcome and those yet to come.

"Let's move," she commanded, her voice filled with determination.

As one, the group set off, leaving the dark embrace of the forbidden forest behind. Ahead lay the next stage of their perilous journey, the trials they had endured forging them stronger, ready to meet whatever destiny awaited in the Chronicles of Erenor.

Lysandra brushed a strand of hair from her face, squinting against the dying light as they trudged along the rugged path leading them to Malachor's stronghold. Aerin kept pace beside her, his gaze scanning the surroundings with the vigilance of a hawk.

"Every step we take," she muttered, "brings us closer to him."

Aerin nodded. "And to the end of this."

"Think we're ready for him?" Feyla chimed in, her eyes wary but determined as she adjusted the pack on her shoulders.

"Ready as we'll ever be," Eolande said, his agile form moving effortlessly across the uneven ground.

"Malachor won't be like the elementals," Lysandra warned, her tone edged with steel. "He knows us. Our strengths and weaknesses."

"Let him know," Aerin replied fiercely. "We've grown stronger with each battle. We're not the same people he once knew."

"True," Feyla added, "he's expecting the broken shards of the past. But we're a blade now—forged in fire and magic."

"Speaking of which," Eolande interjected, peering at Lysandra, "how's the control going? With the whole fire thing?"

"Better," she confessed, flexing her fingers and feeling the familiar warmth dance between them. "It's like a song I'm learning to harmonize with instead of trying to silence it."

"Good," Aerin said, squeezing her shoulder briefly. "We'll need every note of that song against Malachor."

"Remember, he's not just after us," Lysandra reminded them, her thoughts drifting to the greater peril looming over Erenor. "It's the whole of our world at stake."

"Which is exactly why we can't fail," Feyla said, her voice

hardening. "We owe it to Erenor."

"Failure isn't an option," Eolande agreed, his eyes reflecting the fire of the setting sun.

They continued in silence for a moment. Each was lost in their thoughts, the gravity of their quest settling around them like a cloak. The path wound through the foothills, the dark silhouette of Malachor's fortress rising ominously in the distance.

"Whatever happens," Lysandra began, breaking the silence. We stand together—not just for Erenor, but for each other."

"Always," Aerin affirmed, meeting her gaze.

"Then let's make sure we give Malachor a fight he'll never forget," Feyla said, a defiant glint in her eye.

"Here's to hope," Eolande added, "and to us, the ones who'll bring the dawn to Erenor once more."

"Here's to us," they echoed, their voices mingling with the whisper of the wind.

As night fell and stars began to dot the sky above, their resolve shone brighter than any celestial body. Tomorrow, they will meet their fate head-on. Tomorrow, they will face Malachor. And they would do so as one.

Chapter 7

THE TEMPLE OF SHADOWS,

The dense canopy of the Forbidden Forest cast eerie shadows on the forest floor as the group moved cautiously through the undergrowth. Shadow, Lysandra's loyal black wolf, led the way, his keen senses attuned to the dangers lurking in Malachor's territory. Lysandra, Aerin, Feyla, and Eolande followed closely, their weapons ready and their nerves on edge.

As they ventured deeper into the forest's heart, the air grew heavier with an oppressive sense of foreboding. The forest whispered with the remnants of dark magic, a constant reminder that they were in enemy territory. The twisted trees and thick undergrowth created a labyrinthine path, making every step forward a challenge.

Shadow suddenly stopped, his ears pricking up and his nose twitching. With a low growl, he turned and loped back to the group, signaling them to follow.

Lysandra kneeled beside her faithful companion, running a

hand through his thick fur. "What is it, boy?" she murmured, trusting his instincts.

Shadow whined softly, his eyes meeting hers with an intensity that spoke volumes. Lysandra nodded, rising to her feet and turning to the others. "Shadow senses something up ahead," she said, her voice low and tense. "We need to be careful."

Aerin stepped forward, his hand resting on the hilt of his sword. "Do you think it's one of Malachor's traps?" He asked, his brow furrowed with concern.

"I'm not sure," Lysandra replied, "but we can't afford to take any chances. Stay alert and watch each other's backs."

The group advanced cautiously, their senses heightened. Shadow led the way, his nose to the ground as he tracked the source of the disturbance.

As they pressed deeper into the forest, the trees seemed to close in around them, their gnarled branches reaching out like grasping fingers. The air grew colder, and a thick mist began to swirl around their feet, obscuring the path ahead.

Feyla shivered, pulling her cloak tighter around her shoulders. "I don't like this," she whispered, her voice trembling slightly. "It feels like the forest is trying to keep us out."

Eolande placed a comforting hand on her arm. "We've come too far to turn back now," he said, his voice steady and reassuring. "Whatever lies ahead, we'll face it together."

Lysandra nodded, her jaw set with determination. "Eolande's right. We have to keep moving, no matter what."

Shadow suddenly froze, his hackles rising as a low growl rumbled in his throat. Lysandra held up a hand, signaling for the others to stop. "What is it, Shadow?" she murmured, scanning the shadows for movement.

The wolf's ears flattened against his head, and he bared his teeth in a silent snarl. Lysandra's heart raced as she realized they were not alone.

A rustling in the undergrowth made them all spin around, their weapons drawn and ready. Twisted, malformed creatures emerged from the shadows—shadow hounds, their eyes glowing with an eerie red light.

Lysandra cursed under her breath. "Malachor's minions," she spat, her grip tightening on her sword. "Get ready to fight!"

The shadow hounds lunged forward, their jaws snapping and claws tearing at the air. Lysandra met them head-on, her sword flashing in the dim light as she fought to keep them at bay.

Aerin unleashed a blast of earthy magic, sending several creatures flying backward into the trees. Feyla and Eolande fought with deadly precision, their daggers finding their marks.

Shadow leaped into the fray, his powerful jaws clamping down on the throat of a shadow hound and shaking it violently. The creature let out a high-pitched yelp before going limp, its body dissolving into a cloud of black smoke.

Despite their best efforts, the shadow hounds kept coming, their numbers seeming to multiply with every passing moment. Lysandra knew they couldn't keep this up forever—they needed to find a way out of this ambush and keep moving toward their goal.

"We need to break through their lines!" she shouted over the chaos of battle. "Aerin, can you clear a path?"

The former witch hunter nodded grimly, his hands glowing with a fierce green light. With a cry of effort, he unleashed a blast of magic that sent the shadow hounds flying in all directions, creating a temporary gap in their ranks.

"Now!" Lysandra yelled, urging the others forward. "Run!"

They sprinted through the forest, dodging and weaving between the trees. The shadow hounds pursued them, their howls echoing through the air like the cries of the damned.

Lysandra's lungs burned with the effort of running, but she didn't dare slow down. Shadow raced ahead of her, his powerful legs carrying him swiftly through the undergrowth.

At last, they burst into a small clearing. The shadow hounds momentarily fell behind, snarling in frustration. Lysandra leaned against a tree, her chest heaving as she fought to catch her breath.

"Is everyone all right?" she asked, scanning her companions for any sign of injury.

Feyla nodded, her face pale but determined. "We're fine," she said, her voice shaking slightly. "But we can't keep running forever."

Aerin's jaw clenched. "We won't have to," he said, his voice low and fierce. "Look."

He pointed ahead to where the trees thinned out, revealing a towering stone structure in the distance. It was the Temple of Shadows, its dark walls seeming to absorb what little light penetrated the dense canopy above.

Lysandra's heart raced with a mix of fear and anticipation. "That's it," she breathed. "One of Malachor's strongholds."

Eolande stepped forward, his eyes narrowing. "And our best chance at finding a way to stop him," he said grimly.

Shadow let out a low whine, his tail tucking between his legs. Lysandra kneeled beside him, running a soothing hand over his fur. "I know, boy," she murmured. "I feel it, too. The darkness here is stronger than anything we've faced before."

She rose to her feet, squaring her shoulders and facing her companions. "But we can't let that stop us," she said, her voice ringing with conviction. "We've come too far to turn back now. Erenor is counting on us."

Aerin stepped forward, his hand finding hers and reassuringly squeezing it. "We're with you, Lysandra," he said softly. "No matter what happens."

Feyla and Eolande nodded in agreement, their faces set with grim determination.

With a deep breath, Lysandra turned towards the temple, her sword gripped tightly in her hand. "Then let's finish this," she said, her voice low and fierce. "For Erenor and each other."

As one, they moved toward the temple, the weight of their mission pressing down on them like a physical burden. Shadow padded silently at Lysandra's side, his presence a comforting reminder of their unbreakable bond.

The air grew colder as they approached the temple, the darkness thickening with every step. Lysandra could feel the weight of Malachor's malevolent presence pressing down on her, but she refused to let it shake her resolve.

At last, they reached the temple's entrance, its towering stone doors looming like some great beast's jaws. Strange symbols were carved into the rock. Their meaning was lost to time and the ravages of Malachor's dark magic.

Lysandra placed her hand on the cold stone, feeling the pulse of dark energy from within. She glanced back at her companions, seeing the same mix of fear and determination in their eyes that she felt in her heart.

"Whatever happens," she said softly, "we face it together. As one."

Aerin stepped forward, his hand resting on the door beside hers. "As one," he echoed, his voice low and fierce.

With a deep breath, Lysandra pushed against the doors, feeling them give way beneath her touch. Slowly, they swung open, revealing a yawning darkness beyond.

Shadow let out a low growl, his fur standing on end as he stared into the abyss. Lysandra placed a comforting hand on his head, silently urging him forward.

Together, they stepped into the Temple of Shadows, the darkness swallowing them whole. The doors swung shut behind them with a resounding boom, sealing them inside.

Lysandra blinked, her eyes struggling to adjust to the sudden lack of light. She could hear the others breathing heavily beside her, their presence a small comfort in the oppressive gloom.

"Stay close," she whispered, her voice sounding unnaturally

loud in the stillness. "And be ready for anything."

They moved forward cautiously, their footsteps echoing off the stone walls. The air was thick and heavy, laden with the stench of decay and dark magic. As they ventured deeper into the temple, they noticed strange, flickering lights in the distance. Lysandra's heart raced as she realized what they were—torches, their flames casting eerie shadows on the walls.

"Someone's been here recently," Aerin murmured, his hand tightening on the hilt of his sword.

"Malachor or his minions," Lysandra said. "We need to be careful."

They pressed on, the torchlight growing brighter with every step. At last, they emerged into a vast chamber, its walls lined with ancient runes and symbols that pulsed with a sickly green light. In the center of the room stood a massive stone altar, its surface stained with the dark rust of old blood. Hovering above the altar like an evil specter was the Heart of Shadows.

Lysandra's breath caught in her throat at the sight of the dark crystal, its surface swirling with an inky blackness that seemed to absorb all light. This was the source of Malachor's power, the key to his hold over the Shadow Realm.

"By the gods," Feyla breathed, her eyes wide with horror. "The darkness radiating from that thing... it's overwhelming."

Eolande stepped forward, his jaw set with grim determination. "We have to destroy it," he said, his voice low and fierce. "It's the only way to stop Malachor."

Aerin nodded, his hand glowing with the green light of his

earth magic. "I'll create a barrier to contain the blast," he said. "But we'll need to act quickly. Once we start, Malachor will know we're here."

Lysandra took a deep breath, her grip tightening on her sword. "Then let's not waste any more time," she said, her voice ringing with conviction. "For Erenor and the future."

Before they could move, a sudden rumble echoed through the chamber. The ground beneath them shook violently, and they struggled to keep their footing.

"What now?" Feyla shouted, gripping her dagger.

Eolande's eyes darted around the room, his expression filled with alarm. "Something's coming," he warned. "Brace yourselves!"

Without warning, the temple walls seemed to ripple and shift, the runes glowing brighter as the entire structure groaned under an unseen force. The Heart of Shadows pulsed ominously, its energy expanding outward in waves.

Shadow barked frantically, backing away from the altar as dark tendrils emerged from the crystal, writhing and twisting like living shadows.

"Everyone, get back!" Lysandra yelled, her voice cutting through the chaos.

The tendrils lashed out, striking the ground and walls, sending shards of stone flying. Lysandra raised her sword, preparing to attack, but a sudden power surge knocked her off her feet.

Aerin rushed to her side, helping her to her feet. "We need to get out of here," he said urgently. "This place is collapsing!"

Lysandra's heart pounded as she looked around the chamber, realizing the full extent of their peril. The temple was coming apart, and they were trapped in the heart of Malachor's dark magic.

"Follow me!" she shouted, leading them towards a side passage that appeared to offer a way out.

The group scrambled to their feet and followed her, dodging falling debris and avoiding the lashing tendrils of dark energy. Shadow led the way, his keen senses guiding them through the maze of crumbling stone and swirling shadows.

As they fled the collapsing chamber, Lysandra glanced back at the Heart of Shadows, now fully engulfed in a vortex of dark power. They had come so close to destroying it, but now they had to survive.

"Keep moving!" she urged, pushing them forward. "We can't let this place be our tomb!"

With every step, the temple's destruction grew more intense, with the walls buckling and the floor cracking under the strain. But Lysandra refused to give up, and her determination to save Erenor drove her forward. At last, they burst through a narrow opening, emerging into a hidden tunnel leading away from the main chamber. The rumble of the collapsing temple faded behind them as they stumbled into the passage's relative safety.

Lysandra paused, catching her breath, and checked on her companions. They were battered and bruised, but alive.

"We need to regroup and find another way to destroy the Heart of Shadows," Aerin said, his voice filled with resolve.

"Malachor will know we're here by now."

Lysandra nodded, her eyes blazing with determination. "We'll find a way," she vowed. "No matter what it takes, we will stop him."

With a final glance back at the temple, she turned and led the way down the tunnel, the flickering torchlight guiding them towards their next challenge. They had escaped the immediate danger, but their battle against Malachor was far from over.

As they navigated the treacherous path, the forest seemed to converge around them, whispering maliciously and conjuring illusions to disorient them. Their every step was met with hostile resistance, but through determination and unity, they pushed forward.

After what seemed like an eternity, the dark, oppressive shadows faded, giving way to a gentle, golden glow filtering through the branches. They emerged from the clutches of the Forbidden Forest into an open, sunlit clearing, their breaths ragged but triumphant.

Lysandra's eyes met her companions', and she could see the same relief and pride reflected in their expressions.

"We made it," she said, her voice filled with exhaustion and triumph. "We faced the darkness and emerged victorious."

As the tension ebbed away, they shared a moment of hard-earned victory, knowing that they had braved the perils of the forest together and emerged stronger for it. Their journey was far from over, but they knew they were stronger together. With Shadow at their side and their unwavering courage lighting the way, they moved forward, ready to face whatever challenges lay ahead.

The fate of Erenor hung in the balance, and they would not rest until they had secured a future free from Malachor's dark grip. They would fight on for Erenor, each other, and the light that still shone in their hearts.

Chapter 8

THE SHATTERED REALM

Lysandra's heart pounded in her chest as she gripped her sword tightly and stepped forward with determination. Aerin and the others, their faces a mix of fear and resolve, flanked her. Shadow paced beside her, his fur bristling with tension. They had only walked about a mile back into the forbidden forest when they came across this cavern.

"Let's investigate." Lysandra's voice was clear and unafraid, masking her beating heart. Of course, she felt afraid, but she wouldn't show it.

Aerin gave her hand a quick squeeze before grabbing his daggers.

The group of friends carefully matched their steps and, hunched forward, weapons drawn, crept forward.

As Lysandra and her companions stepped further into the dark cavern, they were immediately overwhelmed by Malachor's presence. It was a suffocating darkness, thick with the stench of decay and the weight of malice. The cavern's walls pulsed with unnatural life, the shadows twisting and writhing as if under the sorcerer's control.

Malachor sat upon his conjured throne, a monument of obsidian and dark magic floating above the ground. His face was gaunt and pale, and his eyes glowed like embers in the darkness. A cruel sneer twisted his thin lips, and his long, talon-like fingers tapped an ominous rhythm on the arm of his throne.

"Welcome, heroes," he mocked, his voice a sibilant whisper that echoed through the cavernous chamber. "I must admit, I'm impressed you made it this far. But your journey ends here, at the feet of the true master of Erenor."

Lysandra's strong and defiant voice rang out as she stepped forward, her sword held high. The blade glimmered with an inner light, a beacon of hope against the oppressive darkness. "Your reign ends here, Malachor," she declared, echoing through the chamber.

Malachor's laughter, a harsh, grating sound, set Lysandra's teeth on edge. "You are nothing but insects to me," he spat, rising from his throne in a swirl of dark robes. "I have spent centuries preparing for this moment, gathering power, and bending the very fabric of reality to my will. Do you think you can stop me?" His words hung in the air, heavy with impending doom.

Aerin moved to stand beside Lysandra, his hand resting on the hilt of his sword. His dark eyes blazed with determination, and his voice was steady and unwavering. "We have faced countless challenges to get here, Malachor. We have battled the horrors of the shadow realm and the darkness within our hearts. We will not falter now, not when the fate of Erenor hangs in the balance."

His words, a testament to their unyielding spirit, echoed through the semi-dark cavern.

Malachor's eyes narrowed, and the air around him crackled with dark energy. "Then you will die together," he hissed, raising his arms in a gesture of summoning.

With a wave of his hand, Malachor conjured a horde of shadow creatures, their forms twisting and writhing as they emerged from the darkness. Their eyes glowed with an evil red light, and their claws and fangs dripped with a viscous, black ichor.

The heroes leaped into action, their weapons gleaming in the dim light as they confronted the relentless onslaught. Lysandra and Aerin fought side by side, moving in perfect harmony as they weaved through the chaos. "Stay close, Lysandra!" Aerin shouted, creating a protective wall of earth with his magic as Lysandra's runic sword danced through the shadowy creatures with blinding speed. "I've got your back, Aerin," Lysandra called back, her voice unwavering amidst the fray.

Meanwhile, Feyla and Eolande moved with deadly precision, their daggers finding the vulnerabilities in the creatures' defenses. "Watch your flank, Eolande!" Feyla warned as she darted around, her movements blurry as she expertly landed each precise strike. "I see them, Feyla," Eolande replied, his voice calm as he let his daggers fly with unerring accuracy.

As the battle raged on, Shadow dashed in and out of the

chaotic struggle of wills, his deep growls reverberating in the cavern as he lunged at the shadow creatures. "Good boy, Shadow! Keep them at bay!" Lysandra encouraged him, spurring the wolf on as he fearlessly fought alongside his companions.

Despite their tireless efforts, the relentless tide of shadow creatures seemed never-ending. "They just keep coming!" Aerin shouted, frustration evident in his voice, as he created another barrier to repel the encroaching enemies. "We need to find another way to stem the tide," Lysandra declared, her eyes scanning the cavern for a solution amidst the chaos.

Malachor watched from his throne, a cruel smile playing on his lips. "You cannot win," he taunted, his voice a malevolent purr. "The Shadowrealm and Erenor will soon be one, and darkness will reign eternal. Surrender now, and I may grant you a merciful death." He laughed and suddenly disappeared in a dark cloud of dust and smoke. Of course, he left his creatures behind.

Lysandra gritted her teeth, her arms burning with fatigue, as she fended off another shadow creature. She knew they couldn't keep this up forever. They needed to find a way to strike at Malachor directly, cut off the serpent's head, and end his reign of terror once and for all.

Suddenly, a blinding light filled the cavern, and a familiar figure shimmered before Lysandra. It was Aviara, the redeemed deity, her form shimmering with divine energy. Her eyes were filled with fierce determination, and her voice was urgent as she spoke.

"Lysandra," Aviara said, her words cutting through the chaos of battle. "You must seek the seer's orb. It will reveal the path to victory, the key to unraveling Malachor's power and restoring balance to Erenor."

Lysandra's eyes widened, a spark of hope kindling in her heart. "Where can I find it?" she asked, her voice strained with effort as she dodged another blow from a shadow creature.

"In the Shattered Realm," Aviara replied, her form fading. "But be warned, the path is treacherous. Malachor's influence has spread far and wide, and the fabric of reality is torn asunder in that forsaken place."

With those words, Aviara vanished, leaving Lysandra with a renewed sense of purpose.

A spark of hope kindled in her heart, fueling her determination. She turned to her companions, her voice rising above the chaos of battle, filled with a newfound optimism.

"We need to retreat!" she shouted, her words laced with urgency. "Aviara has shown me the way forward, but we cannot win this battle here and now. We must find the Seer's Orb in the Shattered Realm!"

Aerin nodded, his face grim with determination. "Then let's make our escape," he said, his earth magic surging to create a stone wall between them and the advancing shadow hounds. "We'll cut a path through these abominations and make for the entrance. Together, we can overcome any obstacle."

With a concerted effort, the group fought their way toward the cavern's entrance, their movements desperate and urgent.

The shadow creatures who broke free from the spell clawed at them, their hideous shrieks filling the air, but the heroes pressed on, their resolve unbreakable.

Malachor's laughter echoed unseen behind them, a promise of the darkness that sought to consume Erenor. "Run, little heroes!" he taunted, his voice filled with malicious glee. "Run and hide, but know there is nowhere in this world or any other where you can escape my reach. "In the end, the shadows will consume everything."

As they burst out of the cave, the heroes found themselves again in the heart of the forbidden forest. The air was thick with the stench of decay and dark magic, and the trees seemed to close in around them, their gnarled branches reaching out like grasping claws.

Lysandra leaned against a twisted trunk, her chest heaving with exertion. Her silver-white hair clung to her sweat-drenched brow, and her eyes were filled with fierce determination.

"We need to find the Shattered Realm," she said, her voice heavy with exhaustion but laced with an unwavering resolve. "Aviara said the Seer's Orb is our key to defeating Malachor, unraveling his power, and restoring balance to Erenor."

Aerin placed a comforting hand on her shoulder, his touch steady amidst the chaos. "We'll find it," he said, his voice filled with a quiet strength. "Together, we can overcome any obstacle and face any challenge. Our love and bond are stronger than any darkness Malachor can conjure."

Feyla and Eolande exchanged worried glances, their faces pale in the dim light filtering through the canopy. "The Shattered Realm is a dangerous place," Feyla said, her brow furrowed with concern. "It's said to be a land where the boundaries between worlds are thin and the laws of nature hold no sway. We must be cautious, for the very fabric of reality is fragile there."

Eolande nodded, his eyes scanning the shadows that seemed to press in around them. "Malachor's influence is sure to be even stronger in that forsaken place," he warned, his voice low and urgent. "We'll need to be on our guard, to trust in each other and the strength of our bond."

Lysandra took a deep breath, drawing strength from the presence of her companions. They had come so far, and she knew the road ahead would be fraught with quite possibly even danger and uncertainty, but she also knew they could not give up now.

"We have no choice," she said, her voice filled with a quiet determination. "The fate of our world and the lives of all those we hold dear depend on us. We must find the Seer's Orb and unravel the secrets of Malachor's power, no matter the cost."

As the group set out again, their steps heavy with fatigue and their hearts burdened with the knowledge of the challenges ahead, Lysandra drew closer to Aerin. Amid the chaos and darkness, his presence was a steadying force, a reminder of the love and hope that still existed in the world.

"Aerin," she said softly, her hand finding him in the gloom. "I couldn't do this without you, without the strength of your love and the warmth of your presence. You are my anchor, my guiding light in the darkness."

Aerin's fingers tightened around hers, and he pulled her close, resting his forehead against hers. At that moment, the world seemed to fall away, and there were only the two of them, their hearts beating.

"You'll never have to face this alone, Lysandra," he murmured, his breath warm against her skin. "I'll be by your side, always. Our love is a force that can overcome any darkness, a light that will guide us through the shadows."

For a moment, they stood there, drawing strength from each other's presence. Lysandra closed her eyes, feeling the warmth of Aerin's love washing over her, chasing away the chill of the forest and the lurking dread of the challenges to come.

Lysandra could feel the weight of responsibility pressing down on her shoulders, a burden she carried with grim determination.

Sensing her unease, Aerin grasped her hand, offering a reassuring squeeze. "We're in this together, Lysandra," he said softly, his voice cutting through the oppressive silence of the woods. "No matter what lies ahead, you will never be alone."

Lysandra nodded slightly, feeling grateful for his unwavering support. She knew his words were more than just empty reassurance—they promised solidarity and love that she could cling to in the darkest moments.

Further ahead, Feyla and Eolande exchanged whispered words barely audible over the rustling of leaves and the distant howls of unseen creatures. Their expressions were grave, and their eyes scanned the shadows with wary determination.

"We must be vigilant," Feyla urged, her voice calm but firm. "Malachor's minions could be lurking around any corner, waiting to strike when we least expect it."

Eolande nodded in agreement, his gaze flickering towards the twisting branches overhead. "The Shattered Realm is a place of twisted magic and unfathomable dangers," he warned. "We must tread carefully if we are to emerge unscathed."

Lysandra felt a shiver run down her spine at his words, the reality of their mission settling heavily on her heart. The path ahead was dangerous, but she knew that turning back was not an option—not when so much was at stake.

"We press on," she declared firmly, her voice clear and unwavering in the oppressive silence. "The Seer's Orb is waiting for us and, with it, the power to defeat Malachor once and for all."

Aerin squeezed her hand in silent agreement, his eyes alight with determination. "Here we go again...together," he reiterated, his voice steady with conviction. "We will not falter."

Within the Seer's Orb lay the key to unlocking an unimaginable power that could turn the tide against Malachor, a war that had ravaged the lands for far too long. As they pressed on, her comrades were reminded of the cause they fought for—the dream of a world free from Malachor's tyranny.

Amid the towering trees that stretched towards the sky, the group trekked onward, each step bringing them closer to their goal. The dense foliage around them seemed to hold secrets of its own, and whispers of the past reached their ears as if the very forest was guiding them toward their destiny.

The group stumbled upon a clearing as the sun dipped below the horizon, casting long shadows on the forest floor. At its heart stood a solitary, ancient tree, with its gnarled branches reaching out like twisted but welcoming arms.

"Let's rest here," Lysandra said, sounding weary.

Aerin, Eolande, and Feyla went to gather some firewood as she sat against the tree, gathering her strength.

Their voices carried through the forest as they gathered around the crackling fire that night. They recounted past adventures and remembered their friend, the dragon Harrow, who had sacrificed himself to save them all. Amidst warmth and sadness, they formed bonds that would carry them through the trials ahead.

The call of the Seer's Orb grew stronger, urging them forward. They could feel its power calling to them, encouraging them forward, and they knew that they would not rest until they had found it.

As they sat there, the warmth of the flames dancing in their eyes, Feyla spoke up, her voice steady yet filled with concern. "We cannot afford to let our guard down," she warned, her gaze flickering toward the shadows, growing darker with each passing moment.

Eolande nodded in agreement, his expression grave. "The closer we get to the Seer's Orb, the more treacherous our path will become," he said, his tone somber. "We must remain vigilant and ready for whatever challenges lie ahead."

Aerin's eyes met Lysandra's, a silent understanding passing between them. "We've faced dangers before and always got out on the other side much stronger," he said softly, reassuring Lysandra and the entire group.

Lysandra felt a surge of gratitude for the companions at her side; their unwavering support gave her strength. "Thank you, all of you," she said, her voice filled with determination. "Together, we can overcome anything that stands in our way."

Feyla reached out to place a hand on Lysandra's shoulder, her touch reassuring. "We are a team," she affirmed, her voice unwavering. "And as a team, we will prevail."

Eolande added his own words of encouragement, his gaze unwavering. "Let us face whatever challenges await us with courage and unity," he said, echoing through the clearing.

The group fell into a companionable silence, each lost in their thoughts as they steeled themselves for the trials. The night air was alive with the sounds of the forest, a constant reminder of the dangers lurking in the darkness beyond.

But as they sat together around the fire, a sense of camaraderie and determination filled their hearts, lighting a fire within them that no amount of darkness could extinguish. They were confident they would face it together, no matter what awaited them in the Shattered Realm, because of each other's presence.

"With renewed strength and determination, they set out early the next morning, prepared to confront challenges and emerge victorious over Malachor. Lysandra was adamant that they would be able to overcome any challenge as they made their way toward the center of the Shattered Realm's darkness. "Together, we can conquer anything," she whispered as they continued their dangerous journey."

Chapter 9

THE SEER'S ORB

The day went mostly without incident, although they were constantly on edge. The Shadow Realm was not precisely a restful place to wander around in.

"Where are we heading?" Aerin asked, his breath short, every stride a testament to the urgency that propelled them forward.

"Somewhere safe," Lysandra replied. "A cave Aviara mentioned is linked with the Seer's Orb."

"Right, another cave and the Seer's Orb," Feyla interjected, her eyes alight with curiosity despite the fatigue on her face. "She said it's the key to defeating Malachor for good."

"Exactly," said Lysandra, navigating a particularly thorny bush with ease born from years of combat and flight. "It holds power drawn from the very essence of Erenor itself. If we can find it,

"We'll end this nightmare once and for all," finished Aerin, his determination mirroring Lysandra's.

"Here!" Lysandra signaled, halting before an almost imperceptible crevice in the rock face. She traced her fingers along the angular outline until they came across the cleverly concealed catch—an antiquated moss-covered mechanism.

"Are you sure?" Aerin murmured, his hand instinctively reaching for his sword hilt as he peered into the darkness ahead.

"Trust me," Lysandra said, locking eyes with him. There was no room for doubt, not when they'd come so far.

"Always," he replied, squeezing her hand briefly before letting go.

With a persistent push, Lysandra activated the mechanism, and the rock wall slid aside, revealing a spacious cavern that promised respite from their relentless journey. The group filed in, the walls echoing with their labored breathing and the soft clink of their weapons.

"Secure the entrance," Lysandra ordered, her gaze sweeping the cave's interior, ever vigilant.

"Done and done," Eolande confirmed, his sharp, elven senses already detecting the subtle energies that would conceal their presence.

"Let's ensure we're not followed," Feyla added, tinkering with one of her devices designed to alert them to unwelcome guests.

"Good thinking." Lysandra nodded, her warrior's instincts always planning one step.

"Once we're settled," Aerin began, the memory of their escape receding but not enough to prevent concern from seeping through. We need to talk about what comes next. We won't have much time before Malachor realizes what we are doing."

"And we'll be ready," Lysandra stated, her confidence unshaken. "The Seer's Orb won't remain hidden from us. Not when Erenor's fate hangs in the balance."

"Then let's hope the prophecy is right," Feyla said quietly, her gaze distant. Her thoughts were already racing ahead to the challenges that awaited them.

"Prophecies have a way of fulfilling themselves," Lysandra mused. "But it's our choices that will shape the outcome."

"Agreed," Aerin said, looking around at their makeshift sanctuary. "For now, we rest. When dawn breaks, we move for the seer's orb."

"Rest, strategize, and keep hope alive," Lysandra added, her dark eyes reflecting the flicker of their campfire, a beacon of warmth in the heart of uncertainty. "Together, we're unstoppable."

"Unstoppable," echoed Feyla, a smile touching her lips. The word seemed to hang in the air—a vow charged with magic and the promise of a future they were fighting to reclaim.

Lysandra kneeled beside the flickering campfire, her eyes scanning the dimly lit faces of her comrades. She reached out with a steadiness that belied the tremor in her fingers, unwinding the crudely tied bandage from Aerin's forearm.

"Still playing the stoic, I see," she chided softly, assessing the gash with a practiced gaze.

"Only when it keeps the others focused," he replied, his voice barely above a whisper, betraying none of the pain he must have felt. He could have healed it himself, but he preferred the sharpness of the pain to keep him focused.

"Focus is good. But not at the expense of your well-being." Her touch was light as she cleaned the wound, the warmth from her hands hinting at the magic simmering beneath her skin, ready to mend flesh and bone.

"Is there any sign of infection?" Aerin asked, his eyes never leaving hers. His concern for himself was secondary to the worry reflected in them.

"None. You were lucky," Lysandra answered, the corner of her mouth lifting in a half-smile. She whispered an incantation and a soft glow enveloped her hands, seeping into the cut. "There. That should do it."

"Your magic..." Aerin began, but Lysandra cut him off.

"It is under control. It is always around you." She offered him a reassuring look, though the darkness within her threatened like a storm on the horizon.

"Thanks, Lys," he murmured, flexing his newly healed arm and testing its returned strength. He was still surprised that her elemental magic was continuing to grow. He had the healing powers and the elemental earth magic, yet his beautiful mage was here, healing his arm because he wouldn't.

"Alright, who's next?" Feyla piped up from across the cave, rolling up the sleeve of her tunic to reveal a bruised and swollen wrist. "I might've underestimated that last trap's kickback."

"Let me see," Lysandra said, moving to the younger woman.

As she gently probed the injury, Feyla winced but kept her complaints to herself.

"It looks like a sprain. No broken bones that need magic intervention, thankfully," Lysandra diagnosed, reaching for a salve she'd prepared earlier from their limited supplies. "This should help with the swelling."

"We can't have our resident genius incapacitated," Aerin quipped, moving to sit beside Feyla. They shared a grateful nod. Feyla wasn't offended that Lysandra, or even Aerin, didn't heal her outright—no need to use magic when simple remedies could do the job.

"Genius, huh? I'll add that to my repertoire of titles." Feyla retorted with a grin, her spirits undiminished even by the throes of adventure and danger.

"Rest it for now. And try to avoid using it too much," Lysandra instructed, securing another bandage with deft fingers.

"Right. Because avoiding using my hands is so easy for me," Feyla said sarcastically, but her tone held no bite. "Thanks, Lys."

"Anytime," Lysandra smiled and settled back, taking stock of their meager camp. While not home, the cave provided a momentary respite, a chance to breathe before the chaos that awaited them beyond its protective embrace.

"Are you okay? Truly?" Aerin's question was for her this time, his gaze searching hers for signs of strain.

"Me? I'm fine. Just a few scratches." She shrugged dismissively, brushing away his concern. But Aerin knew better; she saw the fatigue etched in the lines of her face and the slight slump of her shoulders.

"Lys," he murmured, reaching out to cup her cheek, the rough pad of his thumb tracing the path of a faint scar. "You don't always have to bear it alone."

She leaned into his touch, allowing herself this moment of weakness. "I know," she whispered. "That's why I have you."

He made the promise, "Always," and there was a whole world of meaning in that one word—a promise that went beyond the threats they were facing and a bond that was unbreakable in either light or shadow.

"Pass me the salve, will you?" Lysandra's voice cut through the dim silence of the hidden cave as she reached out a hand without looking. Aerin placed the small clay jar into her waiting palm, his fingers brushing over the cuts that marked her skin.

"Here," he said softly. He watched as she applied the healing ointment to a gash along Feyla's arm with practiced ease.

"Does it still hurt?" Lysandra asked, glancing up at Feyla with concern flickering in her eyes.

"Only when I laugh," Feyla quipped, wincing slightly but managing a grin. "Which, given our current situation, isn't likely."

"Your humor remains intact, at least," Aerin observed, allowing himself a small smile. It was a rare moment of fun amid their dire circumstances.

"Someone has to keep spirits up around here," Feyla replied, securing the bandage tightly. She shifted her gaze to the cave entrance, where shadows danced across the jagged rocks. "We've never been this close before. Malachor's Throne Room. We were right there."

Lysandra nodded, her expression turning somber. "And we nearly didn't make it out. But we did, and now we need a plan. We can't rush in blindly next time."

"Agreed," Aerin said, his voice steady. "But any plan we make has to account for the Seer's Orb. Aviara said It's the key to all of this."

"Right, the Seer's Orb." Feyla leaned back against the cool stone wall, crossing her arms. "Aviara said it would be our best shot at taking Malachor down. Any idea where to start looking?"

"Aviara mentioned the Ruins of Althoria in the Shattered Realm," Lysandra recalled, her brows knitting together in thought. "Legends say it's where the First Mage sealed away powerful artifacts. If the seer's orb is half as important as she claimed, it could be there."

"Ruins aren't exactly a rarity in Erenor," Aerin pointed out. "It'll take some narrowing down."

"Then we'll start at dawn," Lysandra decided, rising to her feet with determination. "We have enough supplies for a few days' travel, and if we're cautious, we should be able to avoid drawing attention."

"Speaking of supplies," Feyla interjected, rummaging through her pack. I've got these." She produced a set of small, intricately carved stones. Runestones. They should help mask our trail, at least for a while."

"See? Where would we be without your inventions, Feyla?" Lysandra offered a genuine smile, one that spoke of deep gratitude.

"Lost, or worse," Aerin agreed, earning a pleased nod from Feyla.

"Alright then," Lysandra said, clapping her hands together. "We rest, we heal, and at first light, we move toward Althoria. Together."

"Sounds like a plan," Feyla said. "A dangerous, potentially life-threatening plan... but what else is new?"

"Nothing worth having comes easy," Aerin murmured, meeting Lysandra's eye with a steadfast gaze.

"Especially freedom," Lysandra added, her voice unwavering.

"Especially that," Aerin echoed, and they all settled into a companionable silence, each lost in thoughts of the future—a future they were determined to fight for, no matter the cost.

The flickering flame of the campfire danced in Lysandra's peripheral vision as she unfurled the worn map across the uneven surface of the cave floor—the small group huddled close, their faces a mix of determination and weariness. Aerin knelt beside her, eyes scanning the ancient pathways and forgotten lands crisscrossing the parchment.

"Aviara said the Seer's Orb is hidden where 'the sun's tears cannot reach,'" Feyla recited, tucking a strand of dark brown hair behind her ear. "Any ideas on what that cryptic clue means?"

"Could be underground," Aerin suggested, tracing a finger

over a range of mountains depicted on the map. "Caves, tunnels, some sort of subterranean hideaway."

"Or maybe it's metaphorical," Lysandra mused, her finger hovering over a dense forest known for its perpetual canopy. "A place so shrouded, daylight barely touches it."

"Malachor's got spies everywhere," Feyla pointed out, frowning. "We can't just traipse around the forbidden forest and then the shattered realm, looking for every dark corner."

"Runestones will cover our tracks for a time," Lysandra noted, meeting Aerin's gaze. "But we need to be smart about this. Quick in, quick out."

"Right. So, do we split up and cover more ground?" Aerin asked, though his tone betrayed his hesitance at the idea of separation.

"Too risky," Lysandra dismissed with a shake of her head. "We stick together. One wrong move could lead Malachor right to us—or worse, to the Orb."

"Then we'll need a distraction," Feyla chimed in, her eyes lighting up with the spark of a plan forming. "Something to send Malachor's forces on a wild goose chase."

"Can you handle that?" Aerin asked, an eyebrow raised in challenge.

"Please," Feyla scoffed playfully. "Give me a few gadgets and some time, and I'll have them chasing their tails till next solstice."

"Good," Lysandra said, the corners of her lips twitching upward. "Let's leave the forbidden forest and go to the forests of

Althoria first. It's closest, and if the Orb isn't there, we move to the mountains."

"Althoria it is," Aerin agreed, nodding. "We should leave no trace of our stay here. If Malachor's minions find this place,

"They won't," Lysandra cut in, her voice firm. "Not until we're long gone and the Seer's Orb is in our hands."

"It sounds like you've got it all figured out." Feyla grinned, standing and stretching her limbs. "Just another day saving the world, huh?"

"Something like that," Lysandra replied, carefully rolling up the map. She glanced around at her companions, their faces etched with the same resolve that steeled her heart. Together, they were unstoppable. Together, they would find the Orb and end Malachor's reign.

"Let's get moving," she announced, extinguishing the fire with a swift gesture. The cave plunged into darkness, but not for long. With their path illuminated by purpose, the intrepid band set out, undaunted by the dangers that awaited them in the shadows of Erenor.

As the others fanned out to secure the perimeter, Aerin reached for Lysandra's arm, a silent plea in his eyes. She nodded, understanding his need for solace amidst the chaos. They slipped away, their steps muffled by the mossy undergrowth, until they found themselves secluded and serene at the mouth of a secondary cavern.

"I thought we could use a breather," Aerin murmured, leaning against the cool stone wall. The dim glow from the lichen above painted his features in shades of silvery blue.

"Breathers are a luxury we can seldom afford," Lysandra replied, but her tone was soft, free of the edge it often carried. She joined him against the wall, her gaze fixed on the dance of shadows beyond the cave entrance.

"True." He sighed. "But necessary. You know, back there."

"Hey." Lysandra cut him off, her voice steady despite the tremor she felt inside. "We've faced worse. And we made it. We always make it."

"Because of you," he said, turning to face her. His hand hesitated, then settled on her shoulder, grounding yet gentle. "You're unstoppable, Lyss. Even when everything falls apart."

"Even unstoppable forces need a moment to gather strength," she admitted with a half-smile. Her hand found its way to his, their fingers intertwining instinctively. "Especially with what's coming next."

"Finding the Seer's Orb," Aerin said, his thumb brushing over her knuckles. "It's not just about beating Malachor anymore, is it?"

"No, it's more than that," she confessed, the weight of destiny pressing upon her chest. "It's about restoring balance. About ending this war without losing ourselves in the process."

Aerin pulled her closer, their bodies aligning like two pieces of a puzzle long left unsolved. "I'll be with you every step of the way, Lysandra. Not because I think you need protection, but because I can't imagine facing any of this without you."

"Nor I, you," she whispered, resting her head on his shoulder.

In the quiet of the hidden cavern, with the promise of danger lurking just beyond the horizon, Lysandra allowed the walls she so carefully constructed to crumble, if only for a moment.

Their shared silence was a balm to the chaos of their lives, a space where words were unnecessary and where the simple act of being together spoke volumes. With each breath, they drew strength from one another, fortifying their resolve for the trials ahead.

"Come on," Lysandra finally said, pulling back slightly to look into Aerin's eyes. "We've got an orb to find, and I'd rather not keep fate waiting."

"Lead the way," Aerin said, reluctantly releasing her hand. Together, they stepped back into the fray, their tender moment a fleeting memory but one that would sustain them through the darkness to come.

"Wait!" Feyla's voice sliced through the stillness of the cavern, sharp as a dagger. The urgency in her tone halted Lysandra and Aerin in their tracks.

Lysandra's hand instinctively went to the hilt of her sword, her eyes scanning the shadows. "What is it? Are we not alone?"

Aerin stepped closer, his protective nature flaring despite the absence of immediate danger. Yet there was no fear in Feyla's wide-eyed expression, only wonder. She gestured at the cave wall, where the flickering light from their makeshift torches revealed etchings that danced before their eyes.

"Look!" Feyla breathed out, her fingers tracing the lines of an ancient script. "This is old—very old. It's talking about... the

Seer's Orb!"

"Are you sure?" Lysandra asked, her skepticism born of weariness. They had encountered too many false leads on their journey.

"Positive." Feyla glanced up, her brown eyes alight with excitement. "It speaks of the orb's power to pierce the veil between worlds. To reveal the unseen."

"Could it mean seeing through Malachor's illusions?" Aerin mused, his thoughts aligning with the promise of hope.

"Maybe." Feyla nodded, her usual quirkiness replaced by solemnity. "But it's more than that. This prophecy—it's like a guide. It doesn't just tell us what the orb can do; it hints at how to use it."

"Then it's vital we understand every word," Lysandra declared, feeling the weight of destiny settle upon her shoulders once more.

The trio crowded around the ancient writings. Their heads bobbled together in the study. As they deciphered the cryptic message, the reality of their quest became clearer. But so, too, did the challenges ahead.

"Malachor won't give up easily," Aerin said, breaking the silence. "He'll be hunting for us. For this knowledge."

"Let him come," Lysandra replied, her voice steely. "We've faced worse than his minions."

"Still." Aerin's gaze found hers, the concern evident in his eyes. "Promise me something, Lysandra. Promise me you won't take unnecessary risks. Not for the Orb, not for Erenor."

"Is that your way of saying you care?" she teased, though her heart swelled at his words.

"Deeply," he affirmed, taking her hand and squeezing it gently. "You know I'd move mountains for you."

"Mountains we can handle," she smiled back, intertwining her fingers with his. "It's the shadows that are trickier."

"Then we face them together," he promised, embracing her. "No shadows can withstand our combined light."

"Agreed," Lysandra murmured, resting her head against his chest. "Together."

In that moment, nestled within the safety of each other's arms, Lysandra and Aerin's love was a beacon—a force potent enough to rival the magic they sought to wield. They would need that strength, for the path ahead bristled with thorns and the unknown.

"Rest now," Lysandra whispered, pulling away but keeping her gaze locked with his. "Tomorrow, we chase destiny."

"Rest," Aerin echoed, though they both knew sleep would be fitful, filled with dreams of prophecies and battles yet to come. But tonight, there was solace in their promise—a commitment to see this through, side by side, hearts entwined.

Feyla's fingers traced the glyphs etched into the cave wall, her brow furrowing in concentration. "Eolande, bring the torch closer," she called out, her voice echoing lightly through the cavernous space. The elf complied, moving with silent grace, his curiosity piqued.

"Are you finding something interesting?" Eolande asked,

holding the flickering light steady as Feyla examined the ancient markings.

"More than interesting," Feyla replied, her heart quickening. "I think it's a prophecy. Look here—" She pointed at a sequence of symbols.

Eolande leaned in, his calm eyes scanning the text. "Can you make it out?"

"Mostly," she said, chewing on her lip as she pieced together the fragmented script. "It speaks of a 'Light that pierces Shadow,' and 'The Heart's True Sight shall reveal the path.'"

"Sounds like riddles," Eolande remarked, though his tone held an edge of respect for the ancient wisdom hidden within the stone.

Feyla's gaze didn't waver from the carvings. "Not just riddles. Clues." Her mind raced, connecting the dots between the prophecy and their quest. "Aviara mentioned the Seer's Orb would be essential in defeating Malachor. This could mean that the orb doesn't just hold power; it might also show us how to use it—where to strike."

"Then we're not just searching blindly for a weapon," Eolande mused, his voice low. "We're seeking a guide."

"Exactly!" Feyla exclaimed, excitement bubbling within her. "And if my hunch is right, the 'Heart's True Sight' could refer to someone with a pure heart, or maybe love? That has to be the key to unlocking the Orb's full potential."

"Love as a weapon," Eolande said, almost to himself. His gaze shifted to Lysandra and Aerin, who shared a whispered conversation by the firelight. "That pair might be more crucial than we thought."

"Seems so," Feyla agreed, her eyes never leaving the ancient text. "But let's keep this between us for now. No need to add pressure."

"Agreed." Eolande nodded, casting a protective glance at Feyla. "We'll figure this out together."

"Right. Together." Feyla smiled, buoyed by the newfound hope. The prophecy had given them more than insight—it had reignited the flame of determination that burned within each member of their ragtag group.

Together, they walked back towards the flickering campfire, ready to face whatever challenges lay ahead with a newfound sense of purpose.

"Found something, did you?" Lysandra's voice cut through the darkness as they approached.

"Maybe," Feyla replied, a glint in her eye. "It's just a piece of the puzzle but a start."

"Every piece counts," Aerin added, wrapping an arm around Lysandra's waist.

"That it does," Feyla agreed, her mind already working on the next step of their adventure. They had a prophecy to unravel and a world to save. And with every clue they uncovered, victory against Malachor felt slightly closer.

———————

"Alright, let's not waste another heartbeat," Lysandra declared, her tone steady as she rose from where they had settled around the dimming campfire. "We have a lead on the Seer's Orb now, thanks to Feyla."

"Lead? More like a lifeline," Aerin chimed in, his gaze meeting each of their eyes. "If that prophecy is right, we're closer than ever to turning the tides against Malachor."

"Then we move at dawn," Lysandra said decisively. "We'll need all our strength if we're going to outmaneuver his shadows."

"About that," Feyla interjected, her fingers nervously twirling a strand of hair. "I've been thinking... what if we crafted some magical decoy? Misdirection could buy us time."

"Magic and mechanics?" Aerin raised an eyebrow. "That sounds like a Feyla special. Can you pull it off?"

She grinned, her usual spark reigniting. "Give me a few hours and some quiet. I'll invent something even Malachor's goons won't see through."

"Perfect," Lysandra nodded, appreciating Feyla's ingenuity. "While Feyla works her magic, we should all get some rest."

"Rest?" Aerin chuckled softly, standing behind Lysander, his hands resting lightly on her shoulders. "With everything that's happening, sleep seems like a distant dream."

"Sleep or no sleep," Lysandra replied, leaning back into him momentarily before stepping away. "We can't afford to be sluggish. Tomorrow, we face whatever comes with clear minds and sharp blades."

Aerin watched her, and his admiration was evident in his gaze. "You never cease to amaze me, Lys. Your resilience is—"

"Save it for later," she cut him off, but her lips curled slightly at the corners. "Right now, focus on keeping that healing magic of yours ready. We'll need it."

"Understood," he said, a smile playing on his lips despite the gravity of their situation.

"Hey, don't forget about me," Feyla piped up. "Inventors need their beauty sleep, too, you know."

"Of course not," Lysandra responded, her eyes softening with affection for her friend. "Get some rest, Feyla. And thank you for everything."

"Team effort," Feyla murmured as she gathered her tools and headed toward a quieter corner of the cave.

Lysandra took a deep breath, feeling the weight of leadership heavy on her shoulders. Yet, her companions' presence and unwavering support lightened the load. They were more than a group bound by circumstance; they were a family forged in fire.

"Tomorrow, we fight," she whispered, determination steeling her voice. "For Erenor, for freedom... for us."

As the group settled into their respective corners of the cave, a sense of unity tethered them together—a chain forged from shared purpose and steel will. They were the last hope for Erenor, and as the fire dimmed, their determination burned all the brighter.

Chapter 10

WHERE WORLDS COLLIDE

he air crackled with an electric charge. They were close now; she could feel it in her bones—a tingle that danced along her skin, a pull towards destiny.

"Keep your eyes peeled," she said, her voice low but commanding. "Aviara's guidance was clear: 'Where the sky weeps and the earth sighs, the path to the Shattered Realm shall rise.' We're looking for something unnatural."

"Like Aerin's cooking?" Feyla quipped, brushing a low-hanging branch out of her face.

"Hey," Aerin protested, but his words had no heat. His gaze stayed fixed on the shifting shadows around them, protective instincts on high alert.

Eolande's soft chuckle cut the tension. "Focus," he reminded them gently.

"This place may not welcome us kindly."

Lysandra pressed forward, Shadow padding silently beside

her. The wolf's ears twitched, and his nose worked the air. He suddenly stopped, letting out a low growl. Following his cue, Lysandra halted, raising her hand to signal the others.

"Here." Her eyes narrowed at the space before them, where the air shimmered slightly, like a mirage. "This is it."

"It doesn't look like much," Feyla observed, stepping forward with a frown.

"Appearances can be deceiving," Lysandra replied, feeling the weight of the prophecy on them. "Remember, this is the place where worlds collide."

"Are we ready for this?" Aerin asked, his eyes meeting Lysandra's. There was concern and an unspoken promise—whatever lay ahead, they would face it together.

"Ready as we'll ever be," she answered, reaching to clasp his hand briefly before stepping into the unknown.

The group moved closer to the shimmering air, and a sense of vertigo gripped them as the ground beneath their feet seemed to buckle and twist. Taking a collective deep breath, they crossed the threshold.

The world's vibrant colors faded into muted shades of gray and silver as the air became heavy with the sharp scent of ozone. They had crossed the mysterious Shattered Realm, beginning an unpredictable and dangerous experience ahead.

"Stay close to each other," Lysandra murmured, her voice a steady beacon as the terrain beneath their feet lurched unpredictably. The Shattered Realm unfolded before them, a kaleidoscope of fractured landscapes, each piece a puzzle from another place and time.

"By the stars, it's like walking through a dream," Eolande whispered, nocking an arrow out of instinct more than necessity.

"Or a nightmare," Feyla added, her gaze darting around as she clutched her latest invention—a compass that spun wildly, its bearings lost in this distorted world.

"Focus," Aerin said, grounding himself and reaching for Lysandra's hand. She felt the warmth of his touch and the unwavering strength it offered—her anchor amidst the chaos.

"Can you feel that?" Lysandra's eyes were half-closed, her senses extending outward, skimming the surface of this realm's erratic pulse. "The boundaries between things are thin here, like fabric that time has worn away."

"Thin enough for Malachor to reach through?" Aerin's grip tightened.

"Perhaps. We must be vigilant," she replied, her determination a silent vow against the shadows that danced at the edge of her vision.

They pressed on, the landscape shifting with each step. Trees with silver leaves would vanish, replaced by fields of whispering grasses one moment and towering crystalline structures the next.

"Keep your wits about you," Lysandra instructed, her sword drawn, not against a visible enemy but the unseen forces at play. Her magic thrummed beneath her skin, seeking release against the encroaching dark energy that sought to claim her.

"Stay together," Aerin echoed, his earth-based magic creating subtle vibrations underfoot, a path of stability in the ever-changing realm.

"Look!" Feyla pointed at a clearing where the air shimmered differently, was less volatile, and was more inviting. "There might be something there!"

"Or it could be a trap," Eolande noted, his arrow still ready.

"There is only one way to find out." Lysandra led the way. Her resolve was like steel as they approached the anomaly. The clearing remained constant, a small oasis of calm in the turmoil.

"Is it safe?" Feyla asked, her eyes wide with curiosity and concern.

"Safe is a relative term here," Lysandra said, cautiously stepping into the clearing. She felt a tingle across her skin, but there was no immediate threat. "But we'll make our stand here."

"As a team," Aerin affirmed, sharing a look with Lysandra that spoke volumes. It was a promise, a pledge that their love would be their guiding force even in life-threatening danger.

"Let's figure out our next move," Eolande suggested, joining them in the tranquility circle. Their journey through the Shattered Realm had only begun, and every decision mattered.

"Agreed," Lysandra said, feeling the weight of leadership on her shoulders. "We'll navigate this place one step at a time and find our way to the Seer's Orb."

Feyla said, "Then let's get moving," her usual zeal rekindled by the challenge ahead. "I've got a few tricks that might work here."

"Lead the way," Aerin said with a nod, his faith in their combined strength never wavering.

"Forward it is," Lysandra declared, and together, they ventured deeper into the unpredictable heart of the Shattered Realm.

The air crackled with the discordant hum of shadow energy as Lysandra led the group through the Shattered Realm's ever-changing landscape. The uneven ground shifted beneath their feet, making every step treacherous.

"Watch out!" Feyla shouted, pointing to a sudden fissure that opened up beside them.

Aerin lunged forward, grabbing Lysandra's arm and yanking her back just in time. "That was too close," he said, his breath quick with the narrow escape.

"Thanks," Lysandra replied, her heart racing. She hated how this place made her feel vulnerable—the dark energy trying to seep into her bones.

"Let's keep moving," Eolande said, releasing an arrow into the darkness that seemed to swallow the shaft. "Our path won't stay clear for long."

"Right," Aerin agreed, scanning the horizon. "Lysandra, can you sense which way the shadow energy is less dense?"

She closed her eyes, reaching out with her magic. "This way," she said, pointing towards a faint light shimmering through the gloom.

"Lead on, then," Feyla said, her tone steadier than they all felt. "I've got a gadget or two that might give us an edge here."

"Keep them handy," Lysandra said, taking point once more.

They crept forward, each movement deliberate. The path ahead twisted and morphed, landscapes blurring together like a dream half-remembered. Feyla tossed a small orb ahead of them, which exploded into a shower of sparks, illuminating a safe passage.

"Nice one, Feyla," Eolande praised, his eyes never leaving the shadows that danced just beyond the light's reach.

"Do you think I lugged these tools around for show?" Feyla shot back with a grin.

"Focus, both of you," Lysandra scolded, though she couldn't suppress her smile at their banter. It was a welcome reprieve from the tension.

"Sorry, boss," Feyla quipped, but her gaze was sharp, alert for danger.

"Boss, huh?" Aerin teased, bumping shoulders with Lysandra. "I like the sound of that."

"Quiet, you," she whispered, though her pulse quickened at the touch.

Suddenly, a roar echoed around them, and a wave of shadow creatures emerged from the darkness, their forms shifting and indistinct.

"Stand back!" Aerin commanded, stepping forward to shield Lysandra.

"No, together!" Lysandra countered, drawing her sword, its blade glowing with a pale light. "We fight as one."

"Of course," Aerin agreed, summoning a protective barrier

of earthy magic around them.

"Here goes nothing!" Feyla exclaimed, unleashing another of her inventions—a net that expanded and ensnared several shadow creatures, rendering them immobile.

"Nice shot!" Eolande called out, firing arrows with deadly precision, each tipped with a radiant light that seemed to burn the shadow beings.

"Keep it up!" Lysandra encouraged, slashing through the enemy ranks, her sword singing through the air.

"I can't let you have all the fun," Aerin said, his blade carving a dance of destruction alongside hers.

"Where do they keep coming from?" Feyla gasped as she set another trap.

"It doesn't matter," Eolande replied, calm as ever. "Just keep taking them down."

The last shadow creatures fell after what felt like hours but could have been mere moments in the distorted realm. Their remains dissolved into the air, leaving behind an eerie silence.

"Everyone okay?" Lysandra asked, her eyes scanning the group.

"Still in one piece," Aerin confirmed, his hand finding hers and reassuringly squeezing it.

"Thanks for your quick thinking," Feyla added, wiping sweat from her brow.

"Let's not stick around for round two," Eolande suggested, already scouting ahead.

"Agreed," Lysandra said, taking a deep breath. "Onward we

go. Working as a team, we'll get through this."

"Nothing can stop us," Aerin declared, and they marched on, united against the chaos of the Shattered Realm.

"Watch your step!" Lysandra called out, her voice echoing strangely in the shifting landscape of the Shattered Realm. She caught Aerin's arm just as the ground beneath them lurched, tilting at a precarious angle.

"Thanks," he grunted, steadying himself against her. The terrain here was unpredictable, morphing from solid earth to treacherous chasms without warning.

"Is everyone still with us?" Aviara's gaze swept over the group, her celestial presence a beacon of calm in the chaos. Her form was shimmery and transparent.

"Present," Eolande quipped, nocking another arrow, his eyes darting around the mist that had begun to creep upon them.

"Something's not right," Feyla murmured, eyebrows knitted as she peered into the fog.

"State the obvious much?" Eolande teased, but there was an edge of tension in his voice.

"Quiet," Lysandra hissed, sensing more than seeing a shift in their surroundings. The shadows seemed to draw back, recoiling in fear, and the mist began to glow faintly.

"By the First Mage..." Aerin breathed, and they all witnessed the emergence of ethereal figures, luminous and solemn, drifting toward them through the haze.

"Ancestors," Aviara whispered, her voice laced with reverence. "Warriors of old."

"Are they... friendly?" Feyla asked, taking an involuntary step back.

One spirit spoke, "Peace, children of Erenor." Its voice resonated like a whisper in the wind. We are the Guardians of the Veil."

"Guardians?" Lysandra repeated, feeling a surge of recognition deep within her soul. These were the spirits of heroes who had once stood where they now stood, battling the forces that sought to unravel their world.

"Your arrival has been foretold," another spirit declared, their translucent hands gesturing towards Lysandra. "Bearer of the First Mage's blood, your quest is righteous."

"Foretold?" Aerin echoed, protective instincts flaring as he stepped closer to Lysandra. "What do you know of our quest?"

"Only that the fate of Erenor rests upon fragile threads," the first spirit answered, its gaze piercing despite its incorporeal form. "And you must tread carefully, for not all paths lead to salvation."

"Great. Riddles." Eolande muttered under his breath. "Just what we need."

"Focus," Lysandra said, fixing her eyes on the apparitions. "We seek the Seer's Orb. Can you aid us?"

"Many trials lay ahead," the second Guardian warned. "The Orb's power is not easily won."

"Trials we're ready for," Lysandra asserted, feeling Aerin's supportive presence beside her like a steadfast pillar.

"Then the first spirit said, "Go forth with our blessing," and its light became brighter, surrounding the group in a warm, protective glow.

"Thank you," Aviara said, bowing her head. Thankfully, when the light faded, the spirits were gone.

"Did that just happen?" Feyla asked, looking around and half-expecting the Guardians to reappear.

"Seems it did," Lysandra said, a newfound determination settling in her chest. "Let's move. We've got an orb to find."

As they ventured into the unknown with the guidance of ages past, Aerin confidently nodded and said, "Lead the way."

"Watch your step!" Feyla cried out as the ground beneath them quivered, fissures snaking across the once-solid terrain of the Shattered Realm.

"It feels like the world's splitting apart," Eolande murmured, his eyes scanning the horizon for any signs of stability.

"Because it is," Lysandra replied tersely, gripping her sword hilt tighter. "The boundaries here are thin; reality's fabric is tearing."

Aerin reached out instinctively, his hand finding hers and their fingers entwining. "Stay close to me," he said, a silent promise in the chaos enveloping them.

"Spoken like true hearts in battle," a voice echoed around them, ethereal yet resonant.

"Who goes there?" Lysandra called out, her warrior instincts on high alert as she faced the direction of the sound.

"Friends, not enemies," Another voice joined the first, and slowly, shimmering forms materialized before them: the ancient spirits from legends whispered in the dark.

"Guide us," Aviara implored, her regal composure belying the urgency in her tone. "We must find the Seer's Orb."

"Indeed, but knowledge comes at a price," the first spirit intoned, its translucent hand gesturing toward a towering archway of twisted vines and stone. "Pass through the Arch of Revelations, face what lies beyond, and the path to the Seer's Orb shall be revealed."

"Revelations? What does that mean?" Feyla asked, her brows knitting together.

"Your fears, your hopes, your bonds—they will all be laid bare," the second spirit answered. "Only by confronting them can you prove your worth."

"Confronting our... Wait, are we talking about some sort of trial here?" Aerin demanded, a protective edge sharpening his voice.

"Exactly," the spirit confirmed with a nod that seemed to ripple through the air. "Your love, Lysandra, and the ties that bind this fellowship will be the crucible within which your resolve is tested."

Lysandra squeezed Aerin's hand, her pulse racing, not with fear but with unyielding determination. "Then we have no choice," she stated, her voice cutting through the tension like a blade. "We'll face whatever trials await."

"Bravely spoken," the spirit commended, a spectral smile flickering across its features. "But be warned, the trials are reflections; they cannot harm you unless you allow them to. Trust each other, and remember: Strength is found not just in the might of arms but in the courage of hearts."

"Let's not waste any more time," Lysandra decided, stepping forward, her companions falling into step behind her. They approached the arch, the air growing thicker and charged with anticipation and the weight of unspoken fears.

"Stay close," Aerin murmured, his gaze never leaving Lysandra's profile. The line of her jaw was set in fierce resolve.

"Always," she whispered back before they stepped through the arch together, disappearing as if swallowed by the realm itself.

The Shattered Realm held its breath, awaiting the outcome of a trial that would either forge heroes from mere mortals or shatter them beneath the weight of truths too heavy to bear.

"Which way now?" Lysandra's voice echoed through the ever-shifting landscape of the Shattered Realm. Her hand gripped Aerin's with a strength that belied her calm demeanor.

"Left," Aerin said, his eyes scanning the chaotic swirls of shadow energy that threatened to disorient them. "The spirits spoke of an oasis of clarity amid the chaos."

"An oasis that could vanish at any moment," she countered, but there was no fear in her voice, only the steely resolve that had carried her through countless battles.

They turned left, and the world seemed to ripple around them, the ground beneath their feet undulating like waves on a storm-tossed sea. With each step, Lysandra felt the dark energy pulsing through her veins, a reminder of her heritage that she embraced and feared.

"Remember, it's not real," Aerin reminded her, his presence reassuringly solid at her side.

"Doesn't that make it any less terrifying?" She shot back, though her grip on his hand tightened.

"Hey, we've faced worse," he teased, a smile tugging at the corners of his mouth despite the gravity of their situation. It was this—his ability to find light in the darkness—that drew her to him repeatedly.

"True," Lysandra conceded, smiling briefly before the world shifted again.

Abruptly, the ground fell away, opening into a chasm that yawned wide and deep before them. On the other side, a faint glimmer hinted at their path.

"We jump together," Aerin suggested, looking across the divide.

"Without a doubt," she replied, her heart hammering against her ribs. They backed up a few steps, synchronizing their movements with a glance.

"Ready?"

"Yes."

They ran and leaped, soaring over the abyss as one. For a moment, suspended in mid-air, Lysandra felt a surge of exhilaration. But then doubt crept in, a whispering fear that they might fall short.

"Trust me," Aerin's voice cut through her uncertainty, his hand squeezing hers.

And she did. She trusted him with her life and with her heart. They landed hard on the other side, stumbling but upright, still hand in hand. Eolande and Feyla follow closely after them. Shadow was already prowling around to sniff out the terrain.

"See? We've got this," he said, pulling her close briefly, his breath warm against her ear.

"Let's keep moving," she urged, her pulse steadying.

They continued, the trials testing their physical prowess and the fabric of their relationship. Each challenge laid bare their fears and insecurities, yet with every obstacle overcome, their bond solidified further.

Eolande and Feyla had dropped behind a little, discussing what they regarded as their perfect jump.

"Are you scared?" Lysandra asked during a rare lull, her voice betraying none of the anxiety within her.

"Terrified," Aerin admitted, his gaze meeting hers with unflinching honesty. "But I'm more afraid of losing you than anything these trials can throw at us."

"Then we won't lose," she vowed, words wrapping around them like a shield. "Not to this place, not to Malachor, not to anything."

"No, we won't," he agreed, and in his eyes, she saw not just the dangers they faced but the depth of his love for her.

"Come on," she said, drawing strength from his unwavering support. "We have a Seer's Orb to find and a realm to save."

"Lead the way, my fierce warrior," Aerin said with a defiant and adoring grin.

Lysandra took a deep breath, squared her shoulders, and entered the unknown. Her heart was complete, and her spirit was unbreakable. She knew that whatever lay ahead, they would face it together as equals, partners, and lovers bound by love as relentless as the tide and as eternal as the stars.

"Another dead end!" Feyla exclaimed, panting from exertion as she leaned against the moss-covered wall. The labyrinthine corridors of the Shattered Realm had led them in circles for what felt like hours.

"Keep your voice down," Eolande hissed, peering into the shadows with narrowed eyes. "The walls have ears, and worse."

Lysandra stepped to the wall, pressing her palm against its smooth surface. She closed her eyes, trying to sense the pulse of magic that had led them this far. "There's a pattern here," she murmured. "We're being tested on more than our ability to fight or endure."

"Then let's outsmart it," Aerin suggested, moving beside her. "What does your gut tell you?"

"Up," she breathed, opening her eyes. A faint outline shimmered above them—a platform hidden in plain sight.

"Of course." Aerin chuckled dryly. "Why take the easy path when we can climb?"

"Because the easy path is often a trap," Lysandra quipped, meeting his gaze with a smirk.

"Shall we?" Eolande offered, nocking an arrow to his bow, ready to provide cover from any unseen threats.

"Let's go," Feyla said, determination lighting her brown eyes. With a quick tinkering of her wrist device, a grappling hook shot upward, securing it to the platform's edge. "I'll secure the rope."

One by one, they ascended, their movements swift despite the weariness that clung to their limbs. Atop the platform, they found themselves before an ancient archway, runes glowing softly along its keystone.

"This is it," Lysandra whispered, stepping forward. Her heart hammered in her chest as the air thrummed with power.

"Be careful," Aerin said, squeezing her hand. His touch was grounding, a reminder of all they had endured and the bond that had only grown stronger with each trial.

"I always try to be," she said, returning the squeeze and releasing his hand to approach the archway. She raised her other hand, palm outward, and spoke the words of unlocking, a spell handed down from the First Mage, her ancestor.

The archway pulsed once or twice, then burst into light so brilliant that they had to shield their eyes. When the light faded, floating within the arch was an Orb, pulsing with a soft inner glow. It was neither large nor embellished with jewels, yet its power was undeniable.

"By the ancients..." Eolande breathed, his usual composure slipping.

"Is that...?" Feyla trailed off, awe replacing her usual lively chatter.

Lysandra reached out, her fingers barely brushing the orb before it lifted itself into the air, recognizing the heir of the First Mage. It floated toward her, settling into her open palm like it had always belonged there.

"An artifact from the age of legends," Lysandra said, her voice steady despite the whirlwind of emotions within her.

"Will it help us find the Seer's Orb?" Aerin asked, stepping closer to peer at the object resting innocuously in Lysandra's hand.

"It's part of the key," she replied, feeling the artifact resonate with her magic. "It knows we're worthy."

"Then we'd better not waste this chance," Feyla said, breaking the respectful silence over them. "Malachor won't be twiddling his thumbs while we play treasure hunt."

"Indeed," Eolande agreed, glancing at the shadowy passageways around them. "Our presence has not gone unnoticed."

"Time to move," Aerin decided, his protective instincts flaring as he scanned the darkness.

"Agreed," Lysandra said, closing her fingers gently around the artifact. "We have what we came for. Now, let's get out of this place."

Together, they turned away from the archway, the artifact was secured, and their resolve hardened. They knew that danger lurked in every shadow, but with the artifact in their possession, hope flared anew—the hope to challenge Malachor and save Erenor from the encroaching darkness.

Chapter 11

FAITH AND LOVE

"Are you sure this will work?" Aerin asked, his voice a blend of skepticism and hope as they hurried through the Shattered Realm, a realm known for its twisted, distorted landscapes and chaotic energy that defied the laws of nature.

Lysandra kept her gaze fixed ahead, the weight of the artifact in her hand a constant reminder of its purpose. Her heart beats even faster. This little artifact would be instrumental in removing Malachor once and for all.

"It has to," she replied, a thread of magic twining around her words. "This fragment... it hums with the orb's energy."

"Then let's not disappoint it," he quipped, but his light-hearted tone couldn't mask the tension coiling within him.

"Here," Lysandra said abruptly, stopping by a crystal-clear pool that seemed out of place amidst the chaos. She crouched, dipping the artifact into the water. The surface shimmered, and an image flickered to life—a map of Erenor, with a pulsing light marking their next destination.

"By the gods," Aerin muttered, kneeling beside her.

"See? A key to the seer's orb's power, just like the spirits said," Lysandra said triumphantly. She met his gaze, the reflection of the enchanted pool dancing in their eyes. "The spirits, in their cryptic prophecy, foretold of this artifact. They said it would lead us to our salvation, and now, here it is, guiding us to our next destination."

"Your faith never ceases to amaze me," he said softly, brushing a stray lock of hair from her face. His touch sent shivers down her spine, not from fear but from an electrifying sense of connection.

"Faith is all we have against Malachor," she whispered, leaning into his touch for a moment before pulling away. "We need to keep moving."

He nodded, standing and offering her a hand up. "Together, then."

"Of course, my love," she agreed, gripping his hand tightly.

He struggled to conceal his surprise as she addressed him with an endearing term for the first time. The warmth that enveloped his heart eclipsed any radiance the orb could hope to emanate. In a moment of reciprocating trust, he gave her hand a warm squeeze, acknowledging her willingness to show her feelings.

They set out again with the artifact safely tucked away, and their bond quickly grew as unbreakable as the magic they were using.

A soft breeze rustled through the distorted trees of the Shattered Realm as Lysandra and Aerin found momentary shelter in a craggy alcove. Its jagged walls offered some protection from the ever-present shadow energy. They sat close, their backs against the excellent, smooth stone, catching their breath after the relentless march through the twisted landscape. The air was heavy with the scent of magic, and the distant echoes of their footsteps were the only sounds in the eerie silence.

The air was heavy with the scent of magic, and the distant echoes of their footsteps were the only sounds in the eerie silence.

"Remember when our biggest concern was deciphering the High Elder's cryptic instructions?" Aerin's chuckle was dry, but his eyes held warmth as he glanced at Lysandra.

"Those were simpler times before we discovered the true extent of our powers and the weight of our responsibilities. But we've come so far, Aerin. We can't forget how much we've already overcome."

"True," he said, reaching for her hand and squeezing it gently. "I'm just... I'm scared, Lys. Not of what we're facing now but of what it might take from us. The sacrifices we may have to make."

The shadows danced eerily as if to underline his words. Lysandra felt the familiar surge of darkness within her, a reminder of her fears.

She squeezed his hand back, her grip firm. "I know. But look at what we're fighting for—our love, Erenor, and the future. It's worth everything."

Aerin nodded, the corners of his mouth lifting ever so slightly. "I'd face any trial or any danger for you. For us." His voice lowered, filled with conviction.

"I left my witch-hunter past behind because I believed we could forge something better. And I still believe, despite everything."

"Your faith in us gives me strength," she admitted, leaning her head against his shoulder. "And your love... It's like a beacon, guiding me through the darkest moments, even when this"—she tapped her chest where the dark energy pulsed—"threatens to consume me."

He shifted, turning to face her, his expression filled with unwavering determination. "It won't. I won't allow it. Lysandra, this quest isn't the only thing that binds us. Our souls are intertwined and stronger than any curse or prophecy."

"Even so, we must be willing to make tough choices," Lysandra said, locking eyes with him. "For Erenor's sake, I can't bear losing you, but if it means saving our world..."

"Shh," Aerin interrupted, brushing a thumb across her cheek. The roughness of the pad of his thumb against her smooth skin made her whole body tingle. "Don't talk of loss. Not now. We have each other, and that's all that matters now."

"Sometimes, I think you're too optimistic for your good," she teased despite the heaviness in her heart.

"Maybe," he conceded with a grin. "But optimism is another form of strength. Besides, I've got you to keep me grounded."

"And you always will, no matter what happens," she promised, her voice barely above a whisper. Their foreheads touched, and for an instant, the chaos of the Shattered Realm faded away, leaving only the two of them entwined in their resolve.

"Let's rest for a little longer," Aerin suggested softly. "We'll need all our energy for what lies ahead."

"Agreed." Lysandra closed her eyes, allowing herself to find comfort in his embrace. Here, in the eye of the storm, they drew on the love that had blossomed in the most unlikely of places—a love that was their greatest weapon against the encroaching darkness.

"Hurry," Lysandra urged, her voice tinged with urgency as she nudged Aerin's shoulder. The artifact, a glowing shard no more prominent than her fist, pulsed with the energy of the Seer's Orb in her palm.

"We mustn't linger here. Malachor's minions could be upon us at any moment."

Aerin pushed himself up, the warmth of their stolen moment still lingering between them. His gaze met hers, steady and clear.

"Right. Let's regroup with the others."

The pair emerged from the shadow of an ancient, twisted tree, its bark gnarled by the realm's corrupting influence.

Before them, the Shattered Realm stretched—a mosaic of fragmented landscapes, each piece floating and shifting like flotsam on a chaotic sea. Feyla and the rest of their companions were already preparing to depart, checking supplies and casting wary glances at the unstable terrain around them.

"Did you get it?" Feyla asked, her eyes lighting up at the sight of the artifact in Lysandra's hand.

"We did," Lysandra confirmed, tucking the shard safely into the inner pocket of her cloak.

"Good," Feyla replied, adjusting the straps on her backpack. "Because I don't fancy staying in this place a second longer than necessary."

"Agreed," Eolande said, his calm voice a soothing balm amidst the tension. "Our path is clear. We must move swiftly."

"Then let's not waste any more time," Aerin said, scanning the horizon. "Lysandra, lead the way."

With a nod, Lysandra took the point, her senses alert for any signs of danger. The group fell in line behind her, each member alert and ready for trouble. They navigated the distorted landscape, their steps measured and cautious as they avoided rifts that threatened to swallow them whole.

"Keep close," Lysandra called back to them, her voice carrying over the eerie silence that hung heavy in the air. "And watch your footing."

"Shadow's keeping pace," Aerin murmured, his eyes briefly flickering to the great wolf that loped silently alongside them, a reassuring presence amid uncertainty.

"His instincts are sharper than ours," Lysandra replied, grateful for the animal's companionship.

"Once we're out of here, what's the plan?" Feyla asked, her tone betraying her anxiety.

"Find the Seer's Orb," Lysandra answered without hesitation. "Complete the prophecy."

"Simple enough," Feyla quipped, though the gravity of their task weighed heavily on her small frame.

"Simple doesn't mean easy," Eolande said, his gaze trained on the ever-shifting ground.

"Nothing about this has ever been easy," Aerin said, his hand instinctively finding Lysandra's for a brief moment before letting go, a silent promise passing between them.

"Look!" Feyla suddenly exclaimed, pointing ahead, where a sliver of reality seemed less fractured.

"Is that our way out?" Eolande squinted at the anomaly.

"Only one way to find out," Lysandra said, picking up her pace.

They approached the thinning veil between realms as they advanced with unwavering determination and hope. The artifact in Lysandra's cloak throbbed warmly against her chest as a beacon, guiding them home.

"Brace yourselves," Lysandra warned, her heart pounding with anticipation and fear.

"Don't let go," Aerin replied, grimly smiling.

They stepped through the veil, the familiar yet distant world of Erenor welcoming them back with open arms. Behind them, the gateway to the Shattered Realm was closing.

Lysandra sighed with relief. Everyone behind them was safe.

"Remember when our biggest concern was deciphering the High Elder's cryptic instructions?" Aerin's chuckle was dry, but his eyes held warmth as he glanced at Lysandra.

"Those were simpler times before we discovered the true extent of our powers and the weight of our responsibilities. But we've come so far, Aerin. We can't forget how much we've already overcome."

"True," he said, reaching for her hand and squeezing it gently. "I'm just... I'm scared, Lys. Not of what we're facing now but of what it might take from us. The sacrifices we may have to ma ke."

The shadows danced eerily as if to underline his words. Lysandra felt the familiar surge of darkness within her, a reminder of her fears. She squeezed his hand back, her grip firm. "I know. But look at what we're fighting for—our love, Erenor, and the future. It's worth everything."

Aerin nodded, the corners of his mouth lifting ever so slightly. "I'd face any trial or any danger for you. For us." His voice lowered, filled with conviction.

"Let's rest a while," Aerin suggested softly. "We'll need all our energy for what lies ahead."

"Agreed." They found a shady spot where the grass was soft, and they could smell the calming scent of nature. Lysandra closed her eyes, allowing herself to find comfort in his embrace. Here, in the eye of the storm, they drew on the love that had blossomed in the most unlikely of places—a love that was their greatest weapon against the encroaching darkness.

"Hurry," Lysandra suddenly urged, her voice tinged with urgency as she nudged Aerin's shoulder. The artifact, a warm and glowing shard no more prominent than her fist, pulsed with the energy of the Seer's Orb in her palm.

"We mustn't linger here. Malachor's minions could be upon us at any moment."

Aerin pushed himself up, the warmth of their stolen moment still lingering between them. His gaze met hers, steady and clear.

"Right. Let's regroup with the others."

"Have a nice rest?" Feyla asked, her eyes lighting up at the sight of the artifact in Lysandra's hand.

"We have," Lysandra confirmed, tucking the shard safely into the inner pocket of her cloak.

"Good," Feyla replied, adjusting the straps on her backpack. "Because I don't fancy staying here a second longer than necessary."

"Agreed," Eolande said, his calm voice a soothing balm amidst the tension. "Our path is clear. We must move swiftly."

"Then let's not waste time," Aerin said, scanning the horizon. "Lysandra, lead the way."

As they continued, a low rumble echoed through the air, growing louder with each passing moment. The ground vibrated beneath their feet, and a sense of unease settled over the group. Suddenly, a massive rift tore through the earth, splitting the landscape before them.

"Hold on!" Lysandra shouted as they clung to each other, struggling to maintain their footing. They desperately sought a way to safety as the unexpected rift threatened to swallow them whole.

Just when it seemed all was lost, a brilliant light emanated from the center of the rift, growing brighter and brighter. The ground ceased shaking, and the rift slowly began to close. As the light faded, the once-distorted land returned to its original state. Taking a deep breath, the group realized that they had narrowly escaped certain death.

With their hearts still racing, they resumed their journey through Erenor, knowing they had faced grave danger and survived.

Lysandra led the way with renewed determination, and the group remained vigilant, ready to face whatever other challenges the land might throw at them. They pressed on, knowing that they had to uncover the truth behind the mysterious disturbances in Erenor and restore harmony to their beloved land.

Chapter 12

THE LOST CITY

Sunlight pierced the ancient canopy, casting dappled shadows on the crumbling stone archway that marked the entrance to the lost city. Lysandra's heart quickened as she stepped forward, her boots crunching on the carpet of leaves and debris that nature had reclaimed over centuries of neglect.

"Here it is," she whispered, more to herself than to Aerin and Feyla, who flanked her sides.

"Finally," Aerin muttered, his gaze lingering on the weathered runes etched into the stone. "Let's be cautious. This place reeks of old magic."

Feyla bounced on the balls of her feet, her eyes alight with curiosity. "And old gadgets, I bet! Can you imagine what secrets these stones have seen?"

"There's only one way to find out." Lysandra drew her sword, the sound a clear note in the silence that shrouded the archway. The weapon felt like an extension of her will, a comforting weight against the unknown.

They crossed the threshold together, the atmosphere shifting palpably as they entered the domain of history and legend. The city spread before them, its grandeur undiminished by time's relentless march. Towering pillars stood sentinel over the main thoroughfare, while the remnants of statues and fountains hinted at the splendor that once was.

"Wow," Aerin breathed, his warrior's poise giving way to awe. "This place must have been magnificent."

"Look at this!" Feyla called out, darting towards a partially intact mosaic. She traced the colored tiles with a reverent finger. "The craftsmanship is incredible!"

Lysandra couldn't help but agree.

Despite the encroaching vines and dust layers, the lost city's beauty shone through. It was as if the stones whispered secrets of the past, laughter, and life that once echoed through the halls.

"Keep your eyes open," Lysandra reminded them, though her voice held a note of wonder. "We don't know what else might be lurking here."

"Right," Aerin agreed, the protective glint back in his eyes as he scanned their surroundings. "But for now, let's see what answers we can find amidst these ruins."

"Watch out!" Aerin's call came just as Lysandra stepped forward, her boot hovering above the rubble of what was once a majestic hallway.

With quick reflexes, she pivoted back, narrowly avoiding a loose stone that tumbled down from the precarious pile blocking their path.

"It looks like we've hit our first snag," Feyla observed, her gaze assessing the heap of debris with a tactical eye.

"Nothing we can't handle," Lysandra replied confidently, brushing a strand of hair away from her face. She could feel the pulse of magic within her, yearning to be used. But brute force wouldn't serve them here; they needed to be careful not to bring the rest of the structure down upon themselves.

"Let's clear a way through. We do it as a team and together—carefully," Aerin said, stepping beside her. His protective presence was at once comforting and annoying, but this wasn't the time for their usual dance of independence and concern.

"Here, let me," Feyla interjected, crouching to examine the stones more closely. "If I can find the keystone—the one holding everything else in place—we might be able to pull it free without causing a collapse."

"Good thinking," Lysandra approved, watching Feyla's deft fingers move along the cracks, her sharp eyes searching for the pivotal piece.

"Got it," Feyla finally announced, pointing to an innocuously small rock wedged deep within the pile. "See? If I remove this one, the rest should stay relatively stable. Then we can shift the debris safely."

"Stand back," Aerin warned, readying himself to intervene if things went awry.

With a steady breath, Feyla wrapped her hand around the stone. She tugged gently, the tension palpable in the air. With a soft click, the rock came free a moment later, and the pile remained still as if holding its breath.

"Nicely done," Lysandra praised, stepping forward to help move the larger stones aside. Together, they cleared a narrow path to pass through a single file.

"Looks like the adventure continues," Feyla remarked with a grin, dusting off her hands as they moved into the next chamber.

"Speaking of which…" As they entered a sizable room with shafts of light shining through ceiling cracks, Lysandra stumbled. Mysterious symbols and mechanisms adorned the walls, while pedestals stood at intervals throughout the space, each bearing a mysterious object.

"More puzzles," Aerin muttered, his gaze sweeping over the chamber. "Seems like this city doesn't give up its secrets easily."

"Let's split up and see what we're dealing with," Lysandra suggested. As they dispersed, she approached the nearest pedestal. A series of concentric rings with different symbols etched into them demanded her attention. It was a lock of sorts, one that required aligning the rings in a specific pattern.

"Any ideas?" Lysandra called out, trying to decipher the cryptic symbols.

"Wait, these look like elemental sigils," Feyla said excitedly, joining Lysandra at the pedestal. "See, this is water, and this one's fire. I bet we need to align them with their opposites or complements."

"Earth and air, fire and water," Aerin mused, studying another set of rings. "Elemental Balance. That must be the key."

"Exactly," Feyla agreed, her fingers dancing over the symbols. "Lysandra, you're attuned to the elements. Maybe your magic can sense the correct alignment."

Closing her eyes, Lysandra focused on the energy coursing through her. The dark power within her stirred, but she willed it to guide her hands, not to dominate her mind. When she touched the rings, they hummed under her fingertips, resonating with the flow of her elemental magic.

"Here," she whispered, her instincts taking over as she shifted the rings. With a satisfying series of clicks, the rings slotted into place, and a portion of the wall slid open, revealing yet another hidden passageway.

"Teamwork makes the dream work," Feyla quipped triumphantly.

"Let's keep moving," Lysandra said, her heart racing with anticipation. They were one step closer to unraveling the mysteries of the lost city—and one step closer to facing whatever lay ahead.

"Got it!" Lysandra exclaimed as the last puzzle piece clicked into place. The ground beneath them trembled, and a section of the ancient stone wall retracted, revealing an even older, dust-choked passage.

"Come on," she beckoned, her pulse quickening with each step towards the unknown.

The air in the hidden chamber was stale, heavy with the weight of secrets long buried. As their torches flickered against the darkness, they faced a grand mural sprawling across the cavern's expanse. It depicted a figure shrouded in shadows, its hands outstretched, commanding the very stars.

"Malachor," Aerin breathed, her eyes narrowing at the sight. "But look—there's more to this mural than just his image."

Feyla delicately traced the intricate sigils surrounding him with a slender finger, her eyes filled with intrigue. "These symbols aren't just for show, are they?" she mused. "They represent not only the sources of his power but also his vulnerabilities."

"Let's commit this to memory. It might be our ace in the hole when we face him," Lysandra said, studying the mural intently.

Lysandra could almost taste the thrill of their discovery as she committed the symbols to memory. Unraveling the mysteries of the lost city left a sweet, practically electric taste in her mouth.

As Lysandra focused on the task, her mind was sharp and alert. She felt satisfied and fulfilled, knowing she was one step closer to unraveling the mysteries of the lost city.

Lysandra's mouth was dry, and her nerves and anticipation caused her tongue to stick to the roof of her mouth.

As she carved each detail of the stone into her mind, she felt a deep sense of purpose and satisfaction, watching as the fragments of their arduous journey came together perfectly. With their newfound understanding etched firmly into their consciousness, they made their way out of the chamber, Lysandra pausing for a moment to conjure a potent barrier of protection, shielding them from any evil forces that may have been lurking in the shadows.

The courtyard beyond starkly contrasted with the confined

spaces they had traversed. Sunlight streamed through the gaps in the crumbling canopy, illuminating the encroaching wilderness that had claimed the city. Massive statues of forgotten deities stood sentinel amidst the overgrowth, their expressions eroded by time but no less imposing.

"Watch your step," Lysandra warned, eyeing the ivy-covered ground suspiciously. "This place is too quiet, and I don't trust it."

"Traps, you think?" Feyla asked, her voice calm.

"Almost definitely," Aerin agreed, drawing his sword as if expecting an attack from the shadows.

"Let me lead," Lysandra offered, extending her senses to probe the earth beneath the layers of vines and roots. A subtle shift in the magical currents alerted her to danger—a barely discernible vibration underfoot. "There!" She pointed to what looked like an innocuous patch of moss. "Step around that area."

"Good catch," Feyla said, following in Lysandra's careful footsteps.

They navigated the treacherous terrain meticulously, each wary of triggering a trap that would add their bones to the ruins. Despite the danger, there was beauty in this place, a reminder of the city's former glory that nature has now reclaimed.

"Imagine what this place must've been like in its heyday," Feyla mused, her gaze lingering on an archway entwined with flowering vines.

"Probably less deadly," Aerin quipped, but a note of awe in

his voice matched Feyla's wonder.

"Less deadly and more enchanting," Lysandra agreed, allowing herself to appreciate the scene before them. But the respite was fleeting; their mission weighed heavily on her shoulders, a constant reminder of the stakes.

"Let's keep moving," she urged, leading them through the courtyard's deceptive allure. Every step forward was another toward their destiny, which promised as much danger as romance. And Lysandra knew they could not afford to falter—not now, not when so much depended on their success.

"Over here!" Aerin's voice cut through the thick silence of the courtyard, directing them to a patch of earth nestled between two crumbling statues. The brambles that once concealed it had been cleared away, revealing a stone slab with an intricate sun carving.

"It looks like we found our way in," he said, crouching beside the slab. His fingers traced the grooves of the symbol, feeling for the magic hidden within.

"Stand back," Lysandra warned, the orb glowing with a soft azure light in her hand. With a murmured incantation, she directed a beam of energy towards the slab. It trembled, then shifted aside with a grinding sound, exposing a dark staircase leading into the earth.

"Nicely done," said Feyla with a quick smile before turning her attention to the shadows below. "Let's see what secrets this place is hiding."

The pulsing light of the orb in Lysandra's hand illuminated

their path as they carefully descended as the air grew cooler and mustier. At the bottom, a chamber opened up before them, its walls lined with shelves of dusty tomes and artifacts. In the center stood a pedestal, and on top of it lay their prize—a crystal that pulsed with an inner light as if capturing the very essence of the sun itself.

"That has to be it," Aerin said, his eyes fixed on the crystal.

"Malachor's bane," Lysandra whispered, cradling the artifact. Its warmth spread through her, a comforting promise of hope against the darkness they would face.

"Quickly, Lysandra," Feyla urged. "We don't know what taking the crystal might trigger."

Her words proved prophetic.

She lifted the crystal from its resting place no sooner than a deep rumble echoed through the chamber. Dust cascaded from above as cracks spiderwebbed across the ceiling.

"Move!" she shouted, tucking the crystal safely into her bag while still clutching the orb. They sprinted for the stairs, dodging falling debris as the chamber collapsed.

"Left, there's a gap!" Feyla called out, veering towards a narrow opening in the wall. It was barely wide enough to squeeze through, but it was their only chance.

"Go!" Aerin pushed Lysandra forward, his hand at the small of her back, urging her onward.

Lysandra dove into the aperture, the others right behind her, as the chamber gave a final shudder and caved in with a deafening roar.

They emerged into another corridor, panting and covered in dust but alive, with the artifact in their possession. The danger had not passed, but she felt a surge of triumph for a moment.

"Everyone okay?" Lysandra asked, her voice echoing slightly in the dim passage.

"Still in one piece," Aerin confirmed, brushing dirt from his hair.

"Same," Feyla added, though her brow furrowed with concern. "But we need to keep moving. That collapse could've alerted anyone—or anything—watching."

"Right," Lysandra agreed, clutching the crystal bag close. "Let's find our way out of here and ensure this light can shine where needed most."

They set off down the corridor with renewed determination, ready to face whatever lay ahead. The artifact's glow seemed to reassure them, a beacon of hope amidst the shadows of a long-forgotten city.

Dust swirled around them as they stumbled through the narrow passage, the ancient city walls still trembling with aftershocks. Lysandra's heart pounded in her chest, adrenaline coursing through her veins, and she clutched the orb and the artifact tightly to her. It was a solid weight, a reminder of what they had achieved—and what they still had to face.

"Which way?" Feyla's voice cut through the hazy air, her eyes darting between diverging paths ahead.

"Splitting up is not an option," Aerin said firmly, surveying their choices. "Lysandra, any sense from the crystal?"

She closed her eyes momentarily, feeling the light pulse within the artifact. A warm sensation spread through her fingers, and when she opened her eyes, they were drawn to the left tunnel. "This way. It feels... lighter."

"Good enough for me," Eolande said, nocking an arrow to his bow with practiced ease. Feyla nodded, her expression calm despite the chaos around them.

They moved cautiously, the silence of the tunnels pressing in on them. Their footsteps echoed off the stone, constantly reminding them they weren't alone in this place. That's when the first shadow creature lunged.

"Watch out!"

The clash of steel followed Aerin's shout as he dodged the attack, pushing the creature back into the darkness from which it had emerged.

More shapes materialized, their forms flickering like smoke and just as hard to grasp. Feyla loosed an arrow from her crossbow, and it found its mark with a satisfying thud, but there were too many of them.

"Back to back!" Lysandra called out, swinging her sword in a wide arc. The blade hummed with magic, silver light tracing its path.

"Got it!" Feyla's voice was tinged with excitement rather than fear. She was always ready for a challenge.

"Stay close to one another," Aerin instructed, his voice steady as he fought off another shadow with swift, precise strikes.

"Protect the light!" Aviara commanded, her shimmering form suddenly appearing out of what seemed to be nowhere. With her hands weaving through the air, she summoned a gust of wind, scattering several creatures.

"Use your surroundings!" Eolande added, his calm demeanor unchanged even as he shot arrow after arrow, each finding its target in the dimness.

They fought as a single, well-coordinated unit that had undergone numerous battles. Yet the shadows kept coming, relentless.

"Any bright ideas?" Feyla asked, her words punctuated by the twang of her bow.

"Focus on the ones closest to us!" Lysandra shouted back, slicing through the darkness. "Aerin, draw them in!"

Aerin nodded, understanding immediately. He shifted his stance, daggers glinting as he became the focal point of the creatures' attention.

"Aviara, now!" Lysandra sensed the moment—the opening they needed.

"By the light of Erenor, be gone!" Aviara's voice boomed, and a radiant wave of energy surged from her, illuminating the tunnels with blinding brilliance.

The shadow creatures recoiled, shrieking as the light burned them away to nothing. The battle was over in moments, and the only evidence of their enemies was a few wisps of dark mist fading into the air.

"Is everyone okay?" Lysandra asked, panting slightly as she scanned their group for injuries.

"Still here," Eolande confirmed, his composure unshaken.

"Never better," Feyla grinned, though her eyes were alert, watching for more threats.

"Thanks to you," Aerin said, giving Lysandra a nod of respect that spoke volumes.

"And to Aviara," she said. "Let's keep moving," Lysandra urged, knowing that time was against them. "Malachor won't give up easily this time."

"Lead the way," Aerin replied, and together, they plunged deeper into the labyrinth, the light of the artifact their guide and hope in the suffocating darkness.

"Here," Aerin said, his voice low as he brushed aside a tapestry of cobwebs to reveal an ornate door, its surface etched with time and secrets. "This looks promising."

"Promising or dangerous?" Lysandra countered, but her heart raced with anticipation. With a gesture, the door creaked open, revealing a darkness that whispered of forgotten lore.

"Let's find out." He stepped through, and Lysandra followed.

The room beyond was shrouded in shadow, but it didn't take long for their eyes to adjust to the dim light seeping through the cracks in the stone. Walls lined with shelves of ancient texts and scrolls surrounded them, and at the center stood a pedestal, its surface covered in writings that pulsed faintly with magic.

"Can you make anything out?" Lysandra asked, tracing a finger over the symbols, their meanings elusive yet tantalizingly close.

"Give me a moment." Aerin approached, his eyes narrowing as he studied the text. "Yes. It's the old tongue, but some of these phrases are about Malachor."

"Anything useful?" Lysandra needed to know. They all did.

"Here," he pointed. "It speaks of a ritual, one that could bind his powers. And this—" His finger hovered over a series of intricate runes. "A weakness linked to the lunar cycles. We might be able to use this."

"Perfect." Lysandra's pulse quickened at the prospect of turning the tide against Malachor. But then she noticed the strain in Aerin's eyes—the toll of constant vigilance. "You should rest."

He shook his head. "We can't afford to—"

"Rest, Aerin," Lysandra insisted. "That's an order."

For a moment, neither moved; they were locked in a silent battle of wills. Then, finally, he nodded, the tension easing from his shoulders.

"Only because it's an order," he muttered, but Lysandra caught the hint of a smile on his lips.

"Come here." She guided him to a secluded nook, away from the chilling drafts that wound through the ruins. Shadows danced along the walls, casting them in a private world of soft greys and muted silence. Here, they could pretend, just for a moment, that they were not warriors in a war-torn land but simply two souls seeking solace.

"Sometimes I forget," he began, his voice a whisper against her ear, "what it's like not to be fighting."

"Me too," she admitted, leaning into his warmth. Their armor clinked softly as their bodies drew closer. "But when I'm with you, the fight feels... different. Like, we're not just battling for Erenor, but for us."

"For us," he echoed, his hands finding hers in the gloom. His grip was firm and grounding, an anchor in a sea of uncertainty.

"Promise me something," Lysandra said, her voice barely audible even to her ears.

"Anything," he replied without hesitation.

"Promise me that we'll find our way back together no matter what happens."

"I promise." The words were a vow, sealed with a kiss that tasted of hope and defiance—a proclamation that their light would not be extinguished even in the face of encroaching darkness.

"Good." She pulled back slightly, meeting his gaze. "Because I plan on holding you to that."

"I wouldn't have it any other way, Lysandra," he said, and there was steel in his voice, the same steel that made her believe they could win this war.

"Then let's finish this," she declared, determination surging. Together, they rose, ready to confront whatever lay ahead, their bond unbreakable amidst the ruins of a world that dared to test it.

"It looks like the ancestors didn't want us to leave easily," Feyla remarked dryly, her eyes fixed on the massive stone door that loomed before them.

"Let's just hope this is the last test," Eolande added, nocking an arrow with practiced ease, though his bow remained pointed downward in a gesture of temporary peace.

Lysandra stepped forward, her hand hovering over the smooth, cold surface etched with ancient runes. The magic within her stirred, responding to the latent energies pulsing from the door. "It's not just locked. It's sealed with old magic," she said, feeling the familiar tug of darkness at the edge of her consciousness.

"Can you open it?" Aerin asked, his voice steady—a rock amidst the swirling uncertainties.

"Maybe. But not alone." She glanced back at him, searching for the unspoken assurance they'd come to share. "We'll need to combine our strengths."

"Then let's get started," he said, stepping beside her. His hand found its place atop hers on the door. His warmth bled into her, mingling with her powers.

"Everyone, hands on the door," Lysandra instructed. "Focus on your core, magic, essence—whatever drives you."

Feyla hesitated, a flicker of doubt crossing her features. "But

I'm not—"

"You're one of us, Feyla," Eolande interjected softly, catching her gaze with a look that spoke volumes. "Your intelligence and your inventions have brought us this far."

"Right," she muttered, squaring her shoulders as she placed her palms against the stone, Eolande mirroring her position.

"Imagine the barriers falling away," Lysandra continued, closing her eyes to visualize the task ahead. Envision the path as transparent and open."

"Like walking through tall grass back home," Aerin murmured, and she could sense his thoughts drifting to open fields and sunlit skies.

"Exactly," she whispered.

Together, they pushed for a collective exertion of will and power. The stone remained unmoved, but the air around them crackled with energy. Their combined strengths—Aerin's resilience, Feyla's ingenuity, Eolande's precision, and Lysandra's dual-touched magic—merged into a single force.

"More," Lysandra gritted out, feeling the resistance wane. "Just a bit more!"

With a groan that echoed like the cries of the ancient city itself, the door shuddered. Runes flared to life, casting a brilliant glow that bathed them in light. And then, slowly, the door began to slide open, grinding against the weight of centuries.

"By the gods," Feyla gasped, her voice tinged with awe.

"Keep going," Eolande urged, his usual calm replaced by a hint of urgency.

Then, with an almost imperceptible sigh, the obstacle yielded. Warm daylight flooded in, chasing away the chamber's shadows.

"We did it," Aerin breathed, amazement lacing his voice.

"Let's not start celebrating yet. We still have a war to win," Lysandra said, though her heart sang with the triumph of their achievement.

Stepping through the threshold, they emerged into the world again, the lost city behind them now just another chapter in the Chronicles of Erenor. Clutched in her hand was the crystal imbued with light, their most potent weapon yet against Malachor.

"Forward," Lysandra commanded, her voice ringing with newfound determination.

"Forward," her companions echoed, their footsteps in unison as they left the past behind and faced the future head-on.

"Alright," Lysandra said, glancing around at the group, their breaths visible in the crisp air of freedom. "We've got to move fast. Malachor won't be twiddling his thumbs."

Aerin wiped the sweat from his brow and nodded, his swords already sheathed. "The longer we linger, the more time he has to fortify."

"Fortify, schmortify," Feyla quipped, adjusting her pack with a clang of her ingenious gadgets. "He won't know what hit him."

Lysandra couldn't help but smile at her bravado. "That's the spirit, but let's not underestimate him." Her gaze fell on the crystal, pulsating gently in her palm. "This is our ace card."

"Right. So, where to now?" Eolande asked, his bow strapped across his back as he scanned the horizon.

"North," Lysandra declared, pointing towards the jagged peaks that sliced the sky. "The Temple of Astra. That's where we'll find the last piece of the puzzle."

"Through the Darkling Woods, then," Aerin murmured, her eyes narrowing. "It won't be a stroll."

"Since when have we ever done 'leisurely'?" Feyla smirked, pulling an arrow and inspecting its fletching.

"Shadow?" Lysandra called out softly, and the wolf padded to her side, his presence a silent vow of protection.

"Let's keep a tight formation," Lysandra instructed. "Feyla, you take point with Eolande. Aerin, cover our flank. Shadow and I will lead."

"Here we go again," Feyla sighed, but her grin was fierce. "Adventure calls!"

"Remember," Lysandra said, pausing to look each of them in the eye. "We're not just fighting for ourselves. This is for every soul in Erenor."

"Then let's end this—for Erenor," Aerin echoed solemnly.

"Stay sharp; stay alive," Lysandra added. "And stay close."

"Always," Aerin replied, his hand briefly finding hers before letting go and understanding the unspoken words between them.

With the lost city at their backs, they ventured forth, the weight of responsibility like armor upon their shoulders. The path ahead bristled with unknown dangers, but together, no force could stand against them.

"Keep watch for Malachor's spies," Eolande cautioned as they trudged through the underbrush.

"Let them come," Lysandra muttered, feeling the familiar thrum of magic coursing through her veins. "We're ready."

"Damn right, we are," Feyla chimed in, notching an arrow to her bow.

"Focus on the mission," Lysandra reminded them, though their fighting spirit bolstered her own. "We can't afford any mistakes."

"None will be made," Aerin assured her, his voice a low rumble. "Not by my hand."

"Good," Lysandra said. "Because when we face Malachor, it'll take everything we have and then some."

"Then it's a good thing we're bringing everything," Feyla said, her eyes twinkling with mischief and determination.

"Everything and more," Lysandra affirmed.

"Let's keep going," she whispered to Aerin, her voice barely audible over the rustling leaves.

"I'm with you," replied Aerin, gripping her hand tightly.

As they ventured deeper into the enveloping woods, their

hearts resonated as one. Love and a steadfast determination to save the light from the encroaching darkness that loomed over their world united them in their quest.

Chapter 13

THE TRIALS

Lysandra's breath steadied as she focused inward, her mind a fortress of resolve amidst the whirlwind of emotions threatening to unbalance her.

Each steady heartbeat was a drumbeat of war against Malachor's looming shadow, each pulse a reminder of the power coursing through her veins—a legacy she bore with equal measures of pride and trepidation.

This internal struggle, this battle within herself, was the test of her strength and resilience.

"Ready?" Aerin's voice pulled her from her reverie, his dark eyes searching hers for any sign of the uncertainty that gnawed at the edges of his courage.

"More than ever," Lysandra asserted, her voice sharpened by necessity.

She could sense the undercurrent of concern in his gaze, but there was no room for doubt, not when so much hinged on her mastery of the trials ahead.

Her unwavering determination to conquer these challenges was a beacon of inspiration and a testament to the strength of her character.

"Remember, strength isn't just about force," Aerin said, stepping closer to her side. "It's about knowing when to bend and stand firm."

Lysandra nodded, grateful for the reminder. She glanced past him to the entrance of the trial area, where the air itself seemed to buzz with the energy of untold magic. The weight of anticipation settled over her shoulders, a familiar cloak she wore with ease.

The trials were about to begin, and the air was thick with the promise of challenge and growth.

"Let's see what these trials are made of," she declared, a wry smile pulling at her lips as she squared her shoulders and stepped through the threshold.

The atmosphere shifted immediately, charged with excitement that mirrored the flutter in her chest. Here, at the precipice of destiny, Lysandra felt the full magnitude of her journey—the countless battles fought and the love that had bloomed like a rare flower amid chaos.

"May the First Mage guide you," Aerin murmured, close enough that his breath tickled the nape of her neck, sending a shiver down her spine despite the heat of the moment.

"May we both find what we seek," Lysandra answered, turning to flash him a fierce grin that belied the gravity of her next steps. With a final look of solidarity shared between them, a look that spoke volumes of their unbreakable bond, she turned her attention to the trials awaiting her command.

"Bring it on," she whispered to the unseen forces arrayed against her. Her journey through fire and shadow had prepared her for this moment, and now she would show them the true grit of the Last Mage's heir.

The world flared to white as Lysandra crossed the threshold, her eyes adjusting to the blaze of the sun beating down upon an endless sea of sand. Heatwaves danced across the horizon, and the air was thick with the scent of burning earth. She could almost taste the dryness in her throat, but she held her focus unwaveringly on the trials ahead.

"Alright, desert," she murmured wryly, "let's turn up the heat."

She stepped forward, feeling the scorching sands threaten to singe the soles of her boots. It wasn't about enduring the heat, but wielding it as her own. This was her element, after all.

"Fire obeys no one," A whisper from nowhere and no corporal being. Shadow growled at her side, his amber eyes reflecting a challenge.

"Except me," Lysandra countered, her confidence surging like a flame within her chest.

As if responding to her silent command, Lysandra raised her arm, and with a flourish, fire sprung to life around her wrist. The flames flickered eagerly, awaiting direction. With a deft movement, she sent them cascading forward, creating a trail of flickering fire that hardened the sand into glass, forming a walkable path through the desert.

"Nice trick," Aerin would have teased if he had been there with her, his tone laced with pride. But here, she was alone with her power and resolve.

Obstacles soon rose from the heated mirage—a series of fiery vortexes spiraling with such intensity they seemed capable of tearing the air apart. Heart pounding, she focused on the swirling infernos, extending her palm towards them. Her magic surged forth, meeting the chaos head-on. The flames bowed to her will, parting to reveal safe passage through their deadly dance.

"Too easy," she muttered, though adrenaline sang in her veins. Each step was a testament to her mastery over fire; each conquered challenge was a note in the symphony of her growing power.

Her determination and confidence were unwavering, a sign of her growth and mastery of the trials.

With every obstacle bested, Lysandra felt the dual energies within her flow more harmoniously—the light of the First Mage illuminating the darkness of the demon she harbored. It was a delicate balance, one she'd fought hard to maintain.

"Come on, Malachor," she whispered to the wind, her voice steady despite the blistering heat. "I'm ready for you."

The searing heat of the desert dissolved into an incredible rush of water as Lysandra plunged into the second trial's domain. Eyes snapping open, she saw an underwater cave's serene blues and greens, lit by the ethereal glow of luminescent algae. The sudden change in the element was jarring, yet Lysandra adapted with the fluidity that had become her signature.

"Alright, water," she murmured, her voice peculiarly clear under the magic-laden waters. "Let's dance."

The currents twisted around her, treacherous and wild, eager to sweep away anyone who dared challenge their domain. But Lysandra was no mere challenger; she was a force to be reckoned with. With a graceful sweep of her arms, she commanded the waters with her sea-green eyes, now a deep emerald gleaming with concentration and sparkling with raw power.

"Shift," she commanded, and the currents obeyed, swirling into a vortex at her fingertips. The whirlpool became her compass, guiding her through the labyrinthine cave system. She moved confidently, trusting in her connection to the water as it whispered secrets only a master could decipher.

"Remember the last time we were underwater?" Aerin's teasing voice echoed in her memory, a reminder of their shared adventures and the bond they forged through fire and water.

"Focus!" she scolded herself. This was no time for distractions.

Further ahead, the cave narrowed, and a series of glyphs appeared on the walls, each emanating a soft, pulsating light. Puzzles—she should have expected them. The water held its breath, waiting for her next move.

"Let's see if you're as clever as you are strong, Lysandra," she imagined Aerin would say, his confidence in her abilities a steady anchor.

"Watch me," she replied to the empty water, though her heart warmed at the thought of him.

Aligning her body with the flow, Lysandra stretched out her hands, palms facing the enigmatic symbols. With a series of delicate motions, she coaxed the water into intricate shapes, each matching the puzzle's demands. The glyphs shimmered in response, unlocking further mysteries with every correct pattern.

"Almost there," she breathed as the final glyph ignited with a radiant blue hue, signaling the puzzle's completion.

A path revealed itself, the water parting like a curtain to grant her passage. There was a sense of urgency now, the weight of destiny pressing upon her shoulders. She couldn't afford to lose, not when so much hung in the balance.

"Come on, Malachor," Lysandra whispered as she navigated through the opening. "I'm just getting started."

The canopy closed behind Lysandra with a rustling whisper, plunging her into the dappled shadows of the forest. She barely had a moment to catch her breath before the ground beneath her began to tremble. Clenching her fists, she drew upon the elemental energy coursing through her veins, feeling the pulsating life force of the earth.

"Showtime," she muttered, steeling herself for the trial's challenge.

Roots erupted from the soil, twisting and writhing like serpents intent on ensnaring her. With a fluid motion, Lysandra swept her hand to the side, and a wave of force emanated from her palm, pushing the roots back down into the ground. The earth obeyed, its subservience to her magic as natural as breathing.

"Nice try," she said, smirking despite the adrenaline rush. "But you'll have to do better than that."

Ahead, the path forked, and between the two choices stood a sentinel—a golem of interwoven branches and moss. Its eyes, glowing with a deep emerald light, fixed on her with an unwavering gaze. It was a guardian, one of many, she presumed, tasked with barring her passage.

"Alright, big guy," Lysandra addressed the earthen figure, her voice tinged with resolve. "Let's dance."

She stomped her boot against the forest floor, and the earth responded, rippling in waves toward the golem. It braced itself, but the ground beneath shifted, unbalancing the creature. Seizing the moment, Lysandra thrust her arms forward, palms outstretched, commanding the earth to rise. A thick wall of dirt and stone surged upward, encasing the golem's legs and trapping it.

"Ha! Gotcha!"

But the forest was relentless, and more guardians emerged, one after another, each stronger and more resistant to her powers. Sweat beaded on Lysandra's forehead as she concentrated, her control over the earth tested with every encounter. Refusing to yield, she wove her magic into the very fabric of the terrain, bending it to her will.

"Come on, Aerin would love this," she thought, envisioning his proud nod even as her muscles screamed in protest.

She channeled her magic into the trees, leaves rustling as the branches bent to form a bridge across a gaping ravine. She crossed with swift, sure steps, her heart a steady drumbeat. As the final guardian loomed ahead, larger and more formidable than the rest, Lysandra knew this was the culmination of the trial.

"Time to end this," she declared, clapping her hands together. Energy surged, and the ground erupted, sending rocks hurtling toward the guardian. It shattered upon impact, crumbling to dust that mingled with the forest floor.

Breathless and triumphant, Lysandra allowed herself a brief moment of respite, leaning against a nearby tree. The dense foliage seemed to bow in silent acknowledgment of her victory.

"Is that all you've got?" She questioned the deafening silence around her, but all that responded was the soft rustle of the leaves.

"Guess I'm tougher than I look," she added with a grin before striding forward with renewed purpose. The subsequent trial awaited, and she felt closer to the destiny that called her name with each step.

The earth beneath Lysandra's feet gave way to a sprawling expanse of green, the air alive with the dance of zephyrs and gales. She stood at the edge of the vast open field, her dark hair whipping about her face in wild tendrils as the wind greeted her like an old adversary itching for another round.

"Alright," she whispered, squaring her shoulders. "Let's see what you've got."

With a deep breath, she lifted her arms, her palms facing the tumultuous sky. The gusts responded, swirling around her with increasing enthusiasm as if testing her resolve. Lysandra's eyes narrowed; she wouldn't be toyed with. With a sharp twist of her wrists, she commanded the howling winds, bending them to her will.

"Come on, then!" she shouted into the roar, a smile tugging at her lips despite the strain. This was her element, literally and figuratively—the thrill of battle against nature.

She felt the magic surge within her, the storm's force intertwining with her own. Lysandra thrust her hands forward, sending a powerful gust sweeping across the field, flattening the grass, and sending loose stones skittering away like frightened rabbits.

"Nice try!" Aerin's voice cut through the chaos, his tone laced with admiration and that ever-present hint of worry. He stood a safe distance away, yet close enough to jump in if things went south. His hand rested on his sword, his stance ready, though he knew better than to disrupt her focus.

"Stay back, love," she called over her shoulder, not needing to see him to know he was inching closer out of concern. "I've got this!"

Turning back to the trial, Lysandra spotted the first puzzle—a series of stone pillars of varying heights spaced erratically across the field. The objective was clear: navigate the aerial maze without touching the ground. Her heart pounded with excitement.

"Time for a little flight," she murmured, calling upon the wind again. It swept beneath her, lifting her effortlessly into the air. She soared from pillar to pillar, the wind's steady presence beneath her feet as reliable as solid earth. Every leap brought a rush of adrenaline, and every successful landing brought a spike of triumph.

"Look at you, go!" Aerin couldn't contain his pride, his voice carrying on the breeze. Lysandra grinned, spinning around one particularly tall pillar before alighting atop it like a bird of prey.

"Guess I'm a natural," she retorted, though she knew the trials were far from over. As she prepared for the next challenge, she could almost feel the darkness within her recoil at the lightness of the wind. This was her proving ground, her chance to show that she was more than the sum of her ancestry.

"Show me what's next," she challenged the unseen architects of this trial, with the wind responding with a surge that told her they were all too eager to comply.

The wind whipped around Lysandra, a storm of her own making, as she stood poised on the apex of the stone pillar. Below, the final trial beckoned—a tapestry of windswept obstacles that would test her magic and her bond with the elements themselves.

"Ready, Lys?" Aerin's voice cut through the howling air, steady and sure.

"Of course I am," she called back, feeling the weight of his trust like an anchor in the storm. With a sharp gesture, she summoned a gust, propelling herself forward into the heart of the gale.

The field transformed into a motion blur, with each new challenge met with a dance of wind and will. She wove between slicing currents and twisted away from biting whirlwinds, her body a conduit for the raw power of the sky.

"Left!" Aerin's warning rang out just in time for Lysandra to throw her hands up, diverting a rogue vortex that threatened to sweep her off course. His presence was a constant by her side, unseen but unfaltering.

"Thanks," she panted, acknowledging the guidance that had become their silent language amid the trials. Their partnership was seamless, a symphony of action and reaction that carried them through fire, water, earth, and air.

Finally, as the last puzzle clicked into place—a series of wind chimes that sang in harmony only when the breezes were perfectly balanced—Lysandra landed softly on solid ground. Her chest heaved with exertion, but her eyes sparkled with the thrill of victory.

"We did it," she breathed out, her powers no longer strained but singing through her veins in vibrant accord.

"Indeed, you have." The voice was not Aerin's, but one imbued with ancient wisdom and a familiar power that made Lysandra's blood sing.

Aviara stepped into view, her form ethereal and fading at the edges like a waning shadow. Once radiant and formidable, the goddess now appeared fragile, her energy dimming to a mere whisper of its former glory.

"Aviara!" Lysandra rushed to her side, concern etching deep lines across her forehead. "What has happened to you?"

"Peace, child," Aviara said, her voice a soft caress against the tumult of the winds. "I have chosen to conserve my strength. What lies ahead will require all of us to be at our fullest potential."

"Then we must prepare," Aerin declared, stepping forward, his gaze locked onto the goddess with reverence and wariness.

"Yes, you must make preparations," Aviara consented, her enigmatic, dark eyes reflecting a depth of hidden knowledge. "The imminent battle with Malachor cannot be won through sheer strength alone. The unity of your spirits and the harmony of your souls will ultimately shift the balance in your favor."

"Unity..." Lysandra echoed, glancing at Aerin, feeling the truth of the goddess's words resonate within her. Together, they faced the trials and would face whatever darkness awaited. This was their destiny, woven through the fabric of Erenor itself.

"Rest now," Aviara instructed, her form dissipating like mist at dawn. "Gather your strength, champions of Erenor. When next we meet, it will be on the battlefield where fate itself will be forged anew."

And with those final words, Aviara vanished, leaving behind an echo of power and a solemn vow hanging in the air. Lysandra took Aerin's hand, squeezing it tightly, knowing they were ready—together, whatever came next.

The sun dipped below the horizon, casting a golden glow over the training grounds where Lysandra and Aerin stood facing each other. The silence was pregnant with the day's exhaustion and the weight of what would come.

"Today, we proved ourselves," Lysandra said, her voice steady despite the whirlwind of emotions inside her. She wiped the back of her hand across her brow, smearing away sweat and the remnants of fear.

Aerin shook his head, his eyes reflecting the dying light. "No, you proved yourself, but Malachor won't care about trials or tests. He'll only see enemies standing in his way."

"Then he'll see two enemies united by more than just purpose," she replied, taking a step closer. As their eyes locked, a silent understanding passed between them—a vow deeper than words.

"Are you afraid?" Aerin asked, his voice low.

"Terrified," Lysandra admitted with a half-smile. "But fear won't keep me from fighting. It won't keep us from winning."

"Good. Because I need you sharp and fierce." His hand reached out, brushing a stray lock of hair behind her ear. "Just like I know you are."

She leaned into his touch momentarily before stepping back, her resolve hardening. "We've learned a lot. From the desert sands to the forest's heart, every step has made us stronger. We've adapted and overcome. That's what we'll do against Malachor."

"Adapt and overcome," Aerin repeated, a grin tugging at his lips. "Sounds like a plan."

"More than that," Lysandra said, her gaze unwavering. "It's our promise. To Erenor, to each other."

"Then let's make good on that promise," Aerin said, extending his hand to her.

Lysandra took it, feeling the callouses of countless battles and the warmth that had nothing to do with the fading sunlight. "Together," she affirmed.

"Always," he agreed.

They stood side by side as night fell, the stars appearing one by one like tiny beacons of hope amidst the encroaching darkness. There was danger ahead, and a storm was brewing on the horizon. But at that moment, there was also strength, love, and a bond that not even Malachor could break.

"Rest up," Lysandra murmured, her voice soft but fierce. "Tomorrow, we fight. And we win."

"Rest up," Aerin echoed, squeezing her hand. "For Erenor, for us."

With a final glance at the sky, they turned towards their resting place, leaving the trials behind and walking into the unknown. But whatever lay ahead, they would face it together—warriors, mages, and lovers. United in heart and soul, ready for the final battle.

Chapter 14

A CALL TO ACTION

Ash and ember rained from the sky as Lysandra shielded her eyes, gazing upon the smoldering ruins of what was once a vibrant village on the outskirts of the WestRock Covert and not far from the Silver Mountains.

This was the aftermath of Malachor's latest attack, a potent antagonist whose taint spread daily.

Clutching Aerin's hand beside her, she felt his grip tighten—a silent promise that they faced this devastation.

"Look at it," Aerin said in a raw voice as he gestured toward the charred remnants of homes. "Malachor's taint spreads further every day."

"We can't let this continue," Lysandra stated with determination. "We have to gather everyone who can stand against him." Her words were not just a call to action but also a beacon of resolve that could inspire even the most uncertain of hearts.

After enduring a series of devastating battles and overcoming numerous challenges, a group of determined individuals confronted Lysandra in a barren landscape. Their expressions revealed not just determination but also the scars of past sacrifices. They thoroughly understood that the choices they were about to make held great significance for their collective future.

"Alright, let's brainstorm," Keir, a practical swordsman, called out. They gathered around a fallen log, repurposing it as their makeshift table. Maps and scrolls were spread out, marked with potential allies and resources critical for their impending struggle.

Locations like the hidden Silver Mountains armory, the Crystal Spire's secret library, and the Airborne Fleet's training grounds were among the markings on the maps.

"Rion's family in the Silver Mountains could provide us shelter and weapons," suggested Lysandra, tracing the jagged peaks drawn on the parchment.

"Good." Nara nodded, her eyes shadowed but determined. "I'll go. They know me; trust me."

"Meanwhile, we need the allegiance of the Airborne Fleet," Aerin added, his strategic mind plotting their aerial advantage. "Their sky ships could turn the tide."

"Leave that to me," Keir said, clapping Aerin on the shoulder. "I've got a way with words—and more importantly, I speak their language: coin and courage." With that, he set off to negotiate with the Airborne Fleet, fully aware of the sacrifices he might have to make to secure their allegiance.

"Then there are the mages of the Crystal Spire," Lysandra

mused. "Their magic is potent, even if their numbers are few."

"I'll take that journey," said Thalia, her hands aglow with soft light, ready to commune with her fellow spellcasters.

"Be cautious," warned Aerin, his gaze lingering on Thalia. "They are reclusive for a reason."

"Understood," she replied with a confident smile.

"Time is not our ally," Lysandra said, urgently rolling up the map. "We strike fast, gather our forces, and hit Malachor before he expects it." She looked at them and said, "But first, we seek out Aviara."

"Agreed," they all echoed, standing up from their huddle, the weight of responsibility settling on their shoulders.

"Let's move out," Aerin declared, his arm slipping around Lysandra's waist for comfort. "For Erenor."

As they set forth on their dangerous missions, their steps were heavy with responsibility, but their hearts were light with hope of victory.

"For Erenor," they repeated, their voices woven with hope and conviction as they set forth on their dangerous missions.

"Aviara," Lysandra called out, her voice echoing through the grove as the group approached the ancient deity's sanctuary. The air was thick with jasmine and wildflowers, starkly contrasting the acrid stench of Malachor's corruption that lingered beyond. The ground was soft beneath their feet, a reminder of the life that still thrived in this world despite the darkness threatening to consume it.

The nature goddess emerged from the shadows of her sacred bower, her dark hair flowing like streams of night. "Children of Erenor," she greeted, her voice carrying the whisper of rustling leaves. "What brings you to my refuge?"

"Malachor's darkness is spreading," Aerin said with a frown. "We've all joined forces to ask for your help in the upcoming battle. Your natural magic skills could make a difference in the fight."

"Of course," Aviara replied, her eyes narrowing in thought. "But I can't fix everything on my own. What will you give in return?"

"We'll protect your lands," Lysandra promised, stepping forward. "We'll use your power and strength to keep your home safe."

The others nodded in agreement, their expressions a mix of determination and understanding. They knew that every promise they made was pricey, and they were willing to pay for it.

"Alright," Aviara agreed with a nod. "I'll help you with my powers."

But before they could start celebrating, the ground shook violently. Suddenly, a gigantic creature emerged from a nearby thicket, covered in thorny vines and surrounded by dark magic.

"Malachor's sentinel!" Feyla exclaimed, swiftly preparing her bow. "He's found us!"

"Stand together, people!" Aerin commanded, drawing his

sword as he positioned himself beside Lysandra.

The beast roared, a sound that shook the very earth, its eyes alight with malevolent fire. Lysandra raised her hands, the air crackling with arcane energy as she prepared to unleash her magic.

The others stood ready, their weapons glinting in the sunlight, their hearts filled with determination. They were prepared to face whatever came their way, united in their purpose and resolve.

"Keep it distracted!" she shouted. Feyla let loose a volley of arrows, each tipped with a gleaming design invention. They exploded upon impact, stunning the creature momentarily.

"Your turn, Lysandra!" called Aerin, parrying the whip-like lashes of the vines.

Lysandra unleashed a torrent of magical power, her incantations weaving a tapestry of destruction that severed the dark tendrils binding the beast. It wailed, thrashing against the ethereal bonds that now held it.

"Aviara, now!" Lysandra cried.

The goddess stepped forward, her hands reaching out. Without saying a word, she summoned vibrant roots and vines wrapped around the creature, driving away the darkness. Slowly, the sentinel transformed, returning to its harmless form as a creature of the woods.

"Let's keep going," Aviara said calmly, as if using such powerful magic was just an everyday thing. "There's a lot to get ready, and time is something we don't have."

"Another close call," Aerin muttered, sheathing his sword as the group moved away from the subdued guardian of the forest. Lysandra's hands still shimmered faintly with residual magic, her breath coming in slow but steady waves.

"Too many," Lysandra replied, catching Aerin's eye. They stepped away from the others, busily discussing their next move. She reached out, her hand finding Aerin's. "I feel like every step forward comes with a steep price."

Her words carried a weight of sacrifice, a burden they were all willing to bear for the greater good.

"Then we pay it together," Aerin assured her, squeezing her hand. "That's what we promised each other."

"Sometimes I wonder if it's fair to you," she confessed, her gaze dropping. "I dragged you into this battle, and—"

"Stop." Aerin's voice was gentle but firm. "You didn't drag me anywhere. I'm here because I choose to be. Because I believe in you, in us." His thumb stroked her knuckles, a simple touch that anchored her. "And I'll stand by you until the end."

"Until the end," Lysandra whispered, drawing comfort from his steady presence. Their closeness encouraged her. She straightened up and prepared to face whatever lay ahead.

They found Bialaer Presjyre, a weathered male elf, waiting just outside the village.

"You've seen what Malachor's minions are capable of," Lysandra said, pouring her heart out. "We need your expertise in the ancient forests and skilled archers."

Bialaer glanced at them. "And why should I put my people at risk for your cause?"

Eolande, who had been unusually quiet until now, stepped forward. As an elf himself, he knows how they think. "Because it's not just about us," Eolande jumped in. "It's about Erenor. Your home is in danger just as much as ours."

"Words are cheap, and promises are easily broken," Bialaer said, his voice filled with doubt.

"Look at us," Feyla added, moving closer and taking Eolande's hand. "We're beaten down and tired, but we're still fighting. Not for fame or power, but for the hope of a future. Isn't that worth taking a stand for?"

"Your spirit is admirable," Bialaer conceded, his stance softening. "But it will take more than spirit to defeat Malachor."

"Then let us show you our resolve," Lysandra offered. "Stand with us, even for a day, and see what we're capable of."

"Very well," Bialaer finally agreed, a slow nod marking his decision. "One day. Convince me, and you shall have the support of the elves."

"Thank you," Lysandra said, relief coloring her words. "You won't regret it."

"See that I don't," Bialaer replied. Though his words were blunt, a hint of a smile touched his lips.

As they regrouped, Lysandra felt a renewed sense of purpose. With each ally gained, hope flickered brighter in the darkness. Together, they would face the coming storm. Together, they were unstoppable.

Lysandra and her companions stood back-to-back, the air crackling with dark energy around them. They were surrounded by the snarling visages of Malachor's minions, ready for battle.

The creatures, a grotesque blend of shadow and malice, crept closer, their claws scraping against the cobblestones of the village square, which had never been cleared so fast.

"Looks like we've got company," Aerin muttered, daggers already in hand, his eyes darting between the encroaching enemies.

"More than we bargained for," Lysandra replied, her sword drawn and shimmering with an ethereal light. She could feel the dark energy pulsing within her, begging to be unleashed.

"Let them come," Eolande said calmly, notching an arrow to his bow. "We stand united."

"Here they come!" Feyla exclaimed as the first of Malachor's minions leaped towards them.

"Remember, aim for their hearts," Lysandra shouted, and the battle commenced.

Aerin rolled out of the path with a clawed swipe, precisely driving his dagger into the creature's chest. At the same time, Lysandra's blade danced through the air, slicing through shadows as if they were made of butter. Feyla, nimble and quick, fired explosive bolts from her modified crossbow, creating chaos among the ranks of their foes.

"Watch your left, Aerin!" she yelled as he pivoted, narrowly avoiding a lethal blow.

"Thanks!" he called back, his voice laced with adrenaline.

Eolande's arrows flew true, each finding its mark with deadly efficiency. The minions fell one by one, but still they came, relentless in their assault.

"Is it just me, or are they not getting the hint?" Feyla quipped, reloading swiftly.

"Keep fighting!" Lysandra roared, her magic flaring around her as she cast a spell, sending a wave of force that knocked several attackers off their feet.

"Nice one!" Aerin complimented, slashing through another minion that had gotten too close.

"Behind you!" Lysandra warned, and with a swift pivot, Aerin dispatched another enemy.

"Seems like old times, huh?" he grinned at her despite the danger.

"Less reminiscing, more stabbing," she shot back, though her heart warmed at his words.

The group caught their breath as the last of them crumbled to dust. They looked around, their teamwork having seen them through yet another skirmish.

"Good teamwork," Eolande acknowledged, scanning the area for any remaining threats.

"Teamwork makes the dream work," Feyla said with a wink,

checking the integrity of her gadgets.

"Alright, let's move on," Lysandra commanded, sheathing her sword. "We've got a resource to secure."

They journeyed until they reached the edge of West Oak Grove, where ancient trees whispered secrets and the ground was treacherous with hidden roots. Here, the Crystal of Narael, a crucial element in their upcoming battle, was said to be concealed.

"Legend has it that the crystal is protected by a puzzle that only the worthy can solve," Eolande explained as he led them deeper into the woods.

"Any idea what kind of puzzle?" Aerin asked, wary of the forest's deceptive calm.

"Only that it involves the elements," Eolande responded. "Fire, water, earth, and air."

"Great, a pop quiz," Feyla muttered, adjusting her belt full of tools.

They arrived at a clearing, and in its center stood a stone pedestal with four empty recesses, each carved with symbols representing the elements. Above it hovered a shimmering barrier, within which the Crystal of Narael glowed enticingly.

"Okay, so we find a way to fill these with the right elements, and I'm guessing that barrier drops," Feyla surmised, examining the pedestal.

"Sounds about right," Lysandra agreed. "But how do we go about it?"

"Leave fire to me," Aerin said, conjuring a small flame in his palm and carefully placing it into the corresponding recess.

"Air is my domain." Aviara's voice echoed softly, always appearing when she needed it most. A gentle breeze swirled around the pedestal, settling into the second recess.

"Water," Eolande mused, aiming with his bow. An arrow tipped with a water globule struck the third recess, filling it.

"That leaves Earth," Lysandra noted, focusing her magic. A rumble underfoot preceded a chunk of earth rising from the ground and slotting into place.

As the final element found its home, the barrier dissipated with a melodic chime, and the crystal floated gently down into Lysandra's waiting hands.

"Resource secured," she declared, the crystal's light reflecting in her determined eyes.

"Nicely done," Aerin praised, clapping her on the shoulder.

"Let's keep moving," Lysandra said. "We've got a war to win."

Meeting Althea:

"Another dead end!" Feyla exclaimed, her frustration palpable as she kicked at the rubble blocking their path. The once-hidden passageway, meant to lead them to the reclusive sorceress Althea, was now a collapsed tunnel.

"Easy, Fey," Lysandra said, laying a firm hand on her shoulder. "We'll find another way."

"Time isn't exactly on our side, Lys," Aerin interjected, his gaze dark with concern. "Malachor's forces aren't going to wait for us to rally the troops."

"Then we don't waste time sulking about it," Lysandra snapped, more sharply than intended. She could feel the darkness within her stirring, feeding off her irritation.

"Hey!" Aerin said softly, catching her eye. "We're all on edge. But we've got this."

She exhaled slowly, forcing calm into her voice. "You're right. I'm sorry. Let's backtrack to the fork and try the western passage."

"Agreed." Eolande nodded, nocking an arrow out of habit.

"West it is," Feyla muttered, but her eyes were back to their usual glint of determination.

"Althea," Lysandra addressed the elderly sorceress, who peered down at them from her tower window. "We need your help."

"Help?" Althea cackled, her voice carrying the weight of centuries. "And what could you possibly offer in return?"

"An end to Malachor," Aerin called up. "Your knowledge could turn the tide."

"Knowledge isn't free, young ones," Althea retorted, her eyes unusually sharp for such an elderly person as they assessed the group.

"Nor is the safety of Erenor," Lysandra countered, meeting

her gaze evenly. "We're fighting for more than ourselves here."

"Very well," Althea conceded after a tense moment. "Prove your worth, and we'll talk."

"Prove how?" Feyla piped up, and curiosity piqued.

"Survive the night in my forest," Althea challenged, her smile thin and knowing. "Then we'll see."

"Consider it done," Lysandra stated firmly, leading her companions away from the tower, the heavy gates of the forest looming before them.

"Are we doing this?" Feyla whispered as darkness enveloped them.

"We are," Lysandra affirmed. "And we'll make it through, like always."

The night passed in a blur of shadowy figures and unseen threats, but dawn found them whole and unbroken.

"Persistent, aren't you?" Althea observed as they emerged from the forest, the first light of day casting long shadows behind them.

"Persistent and prepared," Aerin replied, a small smile on his lips.

"Very well," Althea declared. "I will lend my aid to your cause."

"Thank you," Lysandra said, relief flooding her voice. They had secured another ally, another step closer to victory.

"Let's not celebrate just yet," Eolande cautioned. "The real battle lies ahead."

"True," Lysandra agreed. "But today, we are stronger than we were yesterday. And tomorrow, we'll be stronger still."

"Spoken like a true leader," Feyla teased gently, and even in the weariness of their triumph, laughter rippled through the group, binding them tighter in camaraderie and purpose.

Lysandra's laughter mingled with the crackling of the campfire, the warmth of the flames a stark contrast to the cool night air of Erenor. Around her, her companions shared tales of narrow escapes and hard-won battles, each story a thread in the tapestry of their journey.

"Remember the time Aerin tried to outdrink a dwarf?" Feyla said, her eyes sparkling mischievously.

"Hey, I held my own," Aerin protested, though his grin betrayed him. "Until the world started spinning."

"Which was after two ales?" Lysandra added, ribbing him gently.

"True," Aerin conceded, wrapping an arm around her waist. "But I've got other skills that don't involve a tankard."

"Indeed, like getting us out of tight spots with those healing hands of yours," Aviara interjected gently, her voice as soothing as the forest breeze and her eyes alight with pride at their collective strength.

They shared knowing nods and soft smiles; their bond deepened with every challenge they faced together. Even amid the laughter, there was a quiet acknowledgment of what lay ahead—the final stand against Malachor. Yet tonight, they were not warriors or mages but friends, finding solace in shared victories and the promise of tomorrow.

As the fire dwindled, Lysandra caught Aerin's gaze. Their silent communication spoke volumes. They were ready, not just for battle but for whatever life would bring beyond it.

"Let's rest," she suggested, rising to douse the embers. "We'll need our strength."

"Agreed," Feyla said, already gathering her inventive gadgets, the tools of her unique brand of warfare. She always had one more trick up her sleeve.

"Aviara, will you keep watch?" Aerin asked, his tone respectful yet familiar.

"Of course," the nature goddess replied, her form shimmering slightly as if part of her essence remained intertwined with the world around them.

In the quiet that followed, Lysandra felt a surge of gratitude. They had come so far from mistrust and isolation to unity and purpose. They would face Malachor tomorrow; today, they would prepare with every ounce of their being.

"Sharpen your swords, check your arrows, and focus your minds," Lysandra instructed, her leader's voice firm yet filled with an undercurrent of care.

"Of course," Feyla responded, clapping her on the shoulder.

Aerin's voice resonated with fierce determination as he said, "Let's show Malachor what happens when he messes with Erenor." The intensity in his eyes only underscored the resolute determination in his words.

"Tomorrow, we fight," Lysander declared, "not just for ourselves, but for all of Erenor."

"Together as one," they all echoed, their voices melding into the night. It was a vow carried on the wind—a promise of hope and the anticipation of a dawn that would herald the end of darkness.

Chapter 15

FACING MALACHOR

The scent of charred earth and the distant wails of the dispossessed carried on the wind as Lysandra led her companions through the remnants of what was once a thriving village in Erenor. The blackened skeletons of buildings clawed at the sky, a stark contrast to the lush green that used to be.

"Malachor's left his mark," Aerin muttered, his voice a low rumble as he surveyed the devastation. His hand instinctively found the small of Lysandra's back, a silent display of solidarity.

"Too many marks," Lysandra replied, her eyes scanning the horizon, where smoke rose in ominous plumes. "We can't let this go on."

"Agreed. But brooding over scorched land won't stop him," Feyla chimed in, her gaze flicking between the wreckage and her companions with restless energy. "It's time we fight fire with something equally hot."

"Strategy, Feyla. We need a solid plan," Eolande corrected, his tone as crisp as the fresh pages of a book.

"Then let's strategize," Lysandra said, pivoting on her heel with a determination that seemed to ignite the air around her.

They shuffled into what remained of the village's war room, now just four walls desperately holding each other up. A dusty table in the center bore witness to their grim resolve as they huddled around it.

"Okay, no more beating around the burnt bush," Feyla started, tugging gadgets from her belt. "I've been working on new traps that could give us an edge."

"Traps will only get us so far," Eolande interjected, folding his arms. "We'll need more allies than we have gained so far. Strong ones."

"Which means we talk to those who've turned a blind eye until now," Lysandra added, her voice steely. "Time to open their eyes."

"Or give them a reason they can't ignore." Aerin leaned forward. "Show them what's at stake."

"Exactly. If we bring together the fractured kingdoms, show them Malachor's threat is real." Lysandra's words hung in the air like a battle cry.

"Then we stand a chance," Aerin finished, the corners of his mouth lifting in a rare smile that spoke volumes of his faith in her.

Feyla bounced on the balls of her feet, excitement sparking in her eyes. "And my inventions will be the cherry on top! Wait till you see the crossbow I've modified. It shoots magical bolts now!"

"Crossbows and alliances," Eolande nodded approvingly. "A good start. We'll need more than that to counteract Malachor's dark magic."

"Which is why we're going to hit him where it hurts," Lysandra declared, slamming her fist onto the table and making the others jump slightly. "The ley lines. If we can protect them, we cut off his power source."

"Sounds risky," Aerin observed, but his smile didn't falter.

"Since when have we backed down from a risk?" Lysandra retorted, her piercing gaze challenging each of them.

"Never," they said in unison, a testament to the bond forged through fire and darkness.

"Then it's settled," Lysandra said, her eyes ablaze with the promise of retribution. "We gather our forces, protect the ley lines, and take Malachor down—for good."

Lysandra strode into King Theobald Kapakuhaili's high-ceilinged throne room, Aerin at her side, her boots echoing authoritatively against the marble. The air was thick with the scent of beeswax from the towering candles that lined the walls.

"Your Majesty," she began without preamble, "Malachor's shadow spreads across Erenor. Your kingdom will not be spared unless we unite."

King Theobald leaned forward on his gilded throne, a skeptical arch to one brow. "And what would you have of us, Lysandra? Men? Gold? My scouts report nothing amiss on our borders."

"Scouts can be deceived. Aerin interjected, his voice urgent: "We've seen villages reduced to ash, lives torn asunder by his darkness."

"Words are wind, Aerin," the king retorted. "I need proof, not tales."

"Then look to your people," Lysandra countered fiercely. "Will you wait until they cry out in anguish under Malachor's heel?"

The king's eyes flickered with doubt, and for a moment, silence hung heavy between them.

"Very well," he conceded. "I will consider your words. But know this—my kingdom's safety comes first."

"Thank you, your Majesty." Lysandra nodded, masking her relief. As they left, she whispered to Aerin, "One step closer."

"Let's hope it's enough," he replied, his hand finding hers for a reassuring squeeze.

Feyla and Eolande trudged through the Whispering Woods, with gnarled roots and low-hanging fog obscuring their path. Eolande scanned the tree line, his bow ready.

"Stay alert, Feyla. Creatures guard these artifacts, remember?"

"I'm more worried about tripping over my own feet than some mythical beast," Feyla muttered, but her hand was on her gizmo-laden belt, fingers twitching.

As she spoke, a growl rumbled through the trees, summoning a shadowy figure—a dire wolf, its eyes glinting like coals—that crept forward.

"Speak of the devil," Feyla breathed, pulling free a shimmering bolt from her pouch.

"Wait for it." Eolande's voice was calm, even as he drew an arrow and tied it to his bowstring.

The creature lunged, and the pair moved in fluid tandem—Eolande's arrow flew through the air, hitting the beast's flank, while Feyla's bolt released a net of sparkling energy, trapping it.

"Nice shot!" Feyla exclaimed, and Eolande offered her a very rare smile.

"Let's keep moving. The artifact won't just be lying around for us to pick up," he reminded her as they continued deeper into the woods, leaving the incapacitated dire wolf behind.

"Adventure and danger, just how I like it," Feyla said with a grin, though her heart pounded against her ribs. Together, they pressed on, their resolve as strong as the magic they sought to claim.

The wind howled across the barren landscape as Lysandra and Aerin approached the temple's ancient stone steps, worn by time and weather. The air buzzed with a silent energy that raised the hair on their arms—a hum of power that resonated with the core of their being.

"Are you ready for this?" Aerin asked, his voice steady despite the palpable tension knotted in his shoulders.

Lysandra nodded, her eyes set on the colossal doors ahead. "We've come too far to doubt our path now."

Together, they ascended the steps, each footfall echoing against the solemn silence that enveloped the temple. At the threshold, they paused, exchanging a glance that conveyed the gravity of their quest. They pushed open the doors with a collective breath, revealing a chamber lit by flickering torches that cast dancing shadows upon the walls.

"Welcome, seekers of truth," intoned a voice emanating from the stones around them.

"Show us your heart's desires," another voice whispered, ethereal and haunting.

"Prove your worth," a third demanded, its tone commanding.

The temple's trial had begun.

"Stay close," Lysandra murmured, her hand instinctively reaching for the hilt of her blade—not out of an expectation of battle but as a comfort against the unknown.

"You know I will," Aerin promised, extending his senses to feel the earth beneath them, seeking stability where little could be trusted.

As they ventured deeper into the Temple of Seqarus, the air grew thick with enchantment. Illusions sprang forth—phantoms of their deepest fears and greatest regrets. Aerin faced the specters of his witch-hunter past, each wraithlike figure accusing him with hollow eyes.

"Your guilt does not define you," Lysandra said through gritted teeth, fighting her demons—a cascade of dark whispers promising power and urging her to embrace the shadow within.

"I won't let it," he replied, setting his jaw and focusing on the warmth of the earth's embrace to anchor him.

Hand in hand, they pressed forward, their intertwined magic a beacon of combined strength. As the final test loomed—a bridge over a chasm plunged into darkness—they knew this was a crossing of faith.

"Trust me," Lysandra said, stepping onto the trembling bridge.

"With my life," Aerin replied, following her lead as the bridge solidified under their shared resolve.

As they made their way to the other side, a breathtaking scene unfolded: an altar illuminated by celestial light, with the ethereal forms of ancient spirits floating above it, nodding in solemn approval.

"Your unity has proven your worth," the spirits said in unison. "Erenor's fate rests with you." They got the confirmation they needed.

Later, the atmosphere was tense as they gathered around a map littered with markers and scrolls. Feyla fidgeted, her gaze darting between Eolande's calm facade and the furrowed brows of her fellow companions.

"We need to focus on fortifying the eastern pass. Malachor's forces will expect a direct assault," Lysandra stated, her finger tracing the mountainous terrain.

"Direct might be unexpected," Feyla countered, her voice edged with frustration. "Hit 'em where it hurts before they see it coming."

"Rash actions lead to unnecessary risks," Eolande interjected smoothly, though his eyes betrayed his concern for the precarious balance they sought.

"Enough," Aerin cut in, his tone brokering no argument. "We must blend caution with courage. Feyla, your ingenuity is vital. Eolande, your strategic mind keeps us one step ahead. We must use every advantage."

Silence fell the weight of his words settling like a mantle over the room. Lysandra met his gaze, her heart swelling with pride and love for the man who once hunted her kind but now stood as her staunchest ally.

"You're right," Feyla admitted, a sheepish smile tugging at her lips. "I just want to do my part."

"And you will," Lysandra assured her, placing a comforting hand on her shoulder.

"United, we stand," Eolande affirmed, nodding toward each member.

"Then it's settled," Lysandra concluded. "We face this together. For Erenor."

"For Erenor," they echoed, their voices merging into a promise of resilience and hope amidst the gathering storm.

Lysandra's hand flew to the hilt of her sword as the crystal orb in her coat pocket suddenly pulsed with an urgent glow. The makeshift war room fell silent, all eyes on her as she took out the orb and placed her palm over the orb's surface, summoning the message within. Aviara's ethereal visage materialized above the orb, her voice laced with tension.

"Malachor's forces march toward the ley lines. It would be best if you acted swiftly," the deity warned before fading away.

"Damn it," Lysandra hissed, turning to Aerin. "We have little time left. Gather everyone."

Aerin nodded, his jaw set. "To arms! Malachor won't wait for us to be ready," he bellowed, rallying the warriors preparing for this moment.

"Let's show them what we're made of," Feyla said, slinging a satchel of her latest contraptions over her shoulder.

"Remember, stay alert," Eolande added, nocking an arrow to his bow with practiced ease. "These are no ordinary enemies."

"Focus on protecting the lines," Lysandra commanded, her tone leaving no room for argument. "We can't let them fall."

As they hurried out of the castle, the distant rumble of dark magic and clashing steel reached their ears. The battle for the ley lines had begun.

Charging into the fray, Lysandra met the onslaught with ferocity, her blade singing through the air as it cut down shadowy figures. Aerin stood unflinching beside her, his incantations shaping the earth to shield their forces. The defenders of Erenor responded to each spell their enemies cast with equal force.

"Watch your flank!" Aerin shouted as a dark wraith lunged toward Lysandra.

With a swift parry, she dispatched it, nodding her thanks. "Stay close," she told him, her heart racing not just from the fight but from the fear of losing him.

"Always," he replied, understanding the unspoken words.

Feyla darted between combatants, her small frame deceptive in its deadliness. A burst of light from one of her gadgets sent a cluster of enemies reeling, giving the soldiers they had recruited the upper hand.

"Gotcha!" she cried triumphantly, already moving to her next target.

From the high ground, Eolande loosed arrows with deadly precision, each finding its mark among the sea of adversaries. "Hold the line!" he called, offering silent support to the warriors below.

The battle raged—a maelstrom of magic and might. Lysandra could see the ley lines shimmering through the chaos, holding firm against the onslaught. They were Erenor's heartbeat, and she would die before she let that heartbeat falter.

"Push them back!" She roared, rallying her companions and all their new allies. "For Erenor!"

"FOR ERENOR!" the cry echoed across the battlefield, a chorus of determination and defiance.

Together, they fought, side by side, their bonds of friendship and love, forging an unbreakable wall against the darkness that sought to consume their world.

Aerin's hands were planted firmly in the scorched earth of the battlefield, and his dark eyes closed as he channeled the raw energy from deep within. Around him, the ground trembled, a low rumble rising to meet the cacophony of war cries and clashing steel.

"Come on, you can do this," Lysandra whispered from her vantage point beside him, her sword slick with the ichor of their foes.

"I've got it," Aerin grunted, his brow furrowed with concentration. The ley lines responded to his call, the glow beneath the land pulsing stronger, steadying against the dark tide that Malachor's magic had unleashed.

"Look!" Feyla shouted over the din, pointing toward the horizon where a wave of greenery swept across the barren fields—Aviara's doing. Soldiers cheered as twisted vines erupted from the ground, entrapping enemy forces in their unyielding grasp. Trees burst forth, branches swatting at the shadowy creatures that dared to come close.

"Is that... is that supposed to happen?" Eolande called down, incredulity lacing his usual calm demeanor.

"She's improvising!" Aerin replied with a gritted smile, opening his eyes to witness the fruits of Aviara's power.

"Stand strong, Earthshaker," Lysandra said, offering a rare grin of her own. Her heart swelled with pride for the man she loved, his strength becoming the backbone of their resistance.

But the moment of triumph was short-lived. From beyond the newly formed forest barrier, a thunderous roar shook the sky, and a towering beast of shadows emerged, its eyes blazing with malicious intent.

"Damn it," Lysandra cursed, stepping forward. "That thing's headed for the ley lines!"

"Nothing we can't handle," Aerin assured her, though his voice held an edge of uncertainty.

"Brace yourselves!" Eolande warned as he sent a volley of arrows skyward, hoping to slow the creature's advance.

"I can't let them through," Feyla muttered, assembling another contraption with trembling hands. She launched it into the fray, and a brilliant flash momentarily blinded their enemies, buying precious seconds.

"Focus on the beast!" Lysandra commanded, rallying the troops. "Protect the ley lines at all costs!"

"Stay together," Aerin added, rising to his feet, his energy waning but his resolve unshaken.

The battle raged fiercer than ever, with every group member and every soldier pushing themselves beyond their limits. Lysandra felt the dark energy within her roil and churn, threatening to spill forth uncontrollably.

"Easy there," Aerin cautioned, noticing her struggle. "Don't let it consume you."

"Like I have a choice," she snapped back, then immediately regretted her harshness. "Sorry, it's just... hard to keep in check."

"Hey, we've got this," he reassured her, gripping her hand momentarily. "We're a team, remember?"

"Right, together," she echoed, tightening her grip on her sword.

The monstrous shadow beast loomed closer, its presence chilling the air. Their valiant forces began to falter under Malachor's relentless assault.

"By the gods," Feyla breathed, horror-stricken as the beast tore through their defenses like paper.

"Fall back!" Lysandra ordered desperation, clawing at her throat. "Regroup and—"

"No," Aerin interjected, steel in his voice. "We stand our ground here. For Erenor, for everything we hold dear. We end this now!"

"Right behind you, always," Lysandra said, feeling their unwavering bond lend her strength.

"Then let's show this creature what happens when it messes with the protectors of Erenor," Aerin declared, raising his arms once more to the skies and drawing on the last reserves of his magic.

"FOR ERENOR!"

The cry echoed again, fueled by hope, incredible bravery, and togetherness, as they stood against the approaching darkness.

"Stand with me, Aerin!" Lysandra's shout pierced through the tumult of battle as she parried a strike from one of Malachor's shadow minions.

"Always," he replied, his voice a solid anchor amidst the chaos. Earth magic surged around him, green tendrils snaking out to entwine with Lysandra's shimmering aura. Together, they were a beacon of resistance, their combined power pushing back against the tide of darkness.

"Your move," Lysandra grunted, side-stepping a vicious swipe and slicing through another foe.

"Watch this," Aerin said with grim determination. With a roar, he slammed his staff into the ground. The earth responded, rising in jagged spikes and impaling shadows that evaporated into the ether. Their allies cheered, fighting with renewed vigor at the sight.

"Keep it up! We're making headway!" Lysandra called out, her blade singing through the air as it cleaved shadow after shadow, each swing fueled by the love and trust she held for Aerin, Erenor, and all they stood to lose.

"I can't let you have all the fun!" Aerin joked weakly, masking his exhaustion with a smile as he conjured a protective barrier around a group of their fighters.

"Come on, we've got a realm to save," Lysandra said, locking eyes with him. In that gaze was an unspoken promise, a shared understanding that transcended words.

"Lead the way," he replied, and together they fought toward the heart of darkness, where Malachor waited for them.

The Shadow Realm pulsed with malice, a swirling vortex of despair. Here, in this forsaken place, Lysandra faced Malachor. His form was a shifting mass of shadows, tendrils of dark energy reaching out like fingers, seeking to choke life from her world. Evil swirled around them in dark clouds and seeped like thick mud deep into the ground. The stench was overwhelming.

"End this, Lysandra." Aerin's voice reached her, filled with urgency. "You have the power."

"Malachor!" she shouted, stepping forward, blade poised. "This ends now!"

"Insolent child," his voice boomed, a cacophony of every nightmare forged into sound. "You cannot hope to defeat me. I am the Lord of Darkness!"

"Watch me," she retorted, her grip tightening around the handle of her sword. It hummed, resonating with her heartbeat, glowing brightly against the oppressive gloom.

Their powers clashed, light against dark, a symphony of destruction. Lysandra dove and wove through the barrage, each spell cast by Malachor a note in the deadly dance. She chanted, weaving her counter-spells—the incantations passed down from the First Mage. In this moment, she also let go of the darkness she held back. To her, it felt like she was growing in stature and that she would destroy everything in her path. Everything...Including Malachor. Even her voice came out masculine, deep, and hoarse—the voice she heard just before she sent her ancestor to Hell. She uttered the Evocation of Alteration and flung it at Malachor, making him stumble.

"Your tricks are useless here," Malachor sneered, throwing a wave of darkness at her.

"Tricks?" Lysandra spat back, deflecting the assault with a flick of her wrist. "I don't need tricks to take you down."

"Then come, child. Face your doom!"

Lysandra let out a fierce, hoarse cry as she charged forward. Her blade, glowing with her unique magic, cut through the air, creating a silver arc against the dark sky. When it clashed with Malachor's essence, it sent shockwaves through the Shadowrealm.

"Is that all?" Malachor taunted, but there was a tremor in his voice now, a hint of uncertainty.

Lysandra didn't respond with words. Instead, she poured every ounce of her being into the next strike, the blade finding the weakness she had sensed—the flaw in the tapestry of his power.

"You dare—" Malachor's outcry was cut short as the sword pierced through, severing the source of his strength.

"Love dares," Lysandra whispered fiercely. "And it wins." She spun around and decapitated him in one single stroke.

As Malachor's form unraveled, Lysandra felt Aerin's presence beside her, grounding her and reminding her of what they fought for. Together, they watched as the darkness receded, leaving Erenor's future hanging in the balance yet filled with hope again. Darkness seeped like sludge from Lysandra and disappeared with the remnants of Malachor into the dark soil of the Shadowrealm.

The ground quaked beneath Lysandra's boots as the Shadowrealm's fabric tore at the seams. "We have to move, now!" she shouted over the din of crumbling darkness and desperate cries.

Aerin was already pulling a fallen comrade to his feet, his voice steady despite the tremors. "This way! Keep close to us!"

"Aviara, we need an exit!" Feyla yelled, her inventive mind racing for solutions amidst the chaos.

"Follow my light," the deity's voice boomed, gentle yet commanding as a path illuminated before them, cutting through the disintegrating realm.

Eolande notched an arrow, his keen eyes scanning for stragglers. "Hurry, I'll cover the rear."

They sprinted through the labyrinth of shadows, each step a gamble against time's cruel hand. Lysandra's heart pounded in sync with the pulsing energy around them—each beat a reminder of what they'd sacrificed and what still lay on the line.

"Look out!" Aerin's warning came just in time for Lysandra to raise a shield, deflecting a shard of dark magic that splintered like wicked glass.

"Keep moving!" she ordered. The shadow realm is breaking up like a piece of glass or a dark mirror!" Her voice propelled her allies forward with a blend of fear and determination.

As they reached the precipice of realms, a final surge of evacuees stumbled through, gasping for breath, their faces etched with relief and terror.

"Is everyone—" Feyla began, but Eolande cut her off.

"Go! Now!" He loosed one last arrow into the void, its brilliance fading as the Shadowrealm shattered and collapsed upon itself.

They crossed the threshold back into Erenor, the once menacing gateway sealing shut forever with a resonant, dull echo. There was no time for rest; the wounds of their world lay open, festering.

"I never thought I'd be part of rebuilding the very thing I once hunted," Aerin murmured, taking Lysandra's hand. His touch grounded her amidst the turmoil.

"Neither did I," she replied, squeezing back. "But all of us..." Her hand made a sweeping gesture over the tired crowd, who, almost to the person, had tears running down their soot-covered faces. "All of us will heal Erenor together."

Chapter 16

THE AFTERMATH

Day 1 of Erenor's New Destiny

The sunset cast a blaze of orange and pink over the restored city, casting a warm glow on the bustling streets. In the weeks since their victory against Malachor, Lysandra and her companions had worked tirelessly to rebuild what he had destroyed.

The once-broken walls, scarred by the fires of Malachor's wrath, were again fortified, new buildings sprouted from the ashes, and hope, a fragile seed, bloomed in every corner, a testament to their resilience and determination.

"I never thought I'd see this place rise from its ruins," said Eolande, leaning against his bow as he surveyed their progress.

Lysandra beamed, her heart swelling with a sense of accomplishment at what they had achieved together. "Thanks to your unparalleled skills as an archer and protector," she acknowledged Eolande.

Eolande chuckled, a testament to their shared bond. "I couldn't have done it without your guidance and leadership," he admitted to Lysandra.

Together, they turned to watch Aerin. She watched her tall, muscular man, with a gentle smile, train a group of soldiers in combat techniques. His grace and strength were unmatched, even among the most skilled warriors in Erenor.

"He's become quite the leader," Lysandra remarked.

Aerin glanced up at them with a smile before instructing another soldier. Lysandra's gaze lingered on him for a moment longer before turning to Feyla, who was busy tinkering with one of her inventions nearby.

"Feyla's contributions have been invaluable as well," she said with a nod toward the tinkering engineer.

Eolande followed her gaze and grinned. "She certainly keeps us entertained."

Feyla looked up at them with her usual mischievous twinkle in her eye and waved before returning to her work.

"And let's not forget Aviara," Aerin spoke upon joining them, his voice tinged with the memory of their epic battle. "Without her guidance and magic, we wouldn't have been able to defeat Malachor, the dark lord who threatened to plunge Erenor into eternal darkness."

They all nodded in agreement before returning to admire the city again.

The once desolate streets were now filled with life and color. Villages were rebuilt, families reunited, and happiness returned to Erenor, a testament to their resilience and unity.

"Here," Lysandra said, handing Feyla a blueprint of the Arcane Council's proposed future headquarters. "Make it real."

"With pleasure," Feyla grinned, her eyes alight with the spark of creation.

"An assembly of mages, seers, elves, other magical folk, and wizards alike, all working towards a shared future," Eolande reflected, his gaze piercing the horizon. "It is what my village would have wanted."

"More than that," Aviara whispered, enveloping them like a warm breeze. "You are the guardians of balance, the harbingers of the new Erenor."

"Guardians..." Lysandra let the word roll off her tongue, considering the weight of it.

She felt a mix of pride, responsibility, and determination.

"I can live with that."

"Good," Aerin chuckled, wrapping an arm around her shoulders. "Because, my love, we've got a world to protect."

The cobblestone streets of Erenor's capital thrummed with life, the air thick with the scent of roasted meats and sweet mead as banners of victory fluttered from every window and archway. Lysandra moved through the crowd, Aerin at her side, their hands clasped tightly.

"Look at them," Aerin said, his voice a low hum of wonder. "They're...happy."

"Thanks to you," Lysandra replied, nudging him with her shoulder. Her eyes danced over the crowd, absorbing the light of their smiles.

"Us," he corrected gently, squeezing her hand. "We did this together."

A cheer erupted as they passed, and children darted between the legs of their elders, weaving tales of the great battle with stick swords and dramatic flourishes. Elderly mages nodded their approval in their direction while young witches wore cloaks emulating Lysandra's own—a tapestry of respect woven in vibrant threads.

"I never thought I'd be a style icon," Lysandra joked, but her chest swelled with pride.

"Nor am I a role model for future Earthshakers," Aerin laughed, gesturing to a group of youths practicing spells that made pebbles hover above their palms.

"Speaking of shaking," Feyla said, standing beside them with a pouch across her body. "I've got prototypes to make those look like parlor tricks."

"Careful, Feyla," Eolande warned, trailing behind her with a fond smile. "Let's not give the kids too much power too soon."

"Ah, what's the worst that could happen?" Feyla winked, mischief lighting up her eyes.

"Chaos, destruction, the end of the world as we know it," Eolande deadpanned, though the twinkle in his eye betrayed his jest.

"Sounds like Tuesday," Lysandra quipped.

"Speaking of which," Aerin began, his tone shifting as he addressed the group. "Aviara sent word. There are still unstable lines needing attention."

"Then we'll attend to them," Lysandra stated firmly. "After the celebration."

"Agreed." Eolande nodded. "For today, we revel in peace."

"Peace," echoed Feyla, raising an imaginary glass. "May it last longer than our hangovers."

Their tight-knit circle reverberated with laughter, and in that brief moment, the burden of their obligations seemed to dissipate, giving way to the pure joy of camaraderie and achievement.

"Tomorrow, we face whatever comes," Lysandra proclaimed to the city, her voice carrying on the wind. "But tonight, Erenor, we dance under the stars!"

The crowds roared their approval, and the music swelled—a rhythmic pulse that beckoned hearts to beat in time with its melody. As the night descended, the city became a mosaic of light and shadow, each flickering torch bearing witness to their camaraderie and the enduring spirit of Erenor.

"Think there'll ever come a day when we're not fighting for our lives?" Aerin mused as they swayed to the music, his arms encircling Lysandra.

"Maybe," she whispered, resting her head against his chest. "But until then, I'm glad I have you."

"Forever," he vowed, and the promise lingered in the air, a sacred oath mingling with the essence of magic that still clung to the fabric of the world.

As the sun rose with hues of pink and gold, whispers of the future weaved through the lingering celebration. "We've got adventures and challenges ahead, but we're in this shoulder to shoulder," said Eolande.

"Yeah, we're not just wielding power. We're creating a destiny bigger than ourselves," Feyla added.

Feyla's eyes sparkled as she chuckled and gestured to the bustling streets below them. "Look at our people," she said with pride. "We've given them hope and a chance to rebuild their lives after everything they've been through."

Day 2: The Path Back to Tyrannis

Lysandra's breath came out in sharp bursts as she sprinted through the dense forest, her hair like a wild silver mane streaming behind her.

The earthy scent of pine and damp soil was heavy in the air, but her focus was razor-sharp—fixed on the towering figure of Aerin, who led the way, his powerful strides barely avoiding tangled roots.

"Keep up," he called back to her without turning, his voice a mixture of urgency and reassurance.

"Like I need the encouragement," Lysandra shot back, a hint

of a smile tugging at her lips despite the danger nipping at their heels.

Feyla, puffing slightly from exertion, piped up from behind, "I could've designed us some sort of flying contraption for times like these!"

"Quiet." Eolande's clear voice cut through the banter with the precision of an arrow. "We're almost there."

They skidded to a halt before an ancient stone archway, vines draping over it like nature's curtains. Their chests heaved in unison, a brief respite as they all turned towards a shimmering Aviara, whose serene gaze held a glimmer of otherworldly knowledge.

"Through here," Aviara said softly, gesturing to the arch. "This is the path to your answers."

"Answers that better be worth this chase," Lysandra muttered under her breath, but her eyes were alight with anticipation.

Aerin placed a reassuring hand on her shoulder, his touch grounding her swirling emotions. "We'll face whatever comes as one," he said firmly, his scars a stark reminder of their shared struggles.

"Right. Together," Lysandra affirmed, drawing strength from his presence.

"Then let's not keep destiny waiting," Eolande quipped, already moving towards the arch with his usual graceful poise.

They stepped through the archway one by one, the atmosphere shifting around them, charged with magic. A sense of foreboding tingled at Lysandra's skin as they emerged into a clearing bathed in ethereal light on the other side.

"Remember, the road back will be fraught with more than just physical dangers," Aviara warned, her voice echoing strangely like the wind.

"Let's just hope it leads us to Tyrannis without us becoming mincemeat for whatever lurks in these woods," Feyla added, her wit never failing even in the face of uncertainty.

"Whatever it takes," Lysandra said, determination etching her features.

"Whatever it takes," Aerin echoed, squeezing her shoulder once more before they all stepped forward, ready to confront what awaited them with the courage of true warriors and the power of unwavering love.

As the meadow's light waned, the group approached a hollowed, ancient oak that twisted skyward like an arthritic hand grasping the heavens. Lysandra took point, pulling back her hair to reveal the sharp focus in her eyes.

"Are you sure this is the place?" she asked, glancing over her shoulder at the motley crew of warriors and mages flanking her.

"Positive," Aerin replied, stepping beside her. His gaze lingered on the gnarled tree, reading the silent whispers of the forest.

"Let's get on with it then," Feyla chimed in, her hands restlessly twirling a dagger. "Seer or no seer, we're sitting ducks out here."

Aviara nodded solemnly, her robes shimmering faintly with

protective enchantments. "The Oracle of the Glimmerwood has never been wrong before. Trust in the journey."

Lysandra reached out, placing her palm against the rough bark, feeling the pulse of magic beneath. She pushed her arcane energy into the tree with a breath, and the air crackled with anticipation.

"Oracle, we seek your guidance," she called into the silence.

A ghostly wind swept through the clearing as the oak shivered, its trunk splitting with a sound like thunder to reveal a shadowed cavern. They all exchanged wary looks before stepping into the darkness.

"Welcome, seekers," whispered an ageless voice from the shadows. The seer materialized before them, enshrouded in veils of shifting color, her eyes pools of starlight.

"Show us what we must know," Lysandra said, her voice steady though her heart raced with the moment's gravity.

"Behold," the seer intoned, and the space around them filled with swirling mist.

Images began to coalesce: Lysandra standing amidst a storm of chaos, her body radiating an aura of pure, blinding light.

"Your power... it's the key," the seer breathed. "The legacy of the First Mage courses through you, but also something... d arker."

"Speak plainly," Aerin demanded, his hand instinctively moving towards the hilt of his sword.

"Darkness and light, two halves of a whole," the seer continued, locking gazes with Lysandra. "Your demon heritage, the shadow within, can consume or empower. The choice will be yours."

"Wait, are you saying I must embrace that part of me?" Lysandra's voice quivered slightly, betraying her inner turmoil.

"Only by accepting all facets of your being could you hope to live a happy life," the seer clarified, her form fading. "Embrace your full potential; victory was yours because you did just that."

Lysandra's breath caught in her throat as the seer's words sank in. "So, it wasn't just my light that defeated him; it was both."

"Exactly." The seer nodded. "You wield a balance of light and dark. That is your true strength."

"Thank you," Lysandra said, bowing her head slightly. The vision dissipated, leaving them once again in the moonlit clearing.

"Then our path leads us to Tyrannis," Eolande said, breaking the silence. "To establish the new heart of Erenor's future."

"Right," Lysandra agreed, the weight of her destiny settling firmly on her shoulders. She turned to the group, her expression resolute. "To Tyrannis, to build our headquarters and begin anew."

The moon hung low, silently witnessing the turmoil churning within Lysandra as she stepped away from the group. Aerin followed his presence, a comforting shadow in the silver-drenched clearing.

"Hey," he murmured, coming up alongside her. "You okay?"

Lysandra let out a shaky breath, leaning against a gnarled tree. "I'm... it's just a lot, you know? Embracing darkness doesn't exactly sound like a winning plan."

Aerin's hand found hers, warm and steady. "We'll figure it out. You're not alone in this."

She squeezed his hand, drawing strength from the simple touch. "How can you be so certain?"

"Because I've seen what you're capable of. Light, dark—it doesn't matter. You're Lysandra, and that's enough for me."

His words wrapped around her like a protective cloak. Lysandra leaned into him, resting her head against his chest and listening to the solid beat of his heart. It was a stark contrast to the chaos that threatened to engulf her.

"Promise me something?" she whispered.

"Anything."

"Stay with me, no matter what happens," Lysandra pleaded, gripping Aerin's hand tightly.

"Without a doubt," Aerin vowed, her voice steady despite the looming danger, as he returned Lysandra's gaze.

He closed his eyes for a minute. Aerin's eyes suddenly reflected fear and love as he leaned in, kissing Lysandra's forehead tenderly. "I couldn't bear to lose you," he whispered, his voice barely above a breath. "We must always be together, facing whatever comes as one."

Lysandra nodded, her gaze never leaving Aerin's. "Together," she affirmed, the weight of the unspoken battles ahead hovering around them.

The seer's voice, piercing through the night, broke the moment. "Children of Erenor," she called, her form materializing once more before them.

Your path leads back to Tyrannis."

"Back?" Aerin echoed, his brow furrowed.

"Yes," the seer continued. "There, you must establish the seat of the Arcane Council. It is there, at the heart of Erenor, where your guidance and strength will ensure the balance of magic and the protection of our world."

"Then we won't waste another minute," Lysandra declared, pulling away from Aerin with renewed resolve.

"Prepare yourselves, for the road is perilous, and time runs thin," the seer warned, her image flickering like a candle in the wind.

"Thank you," Lysandra said, nodding to where the seer had been. She turned to Aerin, her eyes alight with the fire of determination. "Let's go home and finish this."

"Lead the way, my heart," Aerin replied, his voice laced with pride and solemnity.

Together, they rejoined their companions, their hearts intertwined, ready to face whatever dangers awaited in Tyrannis and to lay the foundations for the future of Erenor.

ERENOR'S DESTINY

PART 2
The Arcane Council

ERENOR'S DESTINY
BOOK 3

The Chronicles of Erenor

Chapter 17

THE ARCANE COUNCIL

The Beginning

The morning sun had barely kissed the horizon when Lysandra's boots crunched on the frost-covered cobblestones. She pulled her cloak tighter against the chill, a stubborn glint in her eyes as she approached the city gates where Aerin and the others waited.

"I thought you'd sleep in," Aerin said, his voice warm like the first sip of spiced cider on a cold day.

"Never," Lysandra replied with a wry smile. "Are you ready for this?"

"Born ready," he answered, swinging his packed satchel over his shoulder. His hand brushed hers momentarily, sending a jolt of warmth through her despite the morning chill—a fleeting connection that spoke volumes about their unspoken bond.

Eolande and Feyla were already bickering about who would lead the way, their usual playful banter sounding like an odd symphony to Lysandra's ears.

"Hey, lovebirds, save it for the road!" Lysandra called out from atop her chestnut mare, grinning ear to ear.

"Who are you calling a lovebird?" Eolande shot back,

His eyes softened as they found Feyla's, a playful retort that masked his true feelings.

"Let's not forget why we're doing this," Lysandra interjected before the teasing could escalate. "We need allies, and we can't afford distractions."

"Right you are," Aerin agreed, looking at Feyla's newest contraption strapped to her back. "Though I reckon those gadgets of yours won't count as distractions, eh, Feyla?"

"Only if you're on the wrong end of them," Feyla quipped, patting the device with pride.

"Focus," Lysandra reminded them gently. "Remember, it's not just our lives at stake."

"Indeed," Eolande acknowledged, his jesting demeanor fading into the gravity of their quest. "To Thalor, then. For alliances, for Erenor, and hope."

The five adventurers stepped beyond the archway, leaving city safety behind. The journey ahead bristled with the promise of danger and the unbreakable thread of their camaraderie—a bond forged in fire and magic, as steadfast as the blades at their sides and the spells within their reach.

"Alright, everyone, double-check your packs," Lysandra

called out, her voice steady and authoritative as she tightened the straps on her worn leather satchel. The once-quiet courtyard was now abuzz with activity. The air was tinged with anticipation and the bittersweet tang of parting.

"Got all the potions and scrolls here!" Aerin announced, patting the side of his bag where the soft clink of glass mingled with the rustle of parchment. His gaze lingered on the faces of the townspeople gathered to see them off, the weight of their expectations evident in his dark eyes.

"Make sure you've packed enough food," Aviara reminded them, walking her fingers over the provisions before stuffing them into her pack. She turned to share an encouraging smile with a group of children who had brought them freshly baked bread for the journey. It was always startling to see her in human form. Dark hair flowing and eyes blazing.

"Food, check. Gadgets, check. Unbearably heavy crossbow," Feyla trailed off, heaving the weapon onto her back with a grunt, her brow raised in mock exasperation. "Why did I think this was a good idea again?"

"Because you're brilliant, and your contraptions will save our hides," Eolande replied, securing his quiver and checking the fletching of his arrows with practiced ease. He caught Feyla's eye and winked, eliciting a reluctant chuckle from her.

"Speaking of saving hides, let's gather around," Lysandra urged, gesturing for the others to join her. The chatter around them quieted as the group huddled close, the gravity of their mission settling upon them like a cloak.

"Thalor is first," she began, unfurling a map and pointing to the kingdom in the northeast. "King Alaric is proud but fair.

They had finally defeated Malachor, the dark sorcerer who had threatened to plunge Erenor into eternal darkness, but their journey was far from over. With the Seer's Orb still in their possession and the weight of their newfound purpose pressing upon them, they set out towards Tyrannis, the heart of the kingdom and the future site of the Arcane Council they were planning to establish.

Aerin stepped up to stand beside Lysandra, his presence a comforting constant amid the uncertainty surrounding them. "It still feels surreal," he murmured, his hand brushing against hers as they walked, sending a spark of warmth through her. "We did it, Lys. We defeated Malachor and will establish the Arcane Council, just like we dreamed since first being together."

Lysandra nodded, a smile tugging at the corners of her lips. "Together, we accomplished what many thought was impossible. But our work is far from over. Establishing the Arcane Council will be a challenge in itself."

"I know," Aerin agreed, his brow furrowing slightly. "Gathering all that knowledge and power in one place, ensuring that it's used for the greater good... it won't be easy. There will be those who seek to use it for their own gain, to manipulate and control."

"That's why it's so important that we do this right," Lysandra said, her voice firm and conviction. "The Arcane Council must be a beacon of hope, unity, and strength. We need to make sure that nothing like Malachor ever threatens Erenor again. It will be our legacy, a guardian against the darkness."

Behind them, Feyla and Eolande were engaged in a lively discussion about the potential applications of the Seer's Orb, their voices carrying on the gentle breeze that rustled through the trees. Feyla's eyes sparkled with excitement as she described the possibilities, her hands gesturing animatedly as she spoke.

"Imagine the advancements we could make in healing magic alone," she gushed, her mind already whirring with ideas. "With the orb's power, we could develop new techniques, save countless lives, and bring hope to those who have lost so much."

With a smile on his face, Eolande was all ears as he watched Feyla's excitement. "And let's not forget what this means for magical research," he added, getting increasingly excited. "The orb could help us uncover secrets lost for centuries, rediscover ancient knowledge, and push the boundaries of what we thought was possible."

Aviara, the nature goddess who played a crucial role in their victory, observed the group. Her ethereal form was now fully human; she seemed to blend with the dappled sunlight that filtered through the canopy. "The forest senses your triumph," she said, her voice a soothing whisper in the breeze. "The balance has been restored, but it must be maintained. Your journey is over, and the challenges ahead will test you in ways you cannot yet imagine."

Lysandra nodded, feeling the weight of responsibility settle on her shoulders like a mantle. "We won't let Erenor down,

Aviara. The Arcane Council will be a force for good, a beacon of hope in the darkness. We will face whatever trials come our way and overcome them together."

As they journeyed on, the terrain grew treacherous, winding through dense forests and over rocky outcroppings. The group encountered narrow, winding paths that hugged the edges of cliffs, the drop below stretching into eternity. The air grew colder as they climbed higher into the mountains, the biting wind whipping at their faces and numbing their fingers.

During a tough stretch, Feyla lost her footing, her pack slipping from her shoulders as she scrambled for purchase on the icy rock. Eolande was at her side in an instant, his hand gripping her arm as he pulled her back to safety, his heart pounding in his chest at the thought of losing her.

"I've got you," he murmured, his voice steady despite the fear in his eyes. "I won't let you fall, Feyla. Not now, not ever."

Feyla nodded, her breath coming in short gasps as she leaned against him, her body trembling with the aftershocks of adrenaline. "Thank you," she whispered, the words feeling inadequate in the face of the danger they had just escaped. "I don't know what I would do without you, Eolande."

A clamor of noise abruptly stopped their descent down the other side of the mountain. The once peaceful forest was now filled with the metallic clangs and clatters of weapons being drawn. The group began to panic as they became aware that mercenaries had ambushed them and used the Seer's Orb as a lure.

"Protect it at all costs!" Lysandra shouted, her voice drowned out by the chaos. The air was thick with the stench of sweat and fear as the clash of weapons echoed through the trees.

Fighting back against their unexpected attackers, the group was engulfed in a whirlwind of conflict. Shouts and battle cries mixed in a racket, drowning out any semblance of tranquility that once existed in the forest.

Lysandra sprang back into action, her sword glinting menacingly in the sunlight as she swiftly engaged the attackers. Her strikes were like lightning, each finding its mark with lethal precision.

Meanwhile, Aerin focused intently, using magic to raise the earth and swallow their enemies. The ground shook and trembled under the force of his power, creating a chaotic battlefield where their enemies stood little chance.

Amidst the chaos, the defenders fought with unwavering determination, the forest echoing with the sounds of their struggle. Each swing of their weapons and burst of magic was a testament to their unyielding resolve to protect the precious artifacts they carried.

Once the skirmish was over and they reached their resting place for the evening, Lysandra pulled Aerin aside. Her brow furrowed with concern as she looked him over. "You're hurt." It wasn't a question.

Aerin tried to shrug it off but winced at the movement. "It's nothing, Lys. I'm fine."

She scoffed, gently probing the tender spot on his shoulder. Her touch was light, but he still sucked in a sharp breath. "This isn't nothing. Sit down and let me take a look."

"Always so bossy," he teased, but obediently sat on a nearby log.

As Lysandra examined the wound, Aerin studied her face—the determined set of her jaw and how she bit her lip in concentration. She was still the most beautiful being he'd ever seen, even though she was covered in grime and blood.

"I wish you'd be more careful," she murmured, not meeting his eyes as she cleaned the gash. "I hate seeing you get hurt."

Aerin caught her hand, entwining their fingers. "Hey. Look at me."

Reluctantly, she raised her gaze to his. In the fading light, her eyes were luminous, shimmering with unshed tears.

"I'm not going anywhere, Lys. Wild horses couldn't drag me away from you. Or demons, dark magic, or anything else this crazy world throws at us."

A weak chuckle escaped her. "Promise?"

"Cross my heart." He pressed a kiss on her knuckles.

She smiled a brilliant, blinding smile, and Aerin felt his heart stutter. Lysandra leaned in, resting her forehead against his. This close, he could count every freckle dusting her nose and feel the damp warmth of her breath on his skin.

"I love you," she whispered. "More than anything."

"I love you too. Always."

Their lips met, soft and sweet. Aerin buried his fingers in her hair, losing himself in her feel and taste. Everything else faded: the aches and pains, the worries about tomorrow. All that existed was this moment, this woman in his arms.

When they finally broke apart, breathless and giddy, the stars had emerged, twinkling merrily above them as if in approval. Lysandra nestled into his side with a contented sigh. Aerin wrapped an arm around her, marveling at how perfectly she fit against him, like two puzzle pieces snapping into place.

"Get some rest, love," he murmured into her hair.

She made a sleepy sound of agreement, already halfway to dreaming. Within moments, her breathing evened out, her body going slack with sleep.

As Aerin gazed down at Lysandra, feeling his heart so complete that it felt ready to burst, he knew the path ahead would be challenging. There would be more battles to fight and more wounds to tend to. But he felt he could face anything as long as he had Lysandra. Pressing a tender kiss to her temple, Aerin held her close and let the steady rhythm of her heartbeat lull him into a peaceful doze. He found contentment in knowing their love would see them through, come what may. With that comforting thought, he closed his eyes, knowing their bond would give them the strength to overcome whatever trials lay ahead.

Chapter 18

UNEXPECTED NEWS

The morning sun filtered through the canopy, casting a warm, golden light over the dense forest path ahead. Shadow padded silently at her side, his dark form comforting amid the towering trees and tangled roots. The fresh, earthy air made her feel alive and ready for whatever came next.

With Aerin close beside her, Lysandra led their group through the treacherous terrain. Each step was a thrilling mix of anticipation and nerves. The sight of Tyrannis on the horizon felt like a promise of new beginnings, yet the unknown challenges that awaited them in the city kept their hearts pounding. As they walked, the looming town reminded them of their battles and the bright future they hoped to build—a future now tinged with the unexpected.

"We're almost there," Aerin said. His voice was filled with relief and excitement, and his eyes were sparkling with anticipation. Last night, he was at a turning point—a moment that, for him, changed everything.

Lysandra turned to him, her silver hair catching the sunlight and her voice barely above a whisper. "Do you think our plan for the Arcane Council will work out?" Her voice was soft, filled with hope and a slight hint of uncertainty.

They stood in the warm glow of the setting sun. "As long as we stick together, it will," Aerin said confidently, the strength in his voice echoing the ancient trees around them.

With a shared look of determination, they continued leading the way in front of their companions. Lysandra's thoughts were a whirlpool of excitement and fear. After days of suspicion, the realization hit her—she was pregnant. The thought brought a rush of emotions: joy, anxiety, and an overwhelming sense of responsibility. She placed a hand on her stomach, feeling a connection to the life growing inside her.

Aerin sensed her inner turmoil and stepped closer, his touch warm and reassuring as he took her hand. "What's on your mind?" he asked gently.

Lysandra hesitated, the words catching in her throat. "Aerin, I'm pregnant," she finally managed to say, her voice trembling.

The words hung in the air, heavy with their implications, and the world seemed to hold its breath.

Aerin's eyes widened, shock and wonder flooding his expression. "Pregnant?" he echoed, barely above a whisper. "We're going to have a baby?"

Lysandra nodded, a smile breaking through her uncertainty. "Yes, we are. It's unexpected, and the timing isn't great, but..."

Before she could finish, Aerin swept her into his arms, his laughter echoing through the trees. "Lys, this is amazing," he exclaimed, his eyes shining joyfully. "We're going to be parents!"

Lysandra and Aerin shared laughter and clung to each other as they let the moment's reality sink in. Despite the challenges ahead, they were confident facing them together, just as they always had.

As the news spread through their group, they received congratulations and good wishes. Feyla and Eolande exchanged knowing glances, their relationship having blossomed amidst the trials they faced. "It looks like we'll have a little one to spoil soon," Feyla teased, her eyes dancing with mischief.

"And to train," Eolande added, his tone serious but his eyes warm. "The child of Lysandra and Aerin will have a destiny that we must all be ready to nurture and protect."

Once again, with her ethereal form shimmering in the dappled sunlight, Aviara placed a gentle hand on Lysandra's shoulder. "The spirits whisper of a bright future for your child," she said melodically. "But the path will be challenging. Lysandra, you must be vital for yourself and for the life you carry."

Lysandra nodded, her determination renewed by Aviara's words. She knew the road ahead would be challenging, but she was ready to face it head-on.

As night fell and they made camp, Lysandra gazed up at the stars, her hand resting gently on her stomach. She thought about the life growing inside her, about the love she and Aerin had created, and she knew she would do anything to protect it.

Aerin settled beside her, wrapping an arm around her shoulders and pulling her close. "I love you, Lys," he murmured, kissing her temple. "And I love our child. I promise I will always be here for you, no matter what."

Lysandra leaned into his embrace, her heart swelling with love. "I know you will," she whispered, her eyes closing as the warmth of his presence enveloped her. "As a family, we can face anything."

The rustling of leaves soon interrupted their peaceful moment. Shadow, constantly vigilant, stood at attention, ears perked and eyes scanning the darkness.

Without warning, bandits emerged from the shadows, their weapons gleaming ominously. "Stand your ground!" Lysandra commanded, drawing her sword. Shadow growled low, positioning himself protectively beside her.

The bandits charged, but the group was ready. Aerin moved with the fluid grace of a seasoned warrior, his blade flashing in the firelight. Eolande's arrows flew and reached their targets repeatedly, each shot finding its mark with deadly precision. Feyla, ever the inventive engineer, unleashed a series of gadgets that exploded in brilliant bursts of light, disorienting their attackers.

Lysandra fought with fierce determination, her blade cutting through the chaos. Shadow, a blur of dark fur and fangs, darted between the bandits, taking them down with swift, lethal precision. The skirmish was over quickly, and the bandits fled or lay defeated on the ground.

Breathing heavily, Lysandra looked around at her companions. "Is everyone okay?"

"We're fine," Aerin replied, sheathing his sword. "Thanks to your leadership and Shadow's keen senses."

Shadow nudged Lysandra's leg, his dark eyes reflecting the firelight. She knelt, ruffling his fur affectionately. "Good boy," she murmured, grateful for his loyalty.

With the immediate threat dealt with, the group settled back around the campfire. Lysandra's revelation about her pregnancy had brought a new sense of purpose to their journey, but the bandit attack had reminded them that danger still lurked in the world, even with Malachor gone.

As the fire crackled and the night deepened, Lysandra and Aerin found a quiet spot away from the camp. The moonlight cast a soft glow over the forest, creating a serene backdrop for their conversation.

"I'm scared, Aerin," Lysandra admitted, her voice barely above a whisper. "Embracing darkness doesn't exactly sound like a winning plan."

Aerin took her hand, his touch warm and reassuring. "We'll figure it out. You're not alone in this."

She squeezed his hand, drawing strength from the simple gesture. "How can you be so sure?"

"Because I've seen what you can do," he said, his voice filled with unwavering belief. "Light, dark—it doesn't matter. You're Lysandra, and that's enough for me."

His words wrapped around her like a protective cloak. Lysandra leaned into him, resting her head against his chest and listening to the steady beat of his heart. It was a comforting contrast to the chaos that threatened to overwhelm her.

"Promise me something?" she whispered.

"Anything," he replied, holding her close.

"Stay with me, no matter what happens," she pleaded, her voice trembling with emotion.

"Always," Aerin vowed, his eyes filled with love and determination.

They shared a tender kiss, the world around them fading away. At that moment, it was just the two of them, their hearts beating in sync, their souls entwined.

Back at the camp, Feyla and Eolande sat side by side, their conversation light and playful. "You've got a knack for this, you know," Feyla said, watching Eolande as he tended his bow.

"And you've got a gift for invention," Eolande replied, his eyes softening as he looked at her. "We make a good team."

Their hands brushed briefly, a silent promise of what might be. Feyla's eyes sparkled with unspoken affection, and Eolande's smile hinted at something more than friendship.

As the fire burned low, Lysandra drifted into a restless sleep. Her dreams were filled with visions of Tyrannis transformed. She saw the Arcane Council's headquarters—a majestic structure rising from the city's heart, a beacon of unity and strength.

As the group approached, the first light of dawn illuminated Tyrannis, filling the city's silhouette with a rush of emotions—nostalgia, hope, and the promise of new beginnings.

"We're home," Lysandra whispered, her voice filled with relief and anticipation.

Aerin took her hand, his eyes shining with pride. "Yes, we are. And this is just the start."

As they entered the city, the familiar cobblestone streets thrummed with life. The air was thick with the scent of roasted meats and sweet mead, and banners of victory fluttered from every window and archway. The sight of Tyrannis, bustling with activity and alive with hope, filled them with a sense of accomplishment and excitement for what lay ahead.

"We've brought hope back to Tyrannis," Eolande said, her eyes sparkling with pride. "Our journey isn't over, but we've already achieved so much."

"And we will achieve even more," Feyla declared. "The Arcane Council will guide Erenor to a future where peace and prosperity reign."

Lysandra looked at her friends, feeling a surge of gratitude and determination. "I'm ready for whatever comes next," she said, her voice carrying a steely resolve.

With their heads held high, the group continued into the city, their spirits buoyed by the warmth of home and the promise of a new beginning.

Chapter 19

APPROACHING THE KING

Lysandra stirred from a restless sleep, the first rays of dawn filtering through the curtains. She turned to see Aerin slumbering peacefully beside her. His face relaxed in sleep. With a sigh, she slipped out of bed and padded softly to the window, gazing at the misty morning.

Her mind churned with worry over the monumental task ahead of them: convincing King Thorian to approve the establishment of the Arcane Council. She and Aerin had fought so hard to bring peace and balance to the realm of magic, but this final hurdle seemed insurmountable. Tears pricked at her eyes as she longed for an easier path.

"Lysandra? What troubles you, my love?" Aerin's gentle voice startled her from her reverie. She turned to see him propped up on one elbow, his dark eyes full of concern.

"I'm sorry I woke you," she said, moving to perch on the edge of the bed. "I couldn't sleep. The thought of our audience with the King today weighs heavily on me."

Aerin sat up fully and took her hands in his. "I know it's a daunting prospect. But we'll face it together, as we always have. Our cause is just; the Arcane Council is vital to maintaining the balance we've fought for."

Lysandra nodded, blinking back tears. "I know you're right. It's just...I'm scared, Aerin. This pregnancy has made it harder for me to rein in my emotions. And after all we've been through, it feels cruel that this kind old man could dash our hopes with a single word."

"Oh, Lysandra..." Aerin pulled her into his arms, cradling her against his chest. "Your fears are understandable. But we can't lose faith now. Remember Aviara's prophecy—our children are destined for greatness. We're building a better world for them."

She clung to him tightly, drawing strength from his solid presence. "You're right. We'll do whatever it takes. I'm so grateful to have you by my side in this."

"Always and forever," he murmured, kissing her head. "Now, let me help ease your mind, hmm?" With a mischievous glint in his eyes, he rolled her beneath him, his mouth finding hers in a searing kiss.

Lysandra gasped as his lips trailed fire down her neck, his hands roaming her curves with reverent familiarity. She arched into his touch, the day's worries fading away as she lost herself in his expert ministrations.

Aerin's strong hands glided over Lysandra's curves, his touch igniting sparks beneath her skin. She sighed into his kiss, her body melting against his as he laid her back against the pillows. His lips traced a fiery path down her neck, teeth grazing her collarbone as she gasped.

"Aerin," she breathed, fingers tangling in his sleep-tousled hair.

He looked up at her through his lashes, eyes dark with desire. "Let me worship you, my love."

And worship her he did, his mouth and hands mapping every inch of her body like a man possessed. He lavished attention on her sensitive breasts, now fuller and heavier with impending motherhood. Lysandra nearly sobbed with pleasure as he sucked and nipped, each pull of his lips sending lightning straight to her core.

Lower, he ventured, pressing open-mouthed kisses along the slight swell of her stomach. "So beautiful," he murmured against her skin. "Growing our child safe inside you."

Tears pricked Lysandra's eyes at the raw adoration in his voice. Never had she felt more cherished, more utterly beloved.

All thoughts fled as Aerin settled between her thighs, his clever tongue delving into her most intimate places. She cried out, her hips lifting to meet his hungry mouth as he lapped and sucked. Pleasure coiled tighter and tighter in her belly as he drove her higher until she shattered with a broken moan.

Aerin gentled her through the aftershocks, pressing soft kisses on her trembling thighs. Then he surged up her body to claim her mouth once more, the taste of her desire on his tongue.

Lysandra reached for him eagerly, needing to feel his skin

against hers. He joined with her in one smooth thrust, and they both groaned at the sublime connection. He rocked into her with deep, measured strokes, stoking the embers of her desire back into an inferno.

They moved together in perfect sync—give and take, push and pull. The world narrowed to the slide of sweat-slicked skin, the harmony of panting breaths, and pleasured cries. Lysandra wrapped her legs around his waist, drawing him impossibly deeper as she urged him on with needy whimpers.

"That's it, my love," Aerin praised, his rhythm growing erratic as he neared his peak. "Come undone for me."

Lysandra let go with a wordless cry, her release crashing over her in dizzying waves. Aerin followed moments later, spilling into her with a guttural groan as he pulsed deep within her welcoming heat.

They clung to each other as they drifted down from the heights of passion, trading tender kisses and murmured endearments. Lysandra had never felt so satisfied or so utterly cherished.

Aerin shifted onto his side, drawing her flush against him, one large hand splayed protectively over the gentle swell of her stomach. "I love you," he whispered, nuzzling her sweat-dampened temple. "Both of you, with everything I am."

Lysandra turned her head to kiss his lips sweetly, pouring all her love and devotion into the caress. "And we love you. Always and forever."

They lay tangled together, limbs heavy with satisfaction.

Aerin smoothed her passion-mussed hair back from her face, his gaze tender. "Feeling better, my love?"

She smiled, tracing his jawline with a gentle finger. "Much. You always know just what I need."

He captured her hand and pressed a kiss on her palm. "As you do for me. Now, we'd best get moving to make our appointment with the King."

They moved about their morning preparations in companionable silence, the easy rhythm of two souls in sync. As Lysandra carefully pinned up her hair and donned her court finery, she caught Aerin watching her in the mirror, love and pride shining in his eyes.

"You look radiant," he said softly, coming up behind her to wrap his arms around her waist. "The King won't be able to deny you anything."

She leaned back against him, savoring his solid warmth. "With you beside me, I can take on the world."

He chuckled. "Let's hope the King is a bit easier to sway than that."

Hand in hand, they made their way to the palace, the streets already bustling in the early morning light. Lysandra breathed deeply, trying to calm the nerves fluttering in her stomach. The guards snapped to attention as they approached the grand entrance, ushering them inside with crisp bows.

Despite her trepidation, Lysandra couldn't help but marvel at the opulent throne room with its soaring ceilings and glittering mosaics. The air hummed with ancient magic, the weight of centuries pressing down on her. At the far end, King Thorian sat on his gilded throne, his expression inscrutable.

With a steady breath, Lysandra stepped forward and curtsied deeply. "Your Majesty, we come before you today to humbly request your approval to establish the Arcane Council. This body will be dedicated to preserving peace and ensuring the responsible use of magic throughout Erenor."

Beside her, Aerin bowed. "We have seen firsthand the devastation wrought by unchecked magical power. The Council will provide crucial oversight to prevent such horrors from ever again threatening our land."

King Thorian leaned forward, his keen eyes examining them closely. "A bold proposition. But what assurances can you offer that this council will not become a source of tyranny? Power has a way of corrupting even the most well-intentioned."

Lysandra met his gaze steadily. "We have put much thought into this very concern, Your Majesty. A strict charter will govern the Council, and its members will take solemn oaths of allegiance to the Crown. Your authority will remain supreme."

"We've prepared a detailed proposal outlining the Council's structure and duties," Aerin added, producing a scroll and presenting it with a flourish. "We believe it will address any reservations you may have."

The room fell silent as the king unfurled the scroll, his eyes scanning the neat lines of the script. Lysandra hardly dared breathe, her heart hammering against her ribs. Everything hinged on his verdict.

After what felt like an eternity, Thorian looked up, his face unreadable. "You present a compelling case. But I cannot decide on such an import without consulting my advisors. Leave the proposal with me. I will summon you when I have reached a decision."

Disappointment warred with relief in Lysandra's chest. It wasn't an outright refusal or the ringing endorsement she had hoped for. Aerin squeezed her hand reassuringly as they bowed and backed out of the throne room.

As the palace doors closed behind them, Lysandra sagged against Aerin's side, suddenly exhausted. "That was more nerve-wracking than facing down a horde of demons."

He chuckled wryly. "Indeed. But we did our best. Now we can only wait and pray that the King sees the wisdom in our plan."

"I know. I want so badly to bring our dream to fruition. For us, for our children, for all of Erenor."

Aerin tilted her chin up, her eyes shining with love and determination. "We will, Lysandra. One way or another, we'll make it happen. I believe that with every fiber of my being."

She searched his gaze, finding strength in his unwavering faith. "Thank you, my love. For always being my rock."

"And you are mine." He kissed her softly. "Now, let's go home. We have a bit of time before the others demand our attention. Perhaps I can provide some distraction from the waiting, hmm?" His eyes gleamed with mischief.

Laughing, she let him lead her down the palace steps and

into the bustling city streets. Whatever challenges lay ahead, she knew they would face them together, secure in their love and shared purpose. The future was theirs to shape, and she had never felt more ready to meet it head-on.

Chapter 20

THE KING'S DECISION

The tension in the air was palpable as Lysandra and Aerin waited for King Thorian's decision. Stacks of parchment and magical artifacts surrounded them as they sat in their cozy living room. Lysandra fiddled with a quill, her eyes scanning the meticulously crafted Charter on the table.

"Do you think we missed anything?" she asked, her voice laced with anxiety.

Aerin shook his head, reaching out to still her restless hands. "We've gone over every detail, Lys. The King will see the value in our proposal."

Just as Lysandra was about to respond, a knock echoed through the room. Aerin exchanged a glance with her before getting up to open the door. A royal messenger stood there, a scroll clutched in his hand.

"The King requests your presence at the castle immediately," the messenger announced, handing over the scroll.

Lysandra felt a surge of nervous energy as she and Aerin quickly dressed and made their way to the castle. The walk seemed longer than usual, each step heavy with anticipation.

King Thorian sat on his throne, his expression unreadable as he regarded them.

"Lysandra, Aerin," he began, his voice resonating through the chamber. "I have considered your proposal for the Arcane Council."

Lysandra took a deep breath and stepped forward. "What is your decision, Your Majesty?" she asked, trying to keep her voice steady.

The king leaned forward, his gaze piercing. "I have decided to approve the establishment of the Arcane Council, but there are conditions. The Council must operate in secrecy, with its members sworn to an oath of loyalty to the crown. I will have the final say in all matters, and your actions will be subject to my oversight."

Relief washed over Lysandra as she exchanged a glance with Aerin. "We accept your terms, Your Majesty. Thank you for this opportunity."

King Thorian nodded. "I trust you will not disappoint me. Ensure that the Arcane Council serves the best interests of Tyrannis and Erenor."

As they left the throne room, Lysandra felt a weight lift off her shoulders. They had secured the king's approval, but she knew the real challenge was beginning.

Back in their quarters, Aerin pulled Lysandra into his arms. "We did it," he murmured, his voice thick with emotion. "We're one step closer to making our dream a reality."

Lysandra smiled at him, tears of joy in her eyes. "Together, we can do anything," she whispered, leaning in for a tender kiss.

A soft knock on the door cut short their celebration. Feyla and Eolande entered, their faces alight with curiosity.

"Well?" Feyla demanded, her eyes wide with anticipation.

"We got the approval," Aerin announced, grinning.

Eolande let out a cheer, clapping Aerin on the back. "That's fantastic news! We have a lot of work ahead of us, but this is a great start."

Feyla threw her arms around Lysandra, her excitement infectious. "I knew you'd do it! The Arcane Council is going to change everything."

Lysandra hugged her back, feeling gratitude for their friends' unwavering support.

They gathered around a large table in the palace library, the atmosphere buzzing with energy. Ancient tomes and scrolls lay scattered around, a testament to the depth of their research.

"We need to lay down the principles that will guide the Council," Lysandra said, spreading a fresh parchment. "Honesty, integrity, and the protection of Erenor."

Aerin nodded. "Let's start with the purpose—to monitor the use of magic, prevent the rise of dark forces, and ensure the safety of Erenor."

Feyla said, "And we need to specify how we'll operate in secrecy. Maybe something about maintaining dual lives—public roles that allow us to gather information and act without drawing suspicion."

Eolande added, "We should include provisions for training new members. The Council's strength will lie in its ability to adapt and grow with each generation."

As they worked, the room fell into a focused silence. Each member lost themselves in their thoughts and contributions. Lysandra's quill moved swiftly across the parchment, the words flowing effortlessly.

"The Arcane Council of Erenor," she wrote, her voice barely a whisper. "A secret order dedicated to the preservation of magic and the protection of our world."

Hours passed, and the charter began to take shape. It was a living document. The words reflected their shared vision for Erenor's future. The parchment was filled with their collective hopes and aspirations when they finally stepped back from the table. Aviara's presence, a comforting reminder of the divine guidance that would watch over them, filled the room with a sense of calm.

Aviara spoke with reverence as she said, "The spirits have blessed your work." "Under your wisdom and integrity, Lys, the Arcane Council will be a force for good."

Lysandra looked around at her friends, a sense of accomplishment swelling in her chest. "We've done it," she said softly. "We've laid the foundation for a better future."

Aerin wrapped an arm around her shoulders, his eyes filled with love and admiration. "And it's just the beginning," he murmured, kissing her temple. "Together, we'll ensure this Council stands the test of time."

Eolande and Feyla exchanged glances, their bond deepening as they shared the experience of creating something that would shape Erenor's future.

As they left the library, the weight of their responsibility settled comfortably on their shoulders. They had taken the first step toward a new era of magic and protection that would ensure the safety of Erenor for generations to come.

"Very well," King Thalor conceded after a heavy silence. "I will support the formation of this Arcane Council, but under certain conditions. First, I want regular reports on its progress, and any major decisions must be brought before me. Second, I retain veto rights—should the need arise."

"Agreed," Lysandra said, a sigh of relief escaping her lips. Beside her, Aerin nodded, his dark eyes reflecting pride.

"Excellent," King Thalor said with a final nod. "Then let us proceed with haste. Time is a luxury we cannot afford."

As the audience dispersed, Feyla lingered behind. Her expression was clouded with uncertainty. Lysandra noticed her friend's unease and approached with a comforting arm around her shoulders.

"Hey," Lysandra said gently, "what's on your mind?"

Feyla glanced up at her, worry etched into her delicate features. "It's just... everyone here has magic. I'm the odd one out—an inventor amidst mages. Where do I fit in all this?"

"Every bit as much as any of us," Aerin said warmly. "You've got a sharp mind, Feyla. Your inventions could benefit the council in ways magic cannot."

Lysandra nodded, squeezing Feyla's shoulder and saying, "Exactly." "You know that grappling tether you invented a while back? I can not even begin to count how many times it has helped us. As an individual, you provide originality and insight. It is hugely beneficial."

"Are you serious?" Feyla asked, seeking validation with her brown eyes.

"Unquestionably," Aerin responded with a firm nod. "You are our hidden weapon, I would say."

Feyla's worry gave way to a smile, and she stepped forward. "A hidden weapon, eh? That sounds good to me."

"Excellent," Lysandra smiled. "Because it's true. Now, back to the others. We need to establish a council."

Feyla answered, her spark rekindled, "Lead the way." They clasped hands and strolled back to reunite with their friends, prepared to face the next obstacle with optimism and resolve, illuminating their way.

Watching Feyla engage with the others made Eolande's quiet voice ring with pride. Her previously furrowed brow was now smoothed with confidence, and her eyes sparkled with new-found vigor. "Look at you!" exclaimed Eolande, deeply impressed by her inventiveness. My dear, you are pretty brilliant."

With a flush of modesty and pleasure, Feyla turned to face him. She asked, tucking stray hair behind her ear, "Do you think so?"

"Without doubt," Eolande assured her, stepping closer. "Your mind is as sharp as any blade in this realm. The council will soon realize that magic or no magic, you are indispensable."

"Thank you, Eolande," Feyla said, squeezing his hand. Your faith in me means everything."

Their shared smile was a silent vow, an unspoken promise of mutual support in a world where the lines between love and duty are often blurred.

The imposing King Thalor, however, interrupted the moment. His gaze swept over the gathering before settling on Lysandra, pregnant and committed—a visible representation of the future they were all fighting for.

"Your bravery is beyond question, Lysandra," he began, his tone laced with concern. "But we must address the elephant in the room—your condition. I fear it may slow our progress with the Arcane Council."

Lysandra met his gaze squarely, the set of her jaw indicating her refusal to be seen as anything less than capable. "Your Majesty, if I may speak frankly, my pregnancy does not render me invalid. It fuels my determination to ensure the council's success."

"Your strength is admirable," the king conceded, "but we

must also consider your well-being and that of the heirs of the First Mage. It is not merely a matter of your safety but the continuity of the magical lineage."

"King Thalor," Aerin interjected, stepping protectively beside Lysandra. "We appreciate your concern, but know this—Lysandra is more than capable of fulfilling her duties. We will take every precaution but not step back from our responsibilities."

"Indeed," Lysandra added, her hand instinctively reaching her slightly rounded belly. "My ancestors carried the burden of their power through wars and trials far greater than this. I am no different. The council needs strong leadership, and I intend to provide it."

"Very well," King Thalor replied after a thoughtful pause. "I will trust in your judgment, but let it be known—I expect constant updates on your condition. Should there be any sign of distress?"

"We understand," Aerin assured him. "And we thank you for your concern and your support."

"Then it is settled," the king declared. "Let us proceed with drafting the charter for the Arcane Council. And let it be a beacon of hope for Erenor—a symbol of unity and strength."

As the meeting adjourned, the group dispersed purposefully, each member carrying the weight of their new-found responsibilities. Eolande glanced at Feyla.

A fierce determination replaced her earlier worries, which mirrored Lysandra's.

"Come," he said softly. "Let's work on your designs." The council will need every advantage we can provide."

"Right behind you," Feyla replied, her hand slipping into his as they walked away. Their steps synchronized in harmony with their shared resolve.

In the quiet that followed, Lysandra leaned against Aerin, her head resting on his chest. "Do you ever wonder about the baby? About what kind of world we're bringing them into?"

"Every day," Aerin confessed, his arms wrapping around her. "But one thing I'm certain of—he'll have the fiercest mother in all of Erenor. And a father who'll do anything to protect him."

"Him huh?"... Then more severe. "Even from himself?" Lysandra mused, tracing patterns on Aerin's chest.

"Especially from himself," he said with a gentle chuckle. "Together, we'll guide and teach him to wield his power with wisdom and courage."

"Promise me, Aerin," Lysandra whispered, "that no matter what happens, we'll face it together—as a family."

"I promise," he vowed, sealing it with a kiss atop her head. "Now and always."

Their embrace was a sanctuary, a moment of peace amidst the storm of uncertainty that raged outside their walls. They stood in a close embrace, their love a bastion against the dangers ahead.

As night fell, the flames from the hearth cast dancing shadows across the room. Shadow the Wolf lay curled up, his steady breathing a comforting presence. Lysandra and Aerin retreated to their quarters, savoring the solace of their cottage—their home that had once felt like a distant memory.

They lay together, entangled beneath the sheets, sharing whispers and warm caresses. Their love was a tender melody that played softly in the silence, a song of hope and enduring passion.

"Everything will be alright," Aerin murmured as he traced the curve of Lysandra's stomach, speaking to the life within. "You've got a mother who's a force of nature and a father who's pretty stubborn himself."

Lysandra laughed softly, the sound mingling with the crackling of the fire. Despite Aviara's reassurances, worry still gnawed at her heart—the fear of the darkness in her blood that might one day touch her children.

"Love," Aerin said, sensing her unease. "No shadow is too deep for us to overcome. Together, we are light. All of our children will know this truth."

"Promise?" Lysandra asked, her eyes seeking him in the flickering light.

"Until the stars fade from the sky," he promised, his words a vow as ancient as time.

She turned within his embrace, looking up at him with love. "Do you think we did the right thing today? With the council?"

"Absolutely," he assured her, his confidence unwavering. "Together, we'll build something enduring. Something worthy of our struggles."

"Even with everything that's at stake?" She pressed, and the worry was never far from her heart.

"Especially with everything that's at stake," he replied, his gaze intense. "We have each other, and we have this." He gestured around the humble room to the life they were slowly reclaiming. "—our sanctuary."

Lysandra nodded, her fears gently quelled by his steadfast resolve. She took a deep breath—she hadn't realized she'd been holding—and allowed herself to lean into him.

"Let's not wake Shadow," she murmured, her lips curving into a smile as she glanced at their companion. "He looks so peaceful."

"Agreed," Aerin said, his voice low. "Besides, there's no need for words when actions speak volumes."

With that, he led her to their modest bed, the wooden frame creaking softly under their combined weight. They lay in a comfortable silence between two souls intertwined by fate and choice.

"Tomorrow," Aerin whispered, breaking the stillness, "we begin anew."

"Tomorrow," Lysandra repeated, her heart swelling with a potent mix of hope and apprehension.

The strength of their bond kept the ghosts of the past at bay as they dozed off, the fire casting dancing shadows on their serene faces—a testament to the love that would lead them through whatever difficulties lay ahead. And as they surrendered to the night, wrapped in each other's embrace, they found strength in their unity—a strength that would carry them through the challenges to come, a beacon for the dawn of a new era in Erenor.

Dawn brought a tapestry of hues that painted the sky outside while quiet still reigned over the cottage. The soft crackling of the fire and Shadow's gentle breaths of sleep, their dependable companion, seemed to cloak the world of worries and wars within the charming walls.

Wrapped in each other's arms, Lysandra and Aerin lay in their warm bed, a sanctuary within their sanctuary. Aerin's fingers traced idle patterns over Lysandra's skin, sending shivers down her spine, not born of cold but of anticipation. She met his gaze, reading the same intense love she felt swelling within her chest.

"Are you sure?" he asked, his voice barely above a whisper, as if even the surrounding air was privy to their shared intimacies.

"More than anything," Lysandra replied, her words laced with the certainty that only comes with complete trust.

They moved together then, a slow and harmonious dance guided by the rhythm of their beating hearts. Lysandra closed her eyes and allowed the tenderness between them to carry her. Aerin's touch was featherlight and worshipful, as though he understood the fragility of the moment—their brief respite from the storm that raged beyond their door.

Their love-making was a deliberate journey, not a race to culmination but an exploration of the depths of their connection. Each caress reaffirmed promises made and kept. Every kiss was a seal upon oaths of protection and passion intertwined.

As the day broke brighter and their ardor reached its crescendo, they clung to each other, a lifeline amidst the emotions that threatened to overwhelm them. When at last they lay quiet, a blanket of serene satisfaction enveloping them, Aerin pressed his lips gently against Lysandra's belly, murmuring sweet nothings to the life they had created together.

"Can you hear me in there, little one?" Aerin's voice was tinged with wonder and an unmistakable note of joy. "Your papa will teach you how to wield a sword, and your mama will show you the magic of the elements."

Lysandra smiled. The simple act was filled with complex emotions. She placed her hand atop his, feeling the warmth of his skin seep into her, yet beneath that warmth lurked the icy tendrils of fear that refused to relinquish their grip on her heart.

"Aviara said it would be alright," she whispered, her voice betraying the turmoil. "But the darkness in my blood..."

"Hey," Aerin interrupted gently, lifting his head to lock eyes with her. "We face everything together, remember? Light, dark, and all shades in between. You are the strongest person I know, Lysandra. If anyone can shield all of our children, this one and any in the future, from the shadows, it's you."

"Even with everything we've seen? Everything we fought?" The doubt lingered, stubborn as the darkness she feared.

"Especially because of it," he assured her, his conviction as unyielding as the earth he now commanded. "You've turned every challenge into a victory. This will be no different. We will be no different."

She wanted to believe him, to cast aside the specter of dread that loomed over her happiness like a precursor. Yet it clung to her, a persistent reminder of the battles yet to come—battles not just for kingdoms and councils but for the future of the family they were building.

"Promise me," Lysandra implored, searching his face for the certainty she desperately needed.

"Every day, I promise for the rest of our lives." Aerin sealed his vow with a tender kiss that spoke of an unbreakable bond and love that transcended their world's trials.

And as they settled into slumber, wrapped in the tranquility of their cottage with only Shadow's soft snores as accompaniment, Lysandra dared to hope. Perhaps, with Aerin by her side, the light within them could outshine any darkness within and without.

Chapter 21

RECRUITING FOR THE ARCANE COUNCIL

The sun dipped low, painting the sky in vibrant hues of orange and pink as Lysandra and Aerin approached Eolande's village. A picture-perfect scene of tranquility welcomed them: cobblestone streets lined with charming houses, freshly baked bread wafting through the air, and villagers going about their daily tasks with warm smiles that belied the recent upheaval in the world.

Eolande stood at the village entrance, his face lighting up with a broad grin as he spotted them. "Welcome, my dear friends, to our humble abode!" he exclaimed, pulling Lysandra into a warm embrace. "It is an absolute honor to be a part of this groundbreaking endeavor from the start."

Lysandra returned his hug with equal warmth, feeling gratitude for his unwavering support. "We're thrilled to have you by our side, Eolande. Your vast knowledge and exceptional diplomacy skills will be invaluable assets to our cause."

As they made their way through the village, curious elven faces and bright, inquisitive eyes followed Lysandra and Aerin's every move. The couple spent the day sharing their ambitious vision for the Arcane Council, meticulously explaining how it would serve to safeguard Erenor from any future magical threats. They held an impromptu town meeting in the village square, as there was no need for secrecy among these mystical beings, who all had the potential to be elected to the Council. Eolande took the lead, introducing Lysandra and Aerin to key figures in the village and facilitating engaging discussions about their new roles and responsibilities.

The villagers' enthusiasm was palpable, and their support came in various forms. A local baker offered them warm, crusty loaves of bread as a gesture of goodwill, while children, eager to show their support, presented the couple with handmade charms imbued with protective spells. The sense of community and unity was contagious, and Lysandra felt her heart swell with pride and renewed hope for the future.

As evening fell, Eolande led them to his home, a cozy cottage with a thatched roof and vibrant ivy climbing the walls. They gathered around a sturdy wooden table, sharing a hearty meal of roasted vegetables and succulent venison. Laughter and the clinking of glasses punctuated the lively conversation, which flowed as smoothly as the rich wine they sipped.

Eolande leaned back in his chair, a thoughtful expression on his face. "The villagers are positively buzzing with excitement.

They wholeheartedly believe in the cause we're building and are ready to support us in any way they can."

Aerin nodded, a satisfied smile playing on his lips. "That's precisely the kind of support we need. Garnering the backing of magical communities from every corner of Erenor will strengthen our council and ensure its long-term success."

Lysandra glanced around the room, her gaze settling on the faces of her cherished friends. "We're off to a fantastic start," she said, her voice brimming with conviction. "This is just the beginning of something truly remarkable."

The following day, Lysandra and Aerin set off for Feyla's workshop, a bustling hub of creativity in the town's heart. The workshop was a vibrant riot of color and sound, with half-finished inventions cluttering every available surface and thick air with the spicy scent of oil and exotic herbs.

Feyla greeted them with a wide grin, her hands streaked with grease and her eyes sparkling with unbridled enthusiasm. "You're just in time!" she called out over the steady hum of machinery. "I have something incredible to show you."

She led them to a cluttered table covered in various prototypes for advanced communication devices. Each invention was a marvel of ingenuity, a testament to Feyla's unparalleled inventive genius. "I've already given Eolande a sneak peek; he believes these will be invaluable to our cause. These devices will allow us to stay connected and communicate seamlessly, no matter where we are in Erenor," she explained, picking up one of the sleeker models and handing it to Aerin for closer inspection.

Aerin examined the device keenly, turning it over and marveling at its intricate design. "This is incredible, Feyla. Your inventions will be a monumental asset to the Council's operations."

Feyla's eyes sparkled with pride as she nodded in agreement. "While I may not be a magic practitioner, I can bridge the gap between magic and technology. My inventions can help us communicate more effectively, strategize more precisely, and defend Erenor from potential threats."

Lysandra nodded in agreement with her admiration for Feyla's inventive creations. "You're exactly the kind of brilliant mind we need, Feyla. Your skills and expertise will be invaluable in elevating our council beyond just a group of magic users."

They spent the remainder of the day discussing Feyla's specific role within the Council and exploring how her inventions could enhance their operations. Feyla eagerly showcased her latest project—a sophisticated device capable of detecting magical disturbances and alerting all Council members simultaneously.

"This is going to be a game-changer for our mission," Aerin remarked, carefully testing the device's functionality. "With this technology at our disposal, we'll be able to respond to threats swiftly before they have a chance to escalate."

Feyla beamed with pride, her eyes shining with unbridled excitement. "I'm so grateful to be a part of this incredible endeavor. I've always yearned to be part of a true family and to make a tangible difference in the world. This Council has given me that once-in-a-lifetime opportunity."

Back in Tyrannis, Lysandra and Aerin dedicated their efforts to establishing the Council's infrastructure. They discovered a hidden chamber within the castle's stone walls, accessible only through a labyrinth of secret passageways. The dimly lit chamber, filled with ancient tomes and powerful magical artifacts, would serve as the Council's clandestine headquarters.

One evening, as they sat in the chamber amidst their ever-expanding library of books and artifacts, Aerin reached for Lysandra's hand, his touch gentle and reassuring. "We've come such a long way, haven't we?" he said, his thumb tracing soothing circles on her skin.

Lysandra leaned into his touch, a small smile playing on her lips. "We truly have. And it's all been worth it. We're building something that will protect Erenor for generations to come."

Aerin gently pulled her into his lap, his strong arms wrapping around her waist in a loving embrace. "And we're doing it together," he murmured against the soft skin of her neck, his voice a soothing balm to her weary soul. "You and me, always and forever."

Their lovemaking that night celebrated their unbreakable bond, their bodies moving in perfect synchronicity, a rhythm as old as time itself. Each tender touch and passionate kiss reaffirmed their unwavering commitment to each other and their shared vision for Erenor's future.

Aerin's hands roamed reverently over Lysandra's body, caressing every curve and plane with a gentle touch that spoke volumes of his love and devotion. His lips traced a fiery path along her skin, igniting a blaze of desire deep within her core. Lysandra arched into his touch, her fingers tangling in his hair as she pulled him closer, desperate to feel every inch of his body against her own.

They moved together, their breaths mingling and their hearts beating perfectly as one. Aerin worshipped her body with a fervor that left her trembling and gasping for his name, his skilled hands and mouth bringing her to the pinnacle of pleasure again and again. Lysandra clung to him, her nails raking down his back as wave after wave of ecstasy crashed over her, leaving her boneless and sated in his arms.

Afterward, as they lay entwined on the plush carpet, their bodies glistening with the evidence of their passion, Aerin skimmed his hand gently over the swell of Lysandra's growing belly. "Our children will be born into a world made infinitely safer by the fruits of our tireless efforts," he whispered in awe, his calloused fingers lightly tracing the precious lives growing within her.

Lysandra covered his hand with her own, her heart thudding wildly at the thought of the beautiful life she was nurturing inside her womb. "And they will grow up knowing that their parents fought tooth and nail to protect this world and ensure their future," she vowed, her chest overflowing with fierce, unshakable love and pride.

"Have you considered where we should house the more sensitive artifacts?" Aerin asked, adjusting his position on the bear's skin and allowing Lysandra to tuck her head comfortably under his chin.

Lysandra thought about it for a moment, her mind racing with possibilities. "I believe our best course of action would be to create a separate, heavily fortified chamber with reinforced walls to ensure the utmost security of these powerful items," she replied, her voice laced with determination.

Much later, they returned to the main Council Chamber, where Eolande and Feyla joined them, carrying trays laden with nourishing food and refreshing drinks. "We thought you might require sustenance," Eolande said warmly, setting the trays on a nearby table. "And we have some exciting ideas regarding the Council's future endeavors."

Feyla handed them each a steaming cup of fragrant tea, her eyes sparkling with barely contained excitement. "We've been brainstorming innovative ways to keep our activities hidden from prying eyes. What are your thoughts on implementing a coded message system and enchanted seals to ensure the utmost secrecy?"

Lysandra took a thoughtful sip of her tea, nodding in agreement. "That could prove to be an extremely effective method. We must ensure that only Council members can decipher our communications and access sensitive information."

Aerin interjected, his mind already working to refine the idea further. "In addition to coded messages, we should also establish a network of safe houses strategically located throughout the different regions of Erenor. These secure locations would serve as our resources' meeting points and storage facilities, allowing us to operate without drawing unwanted attention."

The afternoon passed in a flurry of meticulous planning and lively discussion as the Council members worked tirelessly to construct a robust framework for their covert operations.

Eolande suggested an innovative strategy of forming alliances with influential local leaders and prominent magical practitioners. She said, "We need to strengthen our support base and expand our reach to every corner of the realm."

Feyla, always full of inventive ideas, proposed creating an extensive network of informants to gather vital intelligence on potential threats. She added, "We can't afford to overlook any emerging dangers."

The chamber was filled with an infectious energy as ideas were exchanged and refined, punctuated by moments of laughter and camaraderie. "I love how we all come together and improve each other's ideas," remarked one Council member.

The group decided to venture into a nearby forest renowned for its serene beauty and magical properties to take a break from their intense planning sessions. As they walked along the winding paths, Lysandra and Aerin strolled hand in hand, marveling at the lush greenery and the soothing sounds of nature that enveloped them. "This is so refreshing," Lysandra exclaimed.

Feyla and Eolande followed closely behind, engaging in a spirited debate about the potential applications of Feyla's latest groundbreaking invention. "I think this could revolutionize how we approach magical transportation," Feyla said enthusi-astically.

The stresses and tensions from their earlier discussions seemed to melt away in the calming embrace of the forest's tranquil atmosphere, reinforcing the deep bonds of friendship and trust that had grown between them.

As they stumbled upon a hidden meadow, the perfect spot for a brief rest and reflection, Lysandra took a deep, cleansing breath, feeling a profound sense of peace wash over her. "This place is truly magical," she said softly, her gaze wandering over the sun-dappled leaves and the gentle sway of the ancient trees.

Aerin squeezed her hand, a gentle reminder of his constant love and support. "It is a beautiful reminder of why we're doing all this. To protect precious places like this, where magic and nature exist in perfect harmony."

They spread a soft blanket and shared a simple yet nourishing meal, their conversation flowing as quickly as the babbling brook that meandered through the meadow. As they relaxed in the forest's soothing embrace, Shadow, Lysandra's loyal black wolf, appeared silently at her side, his eyes reflecting the dappled light that filtered through the canopy above. Throughout their journey, Shadow had been a constant, if sometimes hidden, presence, always watching over them and offering his unwavering protection.

Lysandra reached out to scratch behind his ears, a smile playing on her lips as he leaned into her touch, relishing the affectionate gesture. "It's good to see you, old friend," she murmured, taking comfort in the knowledge that their bond remained as strong as ever, a testament to the strength and loyalty that had seen them through countless challenges.

As the sun began to dip below the horizon, casting long shadows across the forest floor, the group reluctantly returned to Tyrannis. The brief respite and the rekindled sense of purpose that now coursed through their veins rejuvenated their hearts and minds.

Once again ensconced within the hidden chamber, they resumed their planning with renewed urgency and determination. Eolande and Feyla shared their ideas for recruiting new members and expanding the Council's reach. At the same time, Lysandra and Aerin focused on refining the council's organizational structure, meticulously accounting for every detail.

As the evening wore on and the candles burned low, they crafted meticulous plans for the coming weeks, each member ready to embark on their respective journeys to different corners of Erenor. Their mission was clear: to recruit new members, establish the Council's presence, and lay the groundwork for a brighter, more secure future for all.

"We must exercise the utmost discretion," Lysandra reminded them, her gaze steady and unwavering. "The Council's existence must remain a closely guarded secret until we have established a solid foundation and are fully prepared to reveal ourselves to the world."

Aerin nodded in agreement, a reassuring smile on his face. "We'll proceed with caution and vigilance. Our ultimate goal is to ensure that the Arcane Council becomes a beacon of hope and protection for all of Erenor."

With their plans firmly in place and their hearts filled with determination and hope, they retired for the night, confident they were ready to face whatever challenges arose. Their unwavering bond and the strength of their shared convictions kept them together.

As Lysandra and Aerin lay in bed, their bodies entwined and their hearts beating as one, they knew that the road ahead would be fraught with obstacles and uncertainties. Yet, in the warmth of each other's embrace, they found the courage and resilience to face whatever the future might hold, secure in the knowledge that together, they could overcome anything.

Chapter 22

EXPANDING THE COUNCIL'S REACH

The sun barely rose over the horizon when Lysandra, Aerin, Eolande, and Feyla set out on their thrilling adventure to establish the Arcane Council's presence across Erenor. The air was crisp and cool, and the dew-covered grass glistened in the early morning light, hinting at the epic journey ahead.

"Where should we start?" Feyla asked, her pack slung over her shoulder and a determined glint in her eye.

Eolande unrolled a map, tracing the various routes they could take. "I suggest we begin in the city of Ravenwood," he said, tapping a spot on the map. "It's a major hub of trade and commerce, and we're likely to find potential recruits there."

Aerin nodded, his hand resting on the hilt of his sword, a grave expression etched on his face. "Agreed. And from there, we can branch out to the surrounding villages and towns, ensuring the safety and security of our people."

Lysandra gracefully mounted her horse, her cloak billowing in the gentle breeze and a sense of anticipation shimmering in her eyes. "Let's ride, then," she said, her voice filled with determination and optimism. "We have a long journey ahead of us; every mile will bring us closer to our goal." She turned to Aerin, her smile warm and genuine. "These horses you bought were the best investment you've ever made," she praised, her eyes glowing with admiration. "Especially now," she added, brushing her belly tellingly.

Aerin's eyes softened as he squeezed her hand. "I wanted to make sure you were comfortable," he said, his voice low and intimate. "Our journey isn't just about the Council. It's about our future, too." He gave her an intimate smile before turning to the others.

"Is everyone prepared for the unknown that awaits us?" Aerin, now the group's undisputed leader, shattered the solemn silence. His unwavering gaze met each of his comrades, hinting at the thrilling adventure ahead.

He winked at Lysandra, Feyla, and the others before passing around some Lucky Bull Ale to all his companions. Lysandra got a cup of water, which she promptly sniffed at.

"To us," he declared, tipping back the Lucky Bull Ale and taking a deep sip, "the misfits who became legends."

They all raised their drinks, smiling as they toasted. "Who could have foreseen that a mage, a witch hunter, an elf, an inventor, and an ancient nature goddess would forge such an indomitable bond of friendship and warriors?" he mused, his smile radiating the unbreakable unity of their diverse group.

Lysandra laughed softly, her eyes sparkling with affection. "We may be an odd mix, but we make a formidable team," she said. "Here's to us and the adventures that lie ahead."

And as their laughter resounded throughout the peaceful dawn, the chilly silence completely broke, giving way to the warmth of friendship and the promise of a thousand tomorrows.

Feyla, with a mischievous glint in her eyes, pulled out a flask from her pack and grinned. "Ready as we'll ever be," she replied, her hand adjusting the sling of her crossbow. The glint in her warm, brown eyes reflected the same fire that burned within all of them. "And I've got a surprise for later—a little invention I've been working on. You'll love it."

The group urged their horses forward, their thundering hooves resonating through the picturesque, serene, emerald countryside. The aroma of dewy grass and the caress of a gentle breeze on their faces were the last comforting sensations they would experience for a while as they bid farewell to the familiarity of their home and embarked on another expedition into the uncharted.

The landscape transformed from serene meadows to impenetrable forests to rugged foothills with each passing mile. Each new landmark they encountered reminded them of the daunting trials and high-stakes nature of their mission, igniting a spark of excitement in their hearts.

"Keep your eyes sharp, everyone. We don't know what awaits us out here," Aerin called out, his tone now serious.

As they pressed on through the treacherous terrain, Eolande shouted back to Aerin over his shoulder, his voice filled with determination, "We are unstoppable now, my friend. This mission will provide us with all the support we need."

In the winding streets of Ravenwood, they searched for the most powerful sorcerers. Under the cloak of night, they tiptoed past guards and slipped into dimly lit pubs and back alleys. Their hearts raced as they whispered in hushed tones, plotting strategies to gain support from others. With each meeting, their trust grew stronger as they discussed the council's mission and carefully crafted their words to inspire loyalty.

"The Arcane Council is not just a group of magic users," Lysandra said, her voice low and intense. "It's a brotherhood, a sisterhood, bound together by a sacred oath to protect Erenor from the forces of darkness."

A young woman with fiery red hair and piercing green eyes leaned forward, her interest piqued. "And what would be expected of us if we were to join?" She asked, her voice tinged with a hint of skepticism.

Aerin met her gaze. His expression was severe. "You would be expected to use your magic for the greater good," he said, his voice firm. "To stand against those who seek to harm the innocent and uphold the Council's values."

The woman nodded, a smile playing on her lips. "I like the sound of that," she said, extending her hand. "I'm Nalia, and I would be honored to join your cause."

As they trekked through the rugged terrain, Nalia pointed out other magic users who had grown tired of hiding and yearned for a purpose. Lysandra and her companions greeted each other with open arms, patiently answering their questions and easing their fears. The ecstasy and relief on their faces when they decided to join was a testament to the hope and courage instilled by the Arcane Council.

In a secluded mountain village, they encountered an older man named Oren, whose face bore the marks of years spent healing others. His eyes revealed kindness and sorrow as he spoke of the devastation caused by dark magic. "I've seen the cruel effects firsthand," he said, trembling. I will offer my expertise if the Arcane Council can stop such tragedies."

Lysandra placed a tender hand on his shoulder, gratitude shining in her eyes. "Thank you, Oren," she said softly. "Your wisdom and compassion will be invaluable to our cause."

As they journeyed, they scouted out potential safe houses and marked them on a map hidden within Eolande's cloak.

Eventually, they came upon an old lighthouse on the coast; its once vibrant red paint faded and chipped. With a flick of Nala's wand, the front door creaked open, revealing a large room with stone walls and dusty furniture.

"This will be our sanctuary," Aerin declared, his eyes scanning the room as he cast protective enchantments around the perimeter.

Feyla's gaze wandered to a corner filled with crates and shelves overflowing with magical artifacts and ancient tomes. "And here is where we'll plan our next move," he continued.

Feyla's lips curled into a mischievous grin, her fingers itching to tinker with the mysterious objects before her. "And I can finally test out my latest invention without worrying about setting anything on fire!" she exclaimed.

The others laughed, the sound echoing through the lighthouse's empty halls. It was a moment of fun during their solemn task, a reminder that even in the darkest times, there was still room for joy and companionship.

As the weeks passed, the Arcane Council began to take shape, with its members scattered across Erenor like stars in the night sky. They communicated through secret channels, sharing information and coordinating their efforts to keep the realm safe from the forces of darkness.

And through it all, Lysandra and Aerin's love for each other grew more intense and passionate. In the quiet moments between their duties, they would steal away to the secluded corners of the safe houses, their bodies intertwined and their hearts beating.

"I never knew it was possible to love someone this much,"

Aerin murmured one night, his fingers tangled in Lysandra's hair as they lay together on a bed of soft furs. "You are my everything, Lysandra. My heart, my soul, my reason for being."

Lysandra smiled, her hand tracing the contours of his face. Her other hand rested lightly on her growing belly. "And you are mine, Aerin," she whispered, her voice thick with emotion. "Together, we can face anything. Together, we are unstoppable."

As they returned to Tyrannis, their hearts were filled with a sense of accomplishment and purpose. They had laid the foundation for something extraordinary—a legacy that would endure long after they were gone.

The flickering light of the torches illuminated their faces as they gathered once more in the hidden chamber deep inside the castle. Lysandra looked around at her friends, her heart swelling with pride and gratitude.

"Lysandra, we couldn't have achieved this without your unwavering dedication and vision," Aerin said, his voice filled with love, pride, and gratitude. "Our council is stronger because of your leadership."

Lysandra smiled, a warm feeling of pride flowing over her upon hearing Aerin's words. "Thank you, Aerin. It's an honor to work alongside all of you. Together, we can accomplish even greater things for our community," she replied, her eyes reflecting her sincerity.

"None of this would have been possible without your bravery, dedication, and unwavering commitment." Aerin's voice was soft and sincere. "You truly are the heart and soul of this council," he said, heartfelt.

Tears pricked at Lysandra's eyes as she gazed at the faces of those who had become like family to her through their shared mission. After years of struggle and personal sacrifice, they had finally achieved their joint objective.

The clinking of glasses and Eolande's shining eyes signaled it was time for a toast. "To Lysandra and Aerin!" he exclaimed with admiration. "And to the Arcane Council," he continued, raising his glass higher, "may it prevail and protect us for generations to come!"

As Lysandra looked around at her friends-turned-family, she couldn't help but smile. They had come so far, achieved much, and survived against all odds. Due to their shared love and desire to make the world a better place, this ragtag group of misfits had grown into a potent force.

"Cheers!" Aerin interjected, clinking his glass against Eolande's before taking a sip. As the night wore on, they discussed their plans: recruiting more allies, setting up safe houses, and fighting against evil. Each member had their ideas and insights, but one thing was sure: they were all in this together.

"We should also throw a party or something," suggested one of the new members with a grin. "We have plenty to celebrate."

"Yeah, like our survival skills," joked another. But deep down, they all knew it wasn't just about parties and jokes. The fight against darkness was ongoing, and every day they stood firm was a small victory towards a brighter future.

As the torches started to flicker out and the room grew darker, someone lit some candles, and everyone huddled closer together. They shared stories of their past victories and challenges, laughing at the silly moments and somberly reflecting on the sacrifices they had made along the way.

Their voices grew hoarse from talking and laughing, and Lysandra couldn't help but feel grateful for this unique group of individuals. They were more than just a team; they were a family, and together, they were unstoppable.

The following day, with renewed determination, the friends mounted their horses and set off again. Their shared aspirations and the promise of the future lifted their spirits. They were ready to face the long road ahead with courage, knowing they could overcome any obstacle together and build a better world for all of Erenor.

Chapter 23

THE BIRTH OF A NEW ERA

The landscape transformed from serene meadows to impenetrable forests to rugged foothills with each passing mile. Each new landmark they encountered reminded them of the daunting trials and high-stakes nature of their mission, igniting a spark of excitement in their hearts.

"Keep your eyes sharp, everyone. We don't know what awaits us out here," Aerin called out, his tone now serious.

As they pressed on through the treacherous terrain, Eolande shouted back to Aerin over his shoulder, his voice filled with determination, "We are unstoppable now, my friend. This mission will provide us with all the support we need."

In the winding streets of Ravenwood, they searched for the most powerful sorcerers. Under the cloak of night, they tiptoed past guards and slipped into dimly lit pubs and back alleys. Their hearts raced as they whispered in hushed tones, plotting strategies to gain support from others. With each meeting, their trust grew stronger as they discussed the council's mission and carefully crafted their words to inspire loyalty.

"The Arcane Council is not just a group of magic users," Lysandra said, her voice low and intense. "It's a brotherhood, a sisterhood, bound together by a sacred oath to protect Erenor from the forces of darkness."

A young woman with fiery red hair and piercing green eyes leaned forward, her interest piqued. "And what would be expected of us if we were to join?" She asked, her voice tinged with a hint of skepticism.

Aerin met her gaze. His expression was severe. "You would be expected to use your magic for the greater good," he said, his voice firm. "To stand against those who would seek to harm the innocent and uphold the Council's values."

The woman nodded, a smile playing on her lips. "I like the sound of that," she said, extending her hand. "I'm Nalia, and I would be honored to join your cause."

As they trekked through the rugged terrain, Nalia pointed out other magic users who had grown tired of hiding and yearned for a purpose. Lysandra and her companions greeted each other with open arms, patiently answering their questions and easing their fears. The ecstasy and relief on their faces when they decided to join was a testament to the hope and courage instilled by the Arcane Council.

In a secluded mountain village, they stumbled upon an older man named Oren, whose face had weathered years of healing others.

His eyes held kindness and sorrow as he spoke of the devastation caused by dark magic. "I have witnessed its cruel effects," he lamented, trembling. "If the Arcane Council can prevent such tragedies, I will gladly offer my expertise."

Lysandra placed a tender hand on his shoulder, gratitude shining in her eyes. "Thank you, Oren," she said softly. "Your wisdom and compassion will be invaluable to our cause."

As they journeyed, they scouted out potential safe houses and marked them on a map hidden within Eolande's cloak.

Eventually, they came upon an old lighthouse on the coast; its once vibrant red paint faded and chipped. With a flick of Nala's wand, the front door creaked open, revealing a large room with stone walls and dusty furniture.

"This will be our sanctuary," Aerin declared, his eyes scanning the room as he cast protective enchantments around the perimeter.

Feyla's gaze wandered to a corner filled with crates and shelves overflowing with magical artifacts and ancient tomes. "And here is where we'll plan our next move," he continued.

Feyla's lips curled into a mischievous grin, her fingers itching to tinker with the mysterious objects before her. "And I can finally test out my latest invention without worrying about setting anything on fire!" she exclaimed.

The others laughed, the sound echoing through the lighthouse's empty halls. It was a moment of fun during their solemn task, a reminder that even in the darkest times, there was still room for joy and companionship.

As the weeks passed, the Arcane Council began to take shape, with its members scattered across Erenor like stars in the night sky. They communicated through secret channels, sharing information and coordinating their efforts to keep the realm safe from the forces of darkness.

And through it all, Lysandra and Aerin's love for each other grew more intense and passionate. In the quiet moments between their duties, they would steal away to the secluded corners of the safe houses, their bodies intertwined and their hearts beating.

"I never knew it was possible to love someone this much," Aerin murmured one night, his fingers tangled in Lysandra's hair as they lay together on a bed of soft furs. "You are my everything, Lysandra. My heart, my soul, my reason for being."

Lysandra smiled, her hand tracing the contours of his face. Her other hand rested lightly on her growing belly. "And you are mine, Aerin," she whispered, her voice thick with emotion. "Together, we can face anything. Together, we are unstoppable."

As they returned to Tyrannis, their hearts were filled with a sense of accomplishment and purpose. They had laid the foundation for something extraordinary—a legacy that would endure long after they were gone.

The flickering light of the torches illuminated their faces as they gathered once more in the hidden chamber deep inside the castle. Lysandra looked around at her friends, her heart swelling with pride and gratitude.

Lysandra's voice rang through the council chamber, filled with determination and pride. Looking around at her fellow members, she felt a surge of emotion in her chest.

They had done it—their dream of an Arcane Council was now a reality. She turned to Aerin, their leader, and he reached for her hand. Their fingers intertwined, cementing their bond and shared accomplishments.

"None of this would have been possible without your bravery, dedication, and unwavering commitment," Aerin said, his voice soft and sincere. "You truly are the heart and soul of this council."

Lysandra smiled, feeling tears prick at her eyes as she looked at the faces of those who had become like family to her through their shared mission.

They finally achieved their joint objective after years of struggle and personal sacrifice.

The clinking of glasses and Eolande's shiny eyes were a clear sign that it was time for a toast. "To Lysandra and Aerin!" He exclaimed, his voice thick with admiration. "And to the Arcane Council," he continued, raising his glass higher, "may it kick butt and protect us for generations to come!"

Lysandra couldn't help but smile as she looked around at her friends-turned-family. They had all come so far, achieved much, and survived against all odds. Due to their love for one another and commitment to changing the world, this motley crew of misfits had grown into a potent force.

"Cheers!" Aerin chimed in, clinking her glass against Eolande's before taking a sip himself.

As the night went on, they discussed their plans: recruiting more allies, setting up safe houses for those fleeing from darkness, and fighting against evil. Each member had their ideas and insights, but one thing was sure: they were all in this together.

"We should also throw a party or something," suggested one of the new members with a grin. "We have plenty to celebrate."

"Yeah, like our survival skills," joked another.

But deep down, they all knew it wasn't just about parties and jokes. The fight against darkness was ongoing, and every day they stood firm was a small victory towards a brighter future.

As the torches started to flicker out and the room grew darker, someone lit some candles, and everyone huddled closer together. They shared stories of their past victories and challenges, laughing at the silly moments and somberly reflecting on the sacrifices they had made along the way.

In the end, as the night wore on and their voices grew hoarse from talking and laughing, Lysandra couldn't help but feel grateful for this group of unique individuals. They were more than just a team; they were a family, and together, they were unstoppable.

past, stirs, threatening to unravel the fabric of magic. Lysandra travels beyond the known boundaries of magic with steadfast allies like Aerin, Feyla, the wise Elarion, and Harrow, the fearless dragon.

This thrilling sequel tests alliances, and passionate love blossoms amidst the chaos. Feyla finds unexpected love with Eolande, an enigmatic elf, while Lysandra and Aerin's bond deepens, and they fall deeply in love amidst the trials.

Lysandra faces her most formidable challenge yet: will her powers be enough to preserve Erenor's delicate balance?

"The Last Mage" is the first book in the Chronicles of

Erenor series, following Lysandra, a hidden mage and skilled swordswoman, on her quest to restore balance to her world. She battles King Draven's oppressive rule and evil forces with the help of her loyal black wolf, Shadow, the hunter Aerin, and the inventor, Feyla. Along the way, Lysandra confronts ancient secrets and combats evil creatures like the Shadow Hounds and the corrupted dragon, The Harrow. In the process, she unexpectedly finds love and embraces her destiny as the last descendant of the First Mage.

After defeating King Draven and restoring Erenor's magic, Lysandra and her allies discover an even greater danger looming—a mysterious evil wielding black magic and the power to summon ancient creatures. In an explosive battle, Lysandra faces the shocking truth about her connection to this demon and the struggle between her light and dark sides. With the help of her companions, she emerges victorious, but the triumph is bittersweet as new threats arise from the celestial fracture.

"The Last Mage" is an enthralling fantasy adventure that intertwines themes of magic, bravery, love, and the eternal battle between light and darkness. This book is ideal for fans of stories featuring mythical creatures, loyal companionship, and the quest for balance in a fractured world. Join Lysandra on her epic journey in The Chronicles of Erenor and discover a realm where the fate of all hangs in the balance.

About the author Kim Bock

KIM BOCK BOOKS

Kim Bock is a successful bilingual Indie author and co-owner of a thriving website design business based in South Africa, which she runs with her husband, Eitel. She has already published a historical romance novel in South Africa and released the final book in her trilogy, "The Chronicles of Erenor," on Amazon—Kim's writing benefits from her varied viewpoints and love of storytelling, which she draws on. While working on a website design with her husband, she dedicates her free time to crafting captivating fiction that draws readers into new realms of imagination. Join Kim Bock on her literary adventure, where her novels reflect her diverse experiences and offer readers a glimpse into her imaginative world.

You can find out more on her website at www.kimbock-books.com

Special Request by Kim Bock

PLEASE BE SO KIND TO REVIEW THE BOOK

Dear Reader,

Thank you for joining me on this journey through *The Chronicles of Erenor*. Your support means the world to me, and I hope you've enjoyed exploring the realms of Erenor as much as I've enjoyed crafting them.

If you found yourself lost in the adventures of Lysandra, Aerin, and their companions, or if the story moved you in any way, I would be incredibly grateful if you could take a moment to share your thoughts with other readers.

Your review can be as brief or detailed as you like. It will help others discover "The Chronicles of Erenor" and embark on a similar journey.

To leave your review, visit the book's page on Amazon.Or at your preferred online bookstore! Here's the revised text:

Again, thank you for your support and participation in this epic adventure!